MW01228785

SLIM'S LAST STAND

I dedicate this book to my husband Earl, the wonderful man who has stood by me through our many years of marriage, loving me unconditionally, cheering me on when I am discouraged, and enduring countless nights without complaint while I tapped away on the computer. I would also like to thank my writing group, the Ladies of Marylin Warner's Round Table in Colorado Springs, CO, who helped me shape the story and bolstered my confidence, my brother Willard who edited and formatted the story for publication and who also designed the cover. And last of all, I would like to thank my husband's Uncle Slim, the person who sparked the idea for this story. He's gone now but Slim was truly a man of the Old West born fifty years too late.

SLIM'S LAST STAND

Carol Stoffel

Chapter One

When Tucson Slim heard the mewing cry of a newborn baby, every fiber in his tired old body screamed for him to ignore it. He was eighty-years-old. He'd had a long hard day, and he was off duty and heading home, for Pete's sake. But an old lawman's instincts die hard, and he turned around, eyes narrowed, senses alert.

Crossing Centennial Square at a half-trot, a young girl pushing a baby stroller hurried toward him. She was dressed in black from her head to her toes...toes encased in heavy black combat boots spewing small clouds of dust behind her. In stark contrast to the punk girl, the screaming baby bouncing along in the fancy buggy, head lolling from side to side, dressed in what appeared to be an old-fashioned Victorian christening gown and bonnet.

But what bothered Slim most was the way the girl kept looking back over her shoulder like she was afraid someone was after her.

She had all the characteristics: shoplifter.

Hoping he could later remember which brain cell he stored it in, Slim made a quick mental note of her appearance; Long black hair, Long black sweater over baggy black shorts, Several rings in one ear, One ring in her nose, makeup like black axle grease smeared on her eyes and lips, and there was something peculiar about her face.

Slim squinted, thinking that this girl had shaved off her brows and wore a line of tiny dagger tattoos over each eye.

The old man shook his head and considered, Even after all he'd seen in his long life, what today's youth actually chose to do to their bodies still shocked him.

When she saw him watching her, Dagger-girl, as Slim now thought of her, ducked her head and tried to hurry past him.

Once again, his lawman's instinct took over. After all, even though Old Centennial Square wasn't exactly a town, the upscale reproduction of early Tucson where he worked as the part-time security guard and a full-time tourist attraction was his domain and it was his responsibility to keep the peace. "Excuse me, Miss," he said, "is there a problem?"

She looked up. Her eyes, twin black holes burned into alabaster skin, darted from the badge on his chest to his face and back again, and she suddenly bolted off the sidewalk, pushing the buggy into the landscaping rocks. The harsh jolt made the baby scream.

Taking a broad step sideways, Slim grabbed the girl's arm and saw another tattoo on the inside of her wrist; An odd design, he thought, The head of a dog maybe.

Slim had a vague recollection of having seen that image someplace before, but the girl jerked away so fast, he couldn't be sure. Naturally, this would be one of those times he found calling up a memory as easy as panning for gold with a strainer.

"Stop her!" A buxom blond, dressed like a saloon girl, came barreling out of The Old West Photography Shop. "Stop her! She's got my baby!"

The antique baby dress suddenly made sense, Slim realized, It was a costume from the shop.

Slim lunged at Dagger-girl, but she drew back and punched him hard in the chest. With a sharp wheeze, he stumbled backwards and hit the ground with a bone-rattling thud, tripping the blond who'd been running full tilt to rescue her child. She fell over Slim's prone body and crashed beside him in a heap of black petticoats and red taffeta.

With both her pursuers down, Dagger-girl saw her chance. She rammed the buggy onto the asphalt parking lot and pushed off like a frightened deer. The woman scrambled to her feet and chased after her.

With scraped palms and an aching backside, Slim stood and hobbled along after the two females as fast as he could on his battered hips. When he finally reached the parking lot, he saw Dagger-girl load the buggy into the back of a black van. She hopped in and slammed the doors behind her, almost catching the blonds' grasping fingertips in the process.

The van roared out onto the street leaving a billowing cloud of smoke in its wake and disappeared into the desert night.

Left standing alone in the nearly empty parking lot, the woman clenched her fists and screamed in frustration. Then she turned, pinned Slim with her eyes, and shrieked, "Why didn't you stop her? I told you she had my baby."

Slim's chest tightened. Spasms of burning pain stole his breath. Fighting the dense fog sweeping him away, he staggered and collapsed to the asphalt with that mother's anguished cries resounding in his head

# # #

Feeling about as useless as a three-legged bull in a rodeo, Slim turned away and left Detective Mark O'Brien and the men from the Desert Valley Police Station to their work. He'd never been so humiliated in all his life; waking up like that and finding that young detective staring down at him, pity shining from his eyes like sunbeams.

Oh, the man had said all the right things, that the mother shouldn't have left her child unattended, that Slim had done the best he could, that sometimes the bad guys simply got the upper hand, completely ignoring the fact that it had been a girl--a very young girl--who'd bested Slim. Then the detective had said, oh so respectfully, that Slim should go home and rest. The Tucson police were on the job. What it all boiled down to in Slim's mind was—-you're a joke, old man. Stay out of our way.

What these youngsters didn't understand was the burden of shame Slim would always carry for having failed in his duty. If only he'd been more alert or faster on his feet. If only he'd gotten the van's tag number. If only he'd had his guns....

That thought brought him up short. Tucson Slim would never draw down on a kid without a weapon. Not even a kid with daggers for eyebrows.

As much as he hated to admit it, Slim was beginning to think he'd lost his edge as a lawman, and what happened tonight proved it. He hadn't helped a single soul. Not the police. Not that mother or her baby. And he'd probably destroyed the Square's reputation as a safe place for families.

Carter Winslow, the young pup who ran Centennial Square, as much as said so when he bawled Slim out for not catching the girl; bawled him out in front of God, the police, and everybody, making Slim feel even more inept than ever.

As he limped out to his car, he passed by an older couple dressed in tank tops, shorts and beach sandals, leaning against the back of a sporty little convertible. With skin the color and texture of well-tanned leather, everything about them screamed snowbird.

The woman whispered; a whisper Slim could plainly hear, "Do you think that's really him?"

The man nodded, "Yep, Aggie, I'd bet a sawbuck, that's Roy Rogers' old buddy, Gabby Hayes."

Gabby Hayes! Outraged, Slim couldn't restrain himself. He stopped and whirled around. "You'd lose that bet, Mister. Gabby Hayes was about a foot shorter than me, and he died a long time ago."

The man grinned sheepishly. "Sorry, but you look so familiar."

Caught off-guard, Slim blustered, "Well, I was in a few movies with stars like Clint Eastwood--."

"Don't try to fool us," the woman chimed in. "You're way too old to be Clint."

Slim held up his hands. "Wait a minute. I'm not saying I am Clint Eastwood. I was sayin' I've been in movies with--."

The man interrupted, "Well, what's your name, then?"

Slim drew himself up to his full height. "Arizona Marshall Tucson Slim Stevens."

"Sorry, old fella," the man said, "but I never heard of you."

The woman grabbed her husband's hand and pulled him toward the Square. "Come'on Henry, I told you if he was anybody important, he'd be wearing pistols. Let's go see what the cops are doing."

Galled to no end, Slim gritted his teeth and watched them walk away, the woman's red flip-flops snapping against her stained, cracked heels. On a better day, he might have fantasized about grabbing Henry and Aggie by the backs of their matching tank tops, hauling them into the security office, and showing them a roomful of this old nobody's movie memorabilia, but he was just too tired. Today all he wanted to do was go home.

The old man eased himself into his '78 Ford Pinto, settled his narrow behind into the comfortable sag in the driver's seat, and fastened his safety belt. In the distance, the brilliant corals and purples of sunset dulled and desert splendor dissolved into flat monochrome.

The scene playing out before Slim seemed almost a metaphor for his own life. How the indignities of age had slipped up on him when he wasn't looking, stealing the glory and challenge of his middle years, leaving his life blighted and colorless, a life where he found his worth in memories captured in shifting sand.

Slim took off his black cowboy hat and ran his hand through his thinning silver hair. It wasn't that he didn't appreciate the eighty years he'd been given. A lot of his friends hadn't been so fortunate. He simply missed his old life; back when he'd been an Arizona marshal and his mind had been sharp as a cactus needle. Back when life had vitality, purpose, a future.

He turned the Pinto's key, and while he waited for Queenie to cough and wheeze her way into running, Slim caught sight of his reflection in the rear-view mirror. His heart sank. Beneath a thatch of bushy white brows, the eyes of a tired old man stared back at him…an old man who'd lost a child to a kidnapper.

And he knew when his decline began; last year when he tangled with that wife-beater right here in this very parking lot. That day Slim's judgment faltered, and he made the mistake that changed his life and shattered his confidence, a mistake that cost him the right to carry a sidearm. All because some woman-hitting jerk looked like he was going for a gun, and it turned out to be his cell phone. It was only luck that Slim's hand wavered when he drew his gun, and he shot the car door and not the man.

Taking a deep breath, Slim tried to calm his anger by focusing on the fact that his old friend Bran Phillips was now looking into his case. If a well-known judge--a hard judge of the old school--deemed Slim mentally fit and responsible, the powers that be would have to let him carry his guns again; and when they did, this downward slide would end. Slim's belief in his own abilities would be restored. His life would be like it used to be; back when everybody respected him.

Back when the name of Tucson Slim meant something.

# # #

Slim didn't sleep much that night with the kidnapping scene playing and replaying in his weary mind, forcing him to review each and every detail until he wanted to scream.

Then, like a bubble rising through murky water, the image of Dagger-girl's wrist tattoo slowly surfaced in his mind. It hadn't been a dog at all. It was a goat's head sitting in the middle of an upside-down five-pointed star. And there were green and red intertwined snakes coiling around it like some blasphemous Christmas wreath.

Slim's eyes popped open. No wonder that tattoo seemed so familiar. Years before, he'd seen that very same design carved on a bloodstained altar up in the mountains.

Now the memory was so clear in his mind, it could have happened yesterday. He'd found that altar back in '69 right after the Summer of Love. The hippies had been flowing through Tucson like a river on their way to that great Nirvana of the West, California.

The old man grunted his disgust. As a decorated veteran of World War Two, he considered the 60s and the 70s--and the activities therein to be pimples on the glorious face of American history. Every time he turned around, it seemed like somebody was protesting something with a bonfire, burning all kinds of things, copies of the Constitution, draft cards, bras, even Old Glory. All that crazy behavior and anti-war sentiment still made the old man's blood run hot. Where had all the heroes been during that time; the John Waynes, the Douglas MacArthurs, the dad-burned cavalry, for Pete's sake?

Slim had done his best to set a few folks straight, even banged a head or two. But when he realized he couldn't change the state of the nation all by himself, he did what he could and when he reached the end of his patience, he'd go prospecting for a few days. Time in the desert always had a cleansing effect, settling his spirit, helping him remember why he became a lawman.

Slim suddenly sat up, briskly shook his head, and when his brain quit sloshing around in his skull, scolded himself. "Stay on track, you old fool," he thought, "You ain't good to nobody if your mind's wandering all over the past."

He crawled out of bed, went into the bathroom, and splashed cold water on his face. He had to stay focused and remember exactly where he'd seen that terrible altar. Coffee would help; nothing like a shot of caffeine to sharpen the senses.

Slim hurried into the kitchen and made a pot of joe. While he waited for it to brew, he attempted to reconstruct those bygone days.

On that particular trip, he'd gone prospecting alone. His onetime partner, Luis Martínez, had stayed home with his wife; Dolores had been expecting their sixth child and wasn't feeling so good.

Dolores. The image of her lovely face swept through Slim's mind like a desert sandstorm, threatening to obliterate everything in its path. With great reluctance, he forced himself to put her aside, filled his mug with strong coffee, and sat at the table. He had to stay on point and find that child.

That prospecting venture had been the first year he'd gone up on Mount...Mount..., tarnation! What was the name of that dad-burned mountain?

He banged his fist on the table. Why did his memory always fail him when he needed it the most? That young detective had wanted Slim to call if he remembered anything. Did that apply to almost remembering something?

Deciding any help he could provide was better than none at all, Slim dialed the telephone number to the local precinct and asked for Detective Mark O'Brien. When he got the man's voice mail, Slim slammed the phone down. He'd vowed a long time ago he'd never leave a message on any machine. You couldn't trust the gol-durn things. He'd go to the station house. This couldn't wait. A baby's life might depend on it.

All the way to the Desert Valley Police Station, Slim struggled to remember the name of the mountain. He could see it in his mind and knew exactly where it was. Way out on old Higgins Ranch Road toward the Mexican border. Mount…Mount….

Swirling around him like campfire smoke, the name continued to elude him, but the vision of that grisly altar remained crystal clear. Slim knew exactly how an altar like that had been used; all kinds of crazies wearing robes, singing and dancing under a full moon; knives flashing, a baby screaming. Sacrifice. He read about it all the time in the tabloids.

# # #

When Slim slid old Queenie to a squealing stop in front of the police station and rushed inside, a young Hispanic night duty officer jumped to his feet, asking "Is there an emergency?"

"Yes," Slim panted. "Call Detective O'Brien. Tell him Tucson Slim remembered something important about the kidnapping at Centennial Square."

Before Slim even finished speaking, the officer had the detective on the line. After a quick explanation, he hung up and ushered Slim into a cluttered office. "Detective O'Brien said you should wait in here. Would you like some coffee?"

Noting his racing heart and the tremor in his hands, Slim decided he'd had enough of the miracle mind refresher. "No, thank you. Will O'Brien be long?"

"No, Sir. He said he'd come right over." The officer smiled——that indulgent smile Slim knew young people saved only for the elderly. "You be okay in here on your own?"

Slim narrowed his eyes and glared at the man. "I think I can manage myself for a minute or two."

A wrinkle appeared on the officer's brow, a brow as soft and smooth as a baby's butt. "Did I say something--."?

Slim suddenly resented the man's youth. "Just git on about your business," he said.

"Well, I'll be right out there if you need anything, sir. I'm Officer Diaz." He pointed to his shiny metal nametag as he backed out of the room, like if Slim couldn't hear, maybe he could read.

"Insolent young pup!" Slim sat on a padded metal chair and looked around the room where Detective Mark O'Brien conducted police business. The desk was standard issue for the Department, but darned if that young cop didn't have more new-fangled contraptions than Slim's boss, Carter Winslow, had in his office.

Although he didn't understand why O'Brien's computer monitor sounded like bubbling water, Slim knew today's law enforcement officers had to use computers. Computers ran the whole dad-gummed world. But why would O'Brien need a TV, a VCR, and a telephone the size of a small copy machine? And that treadmill in the corner, what was that all about? Was the Department turning into a danged day spa? Would they offer him a facial next?

Slim snorted at his little joke and felt good about his own police career. When he'd been an active Arizona marshal, he'd managed to solve all kinds of cases with little more than a notebook, his car, a regular telephone, and his six-shooters.

The sound of burbling water finally got the best of Slim's curiosity, and he turned the monitor where he could see it.

A variety of colorful animated fish swam serenely across the screen. In the sand below the fish, a large clamshell opened and air bubbles escaped—hence the burbling sound.

Slim mumbled, "What-the-Sam-Hill?"

"It's called a screen saver. I find the fish soothing." A bemused smile on his freckled face, Detective O'Brien walked to his desk and returned the monitor to its proper position. His wild red hair, puffy eyes, and the fact he was wearing no socks with his black police oxfords told Slim he'd just crawled out of bed.

"You know how stressful the job is, Slim. We cops have to wind down any way we can."

Slim did remember how it was on the job, but that was before all this high-tech nonsense. He'd relieved his stress the old-fashioned way, with other cops at a bar called The Blue Shield.

O'Brien stifled a yawn. "So what do you have?"

Slim leaned forward. "I recollect what that girl's tattoo looks like; you know, the one on her wrist."

"I'd hoped you'd remembered her license plate number or the make of the van; something worth pulling me down here for in the middle of the night."

"Oh, I think this'll be worth your time. Her tattoo is the symbol of some kind of cult or maybe a witch's coven."

The redheaded cop stared at Slim through slitted eyes and drummed his fingers on his cluttered desktop. "A witch's coven. So tell me what that tattoo looked like again."

"It was a goat's head sittin' in the center of a star."

"You said earlier you'd seen a dog's head."

"I know, but I was mistaken. It was a goat."

O'Brien pulled at his earlobe. "That's a pretty common insignia. You see it in all the occult shops."

"I know, but there's more to this picture. I'll draw it for you." He took a small notebook out of his pocket and chose a pencil from the detective's pencil cup. Licking the lead, Slim tediously sketched part of the design. "It was a goat's head setting in an upside down star like this.

"A pentagram," O'Brien asked.

"Yeah." Slim drew a pair of curved horns on the goat's head. "And it had…." His mind suddenly went blank. Although he fought to recapture the memory, he knew it was useless. The image had vanished like a mirage in the desert. A sharp pain bloomed behind Slim's eyes, and he rubbed his temples.

"Are you okay, Slim? I told you, you should've let a doctor check you over."

"I'm fine." He stared at the paper for a moment, but the image was absolutely gone. Desperate not to look like an old fool, Slim tried to laugh it off. "Well, I ain't no artist, that's for sure. Maybe I should just take you where I saw it."

"You saw it on the girl's wrist. Are you telling me you know where she is?" O'Brien asked.

"No. Didn't that fella out at the front desk tell you I remembered I'd seen that tattoo someplace before?"

"No." O'Brien replied.

"Well it is. I found it years ago, when I was prospecting, out off old Higgins Ranch Road on public land. Up on Mount…Mount…."

"Mount what?"

"That's the crazy part. Right now, I can't rightly remember the name, but I can take you there. Ain't that good enough?"

O'Brien tapped the unfinished drawing with his index finger. "Is this all you dragged me out of bed for?"

Slim stalled. "If you got to have the name of that mountain, I'll give you the name, but I need a minute or two. I do recollect it has something to do with the weather. Maybe Mount Storm Cloud. No, that don't sound right. Mount Lightning. No, that ain't it either. Mount Thunder…Thunder…."

The detective stood and walked to the door. "I'm going home. Call me tomorrow if you remember."

"Wait!" Slim was frantic. He had valuable information locked away in his faulty old memory. If O'Brien would quit pressuring him. "It's comin' to me. It was…"

Then, it hit him. Hallelujah!

Slim blurted out, "Mount Thunderdome," but when the name left his mouth, it still didn't sound right.

"And when did you say you found this place?"

"It was in 1969. And from what I saw that baby won't last long if they take her up there."

"Why do you think that?"

"Because what I found was an old altar stained with blood, and that same design as the girl's tattoo was carved into the sandstone beneath it. That makes sense, don't it? It's almost a full moon. Some freaked-out girl steals a baby, and she has a tattoo exactly like the symbol on some hoo-doo altar way out in the wilderness."

"Slim, I know you want to help, but I can't go dragging a search party out on this kind of information. You can't draw the complete tattoo or remember the correct name of the mountain."

"I told you the name."

"Now, you hold on a minute. I realize that compared to you, I'm still considered a newcomer in the Tucson area, but I've been here long enough to know something about the local landmarks, and I've never heard of a mountain with that name." The cop walked to a large county map posted on the wall and looked it over. "Nope, don't see any Mount Thunderdome up here either."

"The name won't be marked on any map. Only the locals call it Thunderdome."

"Why?"

"Because…because…." The more O'Brien pressed him, the less Slim remembered. He slammed his fist on the desk. The pencil cup flipped over, and a collection of pencils and pens clattered to the floor. "What does it matter why they call the mountain Thunderdome?" But even as Slim repeated the name, it clung to his tongue as if reluctant to be heard.

O'Brien sighed. "It matters to me."

Slim thought he could see contempt building in the younger man's eyes. The old man sagged back into his chair, his bravado draining away; confusion tattered the edges of his memory.

The police officer patted him on the shoulder. "Slim, no one blames you for what happened."

Tears stinging his eyes, Slim turned away. "That mama does."

"Slim, forget about what she said. She made a big mistake, and someone took her child. Now she needs to blame somebody besides herself. You just got in the way."

He took Slim's arm and gently helped him stand. "I want you to go home and get a good night's sleep. You took a bad spill when that girl punched you. When you're positive where you saw this marking, or exactly what it looks like, call me." O'Brien yawned. "Only next time, make sure it's not between the hours of midnight and six a.m. Okay?"

Confused and exhausted, Slim allowed the detective to walk him outside and help him into his car. As he waited for Queenie to warm up, he watched O'Brien drive away.

Didn't that young cop understand Tucson Slim had been in some kind of law enforcement for over sixty years and knew this part of Arizona better than most anyone? How could he doubt Slim's credibility? Didn't he care that a baby might be sacrificed on a lonely mountaintop by a bunch of ghouls? But why was Slim so shocked? Nobody trusted old folks anymore.

As he pulled away from the station, an almost full moon peeked up over the dark silhouettes of the distant mountains and flooded the desert below with soft creamy light, honing down the prickly edges, disguising the danger. For some reason, the moonlight brought Luis Martínez to mind. How many times had they watched the moon rise when they were camping up on Mount Thunderbolt?

Slim slammed on his brakes and ignored the car careening past him with horn blaring. That mountain's name was Thunderbolt, not Thunderdome. Thunderdome was the name of that Mad Max movie; the one with Tina Turner.

And then Slim remembered something he believed might even be more important than the name. After he found that altar, he reported it to the Tucson police. They should have a record of it.

Making a squealing u-turn, Slim raced back to the police station and found Officer Diaz still manning the desk.

The cop frowned when he saw Slim. "Detective O'Brien won't be back until eight a.m."

"This can't wait," Slim said.

"Can't you let the poor guy get some sleep?"

"But you don't understand. I told him the wrong thing. It ain't Mount Thunderdome. It's Mount Thunderbolt, and I remember exactly where that altar is. I got to talk to him."

"I'm not calling the detective, so you might as well go home." The officer pointed to the exit, his index finger making little sweeping motions.

That finger made Slim want to shake this disrespectful kid, but he reined in his temper for the sake of the baby. "I only came back to help O'Brien. Call him and tell him I reported what I saw up on Thunderbolt. There's bound to be a record of it."

Officer Diaz's smile disappeared. "Look, in case you don't get it, the police department is perfectly capable of handling our case load without some windy old fool who's known all over the state for his wild stories butting into our business."

The old man drew himself up to his full six foot four height. "If you weren't wearin' a uniform--."

"Well I am, and you're not. It's time you understood, law enforcement has changed a lot since you were a cop."

"I've seen the change, and I ain't all that thrilled with it and come to think about it, I ain't all that thrilled with you either."

Diaz smirked. "At least I don't go around plugging the tourists' cars. The only reason you aren't serving time on an aggravated assault charge is because Judge Phillips is your friend, and everybody else, including Mark O'Brien, feels sorry for you."

Slim's mouth quickly filled with a variety of colorful expletives. He knew if he said another word, they would all spill out and turn the air blue with a flood of profanity. Whether he liked it or not, this boy was a duly appointed peace officer. Slim's personal code of honor wouldn't allow him to disgrace the brotherhood he—-in his heart--still belonged to. He turned around and stormed out of the police station as fast as his damaged feet allowed.

Revving up the Pinto's engine to a high squeal, Slim peeled out onto Escadero Boulevard. Is this what his life had come to, people feeling sorry for him, laughing at him, thinking he was an old fool they could blow off without a qualm?

There had been a time when old folks were respected for the wisdom of their years, but not now. Not in the glorious New Millennium.

As the miles sped by, Slim's anger hardened into cold resolve. Someone had to rescue that baby, and it looked like the police weren't gonna do a thing. In the old days, when the law failed in its responsibility, the citizens stepped in. They were called vigilantes.

Tucson Slim, lone vigilante; had a nice ring to it.

Chapter 2

At eight the next morning, Slim called the Desert Valley Police Station and wasn't surprised to find out Mark O'Brien wasn't in his office like he said he'd be. Swallowing back his anger, he left a curt message with the officer at the desk, leaving both his home and office telephone numbers.

Having done his civic duty, the old man dressed for work. The moon wouldn't crest until the next night, so he had all day to come up with a foolproof strategy to rescue the child. He wanted to be prepared. Just in case the police failed to do their duty. Just in case the Lone Vigilante was needed.

What bothered the old man was he knew couldn't go up on Thunderbolt without weapons and take on a horde of demonic child killers all by himself. And to have weapons, he would have to break the law. But, in Slim's opinion, that was…."

What did the kids call it? A no-brainer. Yeah, everyone knew a child's life far outweighed any bad court decision. He'd strap on his weapons, bring that baby home to her mother, and show those swaggering pups in the Department who was a joke.

His mood lifted. And who knew what the future held? Maybe he'd do such a bang-up job, the authorities would relent and allow him to be the man he knew he was.

By mid-day Slim had come up with what he thought was a good plan to rescue the baby. Happy to have that out of the way, he stopped by the Mesquite Palace to feast on T-bone steak and baked potato; protein and carbs to stoke the furnace for his night on Thunderbolt. Besides the Palace fed him for free if he hung around and swapped stories with the tourists. Slim was always more than happy to eat steak and shoot the bull.

When he got back to his office, he decided to work on his novel for a while. Weaving the events of his own life into the life of his hero, Hank Stone, was always a challenge, but one he loved. Besides, if he didn't think about something else for a while, he'd start hashing and rehashing his plan, second-guessing himself, ripping his plan to shreds. Seemed like the older he got, the more he did that. Should he wear his jacket? Did he turn off the stove? Had he paid the light bill? Where was his checkbook? What was the name of almost anything?

While he waited for his office computer to boot up, Slim slipped his aching feet out of his moccasins and gingerly rested them on the small ottoman next to his desk. The sight of his crippled feet depressed him. Twisted like old tree roots, his toes overlapped, and his bunions were the size of walnuts. Feet like these came from too many years of wearing narrow, high-heeled cowboy boots.

Carter kept telling him he needed to go buy a pair of those German sandals. Said everyone was wearing "Stocks and socks" these days. Carter should have known, there was about as much chance of Tucson Slim wearing sandals, as there had been of him wearing those open-toed Taiwanese cowboy boots everybody wore in the Seventies. What had they called them? Thongs.

Why today, they called underwear thongs. Made the same way too, and the idea of a strap between his crippled toes sounded about as painful as having a strap between his...

He shuddered as he inserted his floppy disc in the proper slot and opened the file marked "Hank Stone." When the words he'd labored so long over appeared on the screen, Slim put on the half-glasses he hated, curled his gnarled fingers over the keyboard, ready to edit any mistake, to correct any misplaced word, and read his work.

Retribution: The Life and Times of
Marshal Hank Stone

A long, lean wraith of a man, Marshal Hank Stone of the Arizona Territory, stood in the middle of the deserted street and squinted into the blazing sun. Mid-afternoon. Time for Black Jack Billings' reckoning. When that outlaw rode into Hank's town and called down the thunder, Black Jack should have known he'd suffer the lightning that came with it.

A door creaked behind him. The Marshal stopped mid-step. His senses heightened, he turned toward the Hair of the Dog Saloon. A voice he knew all too well--Black Jack's deep, gravelly, bass--boomed out. "Marshal, you ready to meet your Maker?"

"Can't say that I am, Jack, but I can tell you this, you skin that smokewagon, and you'll die regrettin' it."

"Ol' man, that's mighty brave talk for an over-the-hill lawdog."

Bam! Bam! Bam! A barrage of bullets spattered the dust at Hank's feet.

Bam! Bam! Bam! "Gosh darn it, Slim! Open up. I know you're in there."

Slim froze, his mind playing catch-up as it jumped from his novel to reality.

Someone pounded on the door again. "Slim, I got that Special Delivery letter you been looking for."

Feeling like a condemned man who'd been granted a reprieve, Slim's old heart lurched. If Bran had done the right thing, Slim wouldn't have to break the law. He'd be able to legally carry his sidearm when he went for the baby.

He couldn't help but smile, when he slipped his reading glasses into his vest pocket, yanked opened the office door, and grabbed for the letter Don the mailman held in his freckled hand.

Don's thick eyebrows shot up and he jerked his hand back. "Hold your horses, Slim. You know darn good and well, there're procedures with a Special Delivery. First you gotta sign right here." He pointed to the card attached to the letter front and held out a pen.

As Slim scribbled his name across the bottom of the card, Don stood on his tiptoes and peered over the old man's shoulder into his office. "You working on your book again?" Don grinned. "Better not let the boss catch you. Remember what happened last time?"

Slim preferred not to think about that. Carter Winslow had been furious when he discovered Slim used his slack time and the Square's computer to write the great Western novel.

"Golly Ned's," Slim snapped. "Why can't you quit bein' such an all-fired busybody and just gimme my letter?"

The mailman ripped off the official receipt card and grinned. "She's all yours, old timer."

Grabbing the letter, Slim stepped back inside his office and closed the door. His old hands trembled as he put on his reading glasses again and opened the envelope. Taking a deep breath, he read,

Dear Mr. Stevens,

Re: the incident on March 31 of last year.

Judge Phillips has finished reviewing your case and has decided there is nothing he can do to help you regain the right to carry a sidearm in the state of Arizona.

Sincerely,

Sally Johannson

Court Assistant

Scrawled across the bottom of the page:

Slim, you made an agreement with the state. They did their part, now you do yours and stay out of trouble. You get arrested again, and you'll wind up in jail or at the very least, a nursing home.

Your old friend Bran

Slim wadded the offensive letter into a tight ball and threw it in the wastebasket. So much for the law helping him, he thought. He was on his own now, and whether they liked it or not, he'd be wearing his guns when he went to rescue the baby.

Too angry to sit down, he paced back and forth.

What happened to the good old days when every man had the right and the responsibility to protect and serve? Hadn't he fought in W.W.II to preserve the very Constitution that guaranteed its citizens the right to bear arms? And where in the blazes did Bran Phillips get off threatening Tucson Slim with a nursing home? Why, there hadn't been a nursing home built that could hold this old man!

Slim now knew he'd made a big mistake back when the D.A. offered him that deal. He should've lawyered up like any other felon. And God knew, after all his years in law enforcement, Tucson Slim didn't care much for lawyers. At the very least, he should have taken the time to think through all the consequences taking a deal would bring.

He should've taken his chances in court. If he'd won, he'd still be wearing his guns and not feeling like he'd been given a ride on the pointed end of a fence post.

Running out of steam, the old man sat at his desk. He didn't care what anyone said. He'd done the right thing standing up for that woman. No Arizona marshal, retired or not, would let some coward beat up on a female, any female. And they'd been fighting right there on the parking lot of Centennial Square—Slim's beat. But when he stepped in, the man went for what Slim thought was a gun. Slim thought he had to protect himself and did what came most naturally. He drew the Twins.

But then his hands started shaking. His gun went off, and he plugged the guy's Lexis. When the police showed up, they discovered what Slim thought was the tourist's gun was really a cell phone. But the cherry on the top of that whole mess was when the woman denied her husband had hit her and claimed she didn't know why Slim shot at them. No wonder cops hate domestic situations.

He shoved his glasses into his vest pocket and swung his chair around to face the gallery of eight-by-ten glossies hanging behind him. Pictures of all the stars he'd worked with through the years, everyone from Ben Johnson to Sam Elliot. He'd loved making movies and had been a real hot commodity back when he worked as an extra. And why wouldn't he have been? Six feet four inches of lean muscle, dark hair, blue eyes, a crack shot, able to ride, rope, and yodel.

But the years passed so quickly. One day he went to a casting call, and they'd told him he'd come to the wrong place. They were casting cowboys. The old men needed for the church scene were meeting on the other side of the set. Slim went home and never acted in another film. Growing old was such lousy repayment for years of good work

Reaching up, he straightened Clint Eastwood's picture. He and Clint had been in three films together, the last one being Slim's all-time favorite, The Legend of Josie Wales. Of course, Clint always had the starring role and Slim a wrangler/extra, but they'd spoken several times.

Right next to Clint hung a picture of young John Wayne. The first time Slim met the Duke, it had been in Utah. They'd been making a film called The Angel and the Badman. Wayne was a real man's man; even invited Slim to shoot skeet when they had time off. Slim still had the gun Duke had given him when they called it a wrap.

Catching sight of another photograph, Slim stared at the man he used to be, a rugged man, standing with the fabulous Patsy Cline. He'd been her bodyguard then.

Slim sighed. "You know, Patsy, sometimes I almost wish I'd been on that plane with you. Then everyone would remember me like I was in these photos."

Spying the crumpled letter lying on the floor, he got mad all over again. "Dag-nab-it! He yelled, "I'll show everyone no matter how old Tucson Slim is, he's still a man to be reckoned with!"

He yanked open the bottom desk drawer and took out his pair of custom, single action Colt 45's, his Twin Girls, each with a shining sterling silver star embedded in their mother of pearl handles. He'd gotten those pistols July 4th, 1970 for being the "Fastest Draw in the West" for five straight years.

After he thoroughly cleaned each of the Twins, he polished their bright nickel finish. "Tomorrow night, when I come against that kidnapper Dagger-girl and her soulless cohorts, you'll be right where you're supposed to be, in your Buscadero rig, strapped down, ready for service."

The old man put the pistols back in his desk drawer and leaned back in his chair. It was going to be a long next couple of days. A little extra shut-eye couldn't hurt.

The oldest living marshal in the state pulled his determination around him like a Kevlar shield and drifted off to sleep. He dreamed he was dancing with Patsy Cline, holding her in his arms, never doubting for an instant he could keep her safe. The warmth of her young body stirred Slim in a way he hadn't felt in a long time.

"Slim, wake up; the tour bus is here!"

Reluctantly opening one eye, the old man looked into the fashionably stubbled face of the Square's manager, Carter Winslow.

"Dag-nab-it, Carter," Slim grumbled as he sat up. "Can't you knock?"

"I did knock, Harold.

Slim tightened his mouth. Carter only called him Harold when he was going to ream him out about something.

"Harold," Carter said, "I came to tell the tour bus is here. Don't you remember what I said? One more screw up—and that includes being late for any of the tours--and you're outta here."

"I know, I know." Remembering the letter, Slim frowned. "I heard back from the judge. I ain't gettin' my guns back just yet."

Carter almost smiled. "Thank God! Now I can quit worrying you're going to blow some poor tourist away and bring down the mother of all lawsuits against the Square."

Slim bolted straight out of his chair. "I never shot no tourist. You know the bullet only nicked the car door. Why does everybody always make more out of it than it was?"

"Now, Harold."

But it was too late. Slim went on a tear. "You and the legal system--a bunch of weak sisters turnin' on a law-abidin' citizen while the city goes to hell in a handbag. A girl steals a baby right from under my nose and I can't do a thing, because I'm hobbled by a stupid court ruling. What kind of city do we live in? A perfectly reliable citizen can't carry a gun, but every gang kid has four."

Carter's voice dropped to a cold edge. "I did not come here to talk about the nation's gun control problem."

But Slim couldn't let it go. "Tell me what would have happened if I had'na been able to carry my sidearms the day that maniac tried to steal Patsy Cline's Caddie with her right there in the back seat. I stopped a kidnappin' that day, I did. I knew exactly what to do, and my movie star friends knew they could count on me."

Carter rolled his eyes and walked to the door. "For the millionth time, I don't want to hear any more of your windies about the old days and all the famous people you claim to know. Get out there and meet that bus."

# # #

By the time Slim got out to the parking lot, Great Western Tours had already deposited its payload of wide-eyed, whispering Japanese tourists at the front gate, and the driver had moved his bus to the back of the lot where he sat in air-conditioned comfort, his cap pulled low over his eyes. When the tourists saw their guide for the afternoon, their excited chatter stilled. They bowed.

As he returned their bow, Slim felt a little better. He'd learned to like the Japanese and their culture when he served on the staff of the great man himself, General Douglas MacArthur, after WW II. One of the Japanese traditions he'd especially come to admire these last few years was the esteem they held for their elderly. Worshipped them, even. Not that he wanted to be worshipped. He simply wanted to be treated with a little respect.

Smiling his Hollywood smile, Slim tipped his hat.

Twenty-five sets of excited Asian eyes fastened on him as the tourists lifted their cameras expectantly.

Always prepared to give the perfect photo op, Slim stopped dead in his tracks, his expression cold as flint. There was something about a camera that brought out the ham in him.

When the tourists finished snapping pictures, Slim smiled. "Ladies and gentlemen, welcome to Old Centennial Square."

With the interpreter translating in the background, Slim introduced himself. "I'm Tucson Slim, the oldest living marshal in Arizona, and I'm here to take you on a trip back to the year 1885. A time when the West was wild and cowboys were kings.

"Each shop in Old Centennial Square is a true representation of those found in the wild and woolly towns that sprang up across this vast desert in our great country's quest for gold. You'll see a bonafide silversmith at work. Meet the most beautiful saloon girls. Visit an old-timey photography studio where...for a moderate price...you can have your picture made wearing authentic Western duds. And as we make our journey, I'll tell you many true and unusual tales of the West."

He jerked around and looked into the Square. "Did y'all hear that? Sounded like trouble to me."

In a moment of forgetfulness, Slim slapped his thighs where his pistols should have been holstered. His hands came up empty.

Trying to cover his mistake, Slim dusted his hands on his jeans. He'd never get used to not wearing his pistols and felt plum unnatural without them. He took a deep breath to regain his composure, "Best keep your eyes peeled, partners. I hear tell the ghosts of the Clanton gang lurk in the shadows of the Square. They're a-waitin' for the Earp brothers and old Doc Holiday to show up, and I don't doubt that one day, when the spirits are ready, we'll be caught in the middle of a gunfight that would envy the likes of the OK Corral." Back in the flow, he lowered his voice. "Who knows, it might even be today."

A titter of nervous laughter skittered across the crowd.

"Now, y'all follow me. Our first stop'll be the Silver Nugget Cafe where you can fill your canteens or have a frosty cold sarsaparilly. You can also purchase all the film you'll need for our walk through the Old West."

Obediently, Slim's charges queued up behind him. He led them to the Nugget, allowed them to file in, and waited. When he heard the gasps of appreciation the guests always made when they saw the nine-foot-tall portrait of Tucson Slim in full western regalia hanging over the old-fashioned soda fountain, he strolled in. At eighty, he'd take his strokes any way he could get them.

# # #

After his charges were safely on the bus and heading to their next destination, Slim limped back to his office to collect the Twins and go home. Sweat trickled around his nose and into his shaggy mustache. He stopped to swipe his handkerchief across his face. Heat from the scorched walkway radiated through the soft leather of his moccasins, easing his aching feet.

Struck with a burst of literary inspiration, he pulled a small notebook out of his pocket and jotted down a line for his book. "The unrelenting July sun beat down like bright hate straight from the belly of hell." Saying it again slowly, Slim smiled. "Yeah, that's good."

"I'm calling you out, marshal!"

Slim whirled around to face the one that dared to draw down on the law.

In the center of the Square, Carter's six-year-old son, Winston, curly blond hair peeking out from under a red felt cowboy hat, glared at him through squinted eyes. His small hand hovered over the cap pistol stashed in the plastic holster at his side. "Time to face the Arizona Kid."

Slim patted his hips and held up empty hands. "Boy, you know you can't draw down on an unarmed man."

The boy's bright blue eyes darted to the empty spaces on Slim's hips. "You ever gonna wear the Twins again?"

It was hard to explain to a six year old what Slim didn't understand himself. "Seems like there's a new law in the Square, partner. No real guns allowed."

Throwing his hat down in a fit of temper, Winston whined, "Then how are we gonna practice our quick draw?"

Carter stepped out of his office. "Slim, isn't it time for you to punch out? You know how I feel about overtime."

The boy pulled on Slim's hand. "I said, how we gonna practice our quick draw?"

Slim glanced at Carter's stern face, and then down at the boy. "I got to go now. You keep on practicing in the mirror like I showed you, and maybe one day, the Twin's will be back where they belong."

The boy rubbed the toe of his red cowboy boot across the pavement. "Hey, I got an idea. Let's go buy you a cap pistol like mine. Then we can practice and still follow the rule."

Appalled by the very thought of wearing a toy weapon, Slim snapped, "I can't wear no toy gun. I'm a grown man."

Lower lip trembling, Winston picked up his hat and glared at Slim. "You're no fun any more. I'm gonna go find a new friend."

Rejected by his most ardent fan, Slim shuffled back to his office. The rift in his ego grew. His horse was dead. His feet hurt all the time. His friends were mostly gone. Even the Sizzlin' Shooters, a quick draw club he'd help organize, seemed to be avoiding him. The government took away his guns. He'd failed to save that baby, and now, he'd lost his number one fan.

Life had become one indignity heaped upon another.

# # #

Before he left the office that afternoon, Slim tried to call Detective Mark O'Brien one last time and got the man's voice mail again. Still refusing to speak to a machine, he called back and left another brief message and his number with the officer at the desk.

When he hadn't heard anything by early the next morning, Slim knew the police were not interested in anything he had to say. So as he prepared to leave on his mission, he did so in perfect peace. He'd given law enforcement every opportunity to do the right thing. Time for the Lone Vigilante to act.

Everything was in place. His guns were ready. His gear was packed. He had enough food and water for a couple of days. And he'd called the Martínez ranch and borrowed a horse. His Queenie couldn't go where he was headed.

When he was ready to walk out the door, in a last ditch effort to find support in this dangerous endeavor, Slim called Sam Turnbow, the president of the Sizzlin' Shooters Quick Draw Club. Slim would bite the bullet and ask for their help.

He knew the Shooters didn't use their guns except for performance and in contests, but he hoped his old cronies would show up on horseback and look impressive. If they did that much, he thought the bad guys would scatter like the cowards they were, and he could save the baby.

"Hello?" Sam's raspy voice was unmistakable.

"Turnbow, this is--."

"Yee-haw, got you. In case you haven't figgered it out yet, Sam and Dotty cain't come to the phone right now. After you hear the music, leave a message, and if this is my little Tootie, you can call Pap-paw and Mam-maw on our cell phone. You got the number."

Slim fought the urge to hang up. Obviously, if he wanted to get the Shooters' help, he'd have to break the vow he'd made all those years ago and talk to an infernal contraption. He guessed he'd be breaking a lot of vows to save this child.

When the tinny rendition of <u>Tumblin'</u> <u>Tumbleweeds</u> ended, he said, "Sam, this is Tucson Slim. I need the Shooters to meet me at the Martínez ranch at first light. Life and death situation. Bring your horses and your guns."

He paused trying to decide how much truck he wanted to have with all the new doo-dads in today's world, then concluded his message. "And bring that cell phone thing-a-ma-jig. Where we're headin', it sure won't hurt to have a way to get a hold of the police if we need 'em."

After he concluded his call, without a moment's hesitation or a backward glance, he quickly loaded the Twins in his usual manner. Load a cartridge, skip a cartridge, load four more. The old Colts didn't have safeties so he carefully set the hammer on the empty chamber. Only fools would carry a fully loaded six-shooter unless they were heading into a full-fledged firefight. He'd assess the situation up on Thunderbolt and add the sixth round if necessary.

Slim buckled his double Buscadero rig around his waist and pushed the loaded cartridge belt low over his narrow hips. When the holsters hung even with his hands for a quicker draw, he tied them tight against his skinny thighs with the leather leg thongs.

The very act of putting on his guns cleared his mind. For the first time in months, he felt like the real Tucson Slim, and not that namby-pamby milquetoast the state was trying to make him. Today he felt like a real Arizona Marshal.

With that thought, the old man faltered. No, he wasn't an Arizona Marshal any longer. When he strapped on his guns, he'd chosen the path of lawlessness, a path that could and probably would lead straight to jail.

Shaking off those unsettling thoughts, Slim set his jaw. If he went to jail, so be it. He'd vowed to save that baby, and he was gonna bust his butt to do it.

In a quick, polished move, he went for his guns. His skin whispered as it brushed against smooth leather, and the Twins nestled in his hands like they'd never left.

Satisfied, Slim hefted the pistols and coldly smiled. Hard-pressed, he would have to admit he had probably lost some of his edge in the last few months, but even if he was a little rusty, his years of experience would carry him through.

Slim picked up his rifle and sighted down the long, blued barrel. His Winchester 94 with its varnished walnut stock rivaled anything out there. Slinging the rifle over his shoulder, he picked up his double action .41 Colt Thunderer with a bird's head grip and a barrel only three and one half inches long. He slipped the reliable old hideout pistol he'd had for years into the small holster hidden under his arm. Just in case anyone came too close.

He stowed his gear in Queenie's trunk, his heart pounding with excitement and anticipation. The emotions Slim thought every lawman must feel when he set out to right a wrong. And today, Tucson Slim would do just that. By tomorrow, that baby would be back home.

Chapter 3

As Slim drove through the main gate of El Rancho de Sol, Luis Martínez' modest spread on the backside of Thunderbolt Mountain, the staccato brrr of his tires skimming across the cattle guard warmed his heart just like the squeak of his mama's screen door always had when he was a button coming home from school.

He hadn't been out here since four months after Dolores, Luis's wife, passed away two years ago. That was when Luis up and married that <u>chica</u> half his age. Losing Dolores had been bad enough, but to see his best friend for almost fifty years, defiling his own wife's memory, living in Dolores' house, sleeping in her bed with that strange female--well, it simply made Slim sick.

He'd been glad when that faithless Luis and his woman moved down old Mexico way to Guadalajara and left his son Raúl in charge of the ranch.

Rounding the last bend in the drive, Slim was unable to stifle the futile surge of hope he felt. But just as he'd known she wouldn't be, Dolores wasn't in her beloved garden filled with cactus, native plants and flowers, not on the shady porch, not in this world.

The ranch house sprawled out across the landscape like an adobe fortress. Slim had helped build this house, one new room for each of Dolores' six kids. Helping Luis through the years, Slim had strung enough fence to encircle the place a couple of times, broke more than his fair share of horses, and attended more christenings, weddings, birthdays, and wakes out here than he cared to remember. The Martínez ranch would always feel like home. Dolores had lived here; sweet little Dolores, how he missed her bright eyes and soft voice.

As he pulled up in front of the house, a red and white blur darted out from under a lantana bush, barking like crazy. Paco, a border collie/Australian Shepherd mix, was the ranch watchdog and one of top cow dogs in the county.

Jumping up on the side of the car, Paco yapped until Slim reached out and let him sniff his hand. The barking stopped, and Paco, his tailless backside wriggling with delight, whined and nuzzled the old man's fingers.

Slim scratched behind the dog's red merle ears. "Good to see you too, Paco old boy."

"Paco, leave Tío alone." A welcoming smile on her lined face, Raúl's wife, María ran out of the house carrying foil-wrapped bundle in her hands. The hot wind lifted her swirling skirt, exposing her bare feet and pudgy thighs. Silver strands reflected the morning sun throughout her thick, black hair.

Melancholy crept over Slim like a shadow. María had been a drop-dead gorgeous girl thirty years and four kids ago. Now, she looked old and a little too fat. At what age does time become such a hateful thing--sneaking up on you--like a thief in the night? One day you wake up and find your beauty and strength and clearness of mind have all slipped away, like sand through your fingers.

Still smiling, María pushed the dog aside, leaned her forearms on the car, and peeked in the open window. "<u>Buenos días</u>, Tío Slim."

María called him Tío like all Dolores' girls did. "<u>Buenos días</u> to you, Marícita."

"It is good to see you."

Her melodious Spanish accent rested easy on Slim's old ears. He tipped his hat. "And if you aren't a sight for sore eyes, I'll give it up."

"Then shame on you, old friend, for neglecting us."

Slim ducked his head. "I know, Marícita. I'm sorry."

"It's okay. You visit soon, <u>sí</u>?" María, a Yauqui Indian from northern Mexico, patted his shoulder with a hand that was broad and brown.

Slim drifted back to another time a woman had leaned against his car and patted his shoulder. The last time he saw Dolores, right before she had that stroke. Only Dolores, descended from high-blood Spanish, had pale, delicate hands.

"Tío Slim, you okay?"

Snapped back to the present, Slim answered gruffly. "Of course, I'm okay. Why wouldn't I be?"

The woman winced at his sharp response. Instantly ashamed, Slim apologized. "Sorry, María. The last few days have been hard. I guess I'm a little tired."

"I understand. She gave him the flat foil bundle. "For you, she said, "Hand-patted, still hot from the griddle."

Determined to end their conversation on a high note, Slim grinned and said, "Muchas gracias, Miss María. My mouth started watering for a bite of your tasty tortillas the minute I turned off the highway."

Giggling like a girl, María blushed. "I don't forget how much you love them. Come in. We'll have café con leche, my friend." She raised an eyebrow and gave him an alluring look. "I make huevos rancheros for breakfast."

The thought of eggs lavished with fiery Mexican salsa made Slim's stomach growl. He hadn't eaten since yesterday noon. "I'd sure love that, but I can't today." He nodded toward the foil-wrapped tortillas. "I'll just eat on these while I ride up to Thunderbolt."

María's expressive face clouded and she crossed herself. "Why you want to go up on that evil mountain for? Father Paul says it is a place where many strange things happen."

"Don't worry, Marícita. I can handle myself. Now, where is that hombre, Raúl?"

"He is at the barn. He said I am to keep Paco here with me."

"That's good thinking. I don't need him following me up the mountain. Has anyone else shown up yet?"

"No, Tío. You are the only person I've seen."

"Gol-durned answering machines," he mumbled. He knew they couldn't be trusted. His hopes of having Sam Turnbow and the Sizzlin' Shooters waiting at the barn, all mounted and ready to ride like an old-fashioned posse, evaporated. If he hadn't been so tired, he would have blown-up. He helped start that club. They had a lot of nerve ignoring his plea for help.

Anxiety gnawed at Slim's confidence. He was only a frail old man. What good would he be all by himself fighting a swarm of crazies? Maybe he should go on home and let the cards fall where they may.

But if he went back home without trying, he would always hear the sound of a baby's cry and know what had happened to her on that altar. He had no choice. He had to go.

# # #

Slim's old heart lurched when he saw the silhouette of a man standing in the shadow of the barn. Short and stocky, bowed legs, an ample belly—Luis! Why hadn't María told him that old tomcat was out here?

The man stepped into the sun. Luis disappeared and there stood the only man Slim ever thought he would have liked to have as his very own son. With his mother's smile and gentle disposition, Raúl was a good boy.

Slim got out of the car. "Hola, amigo."

"Good to see you, Marshal Slim." Raúl grasped his hand and pumped it. "Just because Papá lives in Mexico now, don't mean you can't come to visit me and María."

"I know, I know. Your woman already busted my chops on that account."

Raúl's grin broadened. "Just as she said she would. María don't let no one get away with nothing. She is like mi madre."

Afraid his raw emotions would show if they continued to discuss Dolores, Slim said, "Look, Raúl, as much as I'd like to stand around and shoot the bull, I gotta get out of here before the sun gets too high. I'll get my gear, and head on out, if it's okay with you."

He unlocked the trunk of his car. Canteens clanking dully, he shifted them onto his shoulder and picked up his rifle and his black canvas duster.

Raúl laid his hand on Slim's arm. "I maybe should go with you."

Slim shrugged the younger man off. "Not this time, okay?"

"It is not good for a man your age to ride off into the desert alone. Papá called and when I told him you were coming, he said if you refuse for me to come, I cannot loan you the horse."

"He said what," Slim slammed the trunk lid down with a hollow bang.

Raúl hung his head. "Papá is right. Such a trip is too dangerous for even a younger man to make alone. I have two of our best all saddled and ready to go. Por favor, amigo, it would honor me to go with you."

Narrowing his eyes, Slim stared at Raúl. Did this boy think Slim was too feeble to take care of himself?

Raúl's steady black eyes held Slim's gaze.

The old man's anger dissipated. Since the Shooters didn't bother to show up, maybe he could use Raúl's help. What if he ran into more of those devil worshipers up there than he figured?

"Raúl, I hope you got your rifle and plenty of water and grub. I only brought for one. I didn't plan on having to take Luis's niño with me."

"I packed well...like you taught me." Raúl grinned good-naturedly. "And you forget I am fifty-six, Marshal Slim. I'm no longer a niño, now I am a grandfather, un abuelo.

"Great! Now I've got to baby-sit an old man. I have a hard enough time keeping myself out of trouble." He slapped Raúl on the back. "Well, let's get a move on, abuelito. Daylight's burning, and we got business up on Thunderbolt."

Even though the morning was still young, the sun had already turned the desert into an outdoor oven, baking all who dared to trespass. Sweat trickled down from under Slim's black hat and stung his eyes as he munched on one of María's tortillas, savoring the taste of freshly ground corn. "Raúl, your María is truly an expert tortilla maker."

"Sí," Raúl agreed. "Mamá taught her well."

Slim stuffed another tortilla in his mouth and spurred his horse to a faster gait. He didn't want to be distracted talking about Dolores.

"Marshal Slim," Raúl called after him, "you did not explain to me what you are looking for on this old montaña. You think maybe there is still gold to be found?"

Slim turned in his saddle. "If you aren't a mystery to me, Raúl Martínez. You ride out here--into this inferno--with a old man most of Tucson thinks is crazy, and you're just now getting around to asking me what we're going to do."

"If you think it is important, it must be. Besides, I have always trusted you. I know you are not loco."

Slim took a moment to bask in the compliment. There were so few left who really trusted him. "I hope you feel the same way when I tell you why we're making this trip. It ain't a pretty story."

After explaining why they were there and what they had to do, Slim swallowed his pride and told Raúl how the police had acted when he tried to tell them about Thunderbolt. He was sure he saw a look of pity cross Raúl's agreeable face more than once, but decided to ignore it. He guessed if Raúl had crossed-over to join the club for those who patronized old men, Slim could learn to deal with it. Maybe in the morning, when this whole shebang was settled and the baby was back home with her mother, things would be as they once were, back when he garnered respect, back when people looked up to him.

Slim led Raúl through a forest of saguaros casting thready shadows that offered little respite from the blazing sun. He pointed to an old animal trail. "We're gonna follow this on up the backside of the mountain, so's no one can see us. As I remember, the actual road crisscrosses across the north face of Thunderbolt and ends somewhere near where I saw the altar."

Raúl nodded. "I know which road that is. I have seen where it cuts off the main highway. It is fit only for four-wheel drives and desert buggies."

"Yep, that's the one, all right." Slim coaxed his mount up the narrow trail. "Abuelito, I hope these horses are as good as you say."

The farther up the mountain they rode, the more nervous the horses became, jumping at every noise, walling their eyes and snorting. By the time they reached the high rocks on the south side of the mountain, the sun loomed straight over their heads. Tired from fighting his horse, saddle sore, and bleary-eyed from the lack of sleep, Slim felt every one of his eighty years.

They found a spot where the horses could wait in the shade. His old bones creaking and complaining, Slim slid out of the saddle, and he and Raúl tied the nervous horses on picket lines.

Slim's roan gelding whinnied and moved closer to Raúl's fat mare. "What's gotten into him?" Slim grumbled.

The younger man looked at Slim with big, round eyes. "Do you not feel it, Marshal Slim? I fear there is great evil here."

Slim didn't feel anything except tired, but he knew Raúl was his mother's son. Dolores had grown up in El Paso, Texas, where she became an accomplished curandera, a folk healer. Sensitive to the spiritual forces at work around her, she'd had great success healing the mal puestroes, illnesses of the spirit caused by curses from Indian brujas, witches. Maybe the boy inherited his mother's gift. If he had, he might be a target for evil spirits as she had been, only as far as Slim knew, Raúl knew nothing about the healing arts.

Slim wanted the younger man's help and company, but not as much as he wanted Raúl to be safe. "Look, amigo, this ain't your problem. You don't have to stay. I don't want to be responsible for dragging you into a dangerous situation."

Squaring his shoulders, Raúl took a deep breath and slowly exhaled. "I will stay. In these last months I have heard many rumors along the border about worshippers del Diablo, you know, the ones who serve the devil, mixing drugs with sacrifice. But now, to know they may be true and so close to my home, to my grandchildren. I will not leave. Besides, María sent protection."

He pulled several silver medallions out of his pocket, crossed himself with them, and kissed one. "She is at the church this very minute lighting candles and praying to the Blessed Virgin de Guadalupe, and San Miguel, and even though it may not help much, our old friend Saint Christopher that we may be safe in this wicked place."

He selected a medal and offered it to Slim, but the old man waved him away.

Raúl crossed himself again and returned the talismans to his pocket. "I'll keep it for you. With divine help we will save the baby and inform the police."

Raúl puffed out his chest and tapped it with his fist. "Tomorrow, the grandfather and the old marshal will have made Arizona a safer place, and you, my old friend, will have regained the respect they have stolen from you."

Wishing he felt as confident, Slim smiled weakly. Who knew, maybe María's prayers would help, and they certainly couldn't hurt. Now, if only the members of the Sizzlin' Shooters Quick Draw Gun Club were as loyal.

With great flourish, he added the club's name to the long list he was forming in his mind under the heading: Things and People I No Longer Have Any Use For.

What was that old saying? Fail me once, shame on you. Fail me twice, shame on me. Well, in Slim's world it was, fail me at all and it's all over between us. That's what had happened to his relationship with Luis, Raúl's father and Slim's oldest friend. Luis had let everyone down.

Slinging his rifle over his shoulder, Slim picked up the rest of his gear, and watching for rattlesnakes and scorpions, led Raúl up the narrow path. Sharp stones jabbing into the soles of his leather moccasins tortured his damaged feet. The old man set his jaw and pressed on, hoping Raúl could not see how he winced with pain, how he fought to stay on his feet, how worthless he'd become.

Cursing his bad luck, his age, and his feet with every step, Slim picked his way through the cactus plants and rocks hoping to find a good place to hide, one where they could see the altar, but not be seen.

Hearing the younger man's labored breathing brought Slim to a stop. He turned.

Red-faced and sweating, Raúl struggled up the steep mountainside. When he saw Slim staring at him, he leaned against a boulder and wiped his face. Still huffing, he said, "You move like a goat of the mountains, old friend."

"A goat with bad feet," Slim mumbled. They waited until Raúl caught his breath and continued up the mountain, not stopping until they were above the place he'd seen the altar. After they found a large flat ledge where they could hide but still see the clearing below, Slim made sure the place was rattlesnake free and crawled to the edge of the high cliff. Raúl followed close behind.

Below them, in an almost perfect circle of large boulders and thick desert underbrush, a natural sandstone amphitheater littered with trash baked in the hot sun. Pocked-marked and holey, several giant saguaros with their arms held high in silent supplication, had been used for target practice. In the center of the clearing stood the stained rock altar Slim remembered.

"Looks like we're the first ones to arrive for this here soiree," Slim said.

Raúl nodded. "And now I understand why they've been able keep their evil ways hidden. You cannot see this side of the mountain from the road."

Dropping the canteens, Slim lowered himself into a spot of shade. Raúl plopped down across from him and opened his saddlebag. He pulled out a plastic container filled with tamales wrapped in cornhusks. "Take one."

"No need," Slim said. "I brought my own food."

"Don't matter. María said to share these with you. She says since Mamá passed on, you are thinner each time we see you."

"Don't much like cookin' for myself." Slim unwrapped María's offering and took a bite. He closed his eyes and sighed as he savored the delectable morsel, a perfect blend of masa, pork, and spice.

He swallowed and smiled at Raúl. "I tell you what. That María is a true tamale artiste."

Raúl beamed. "She learned from the best."

"Your mama," Slim,asked.

Raúl nodded.

Taking another bite, Slim thought about the first time he had tasted Dolores' tamales in 1942.

Raúl wolfed down his share, while Slim slowly chewed, taking pleasure in the memories the taste of tamale resurrected in his mind.

Raúl said, "I always wondered. Why did you never marry?"

The image of Dolores Martínez' exotic beauty, sparkling eyes, and thick, curling auburn hair lingered in Slim's mind. Despite the fact his bittersweet love for Raúl's mother had never been about carnal desire or the need to possess, Slim's face burned with embarrassment. He'd always considered his devotion to Dolores a sacred thing to be hidden in his heart forever, cherished, revered, but never revealed.

Slim shrugged. "What woman in her right mind would want to marry an old codger like me?"

"You weren't always old. Mamá used to say that when you and Papá were in the movies together-- for a gringo, you were a very good-looking vaquero. Why didn't some beautiful senorita catch you then?"

Slim's heart pounded as he latched on to the revelation that his sweet Dolores thought he was good-looking. Suddenly afraid he'd give himself away, Slim averted his gaze and concentrated on his tamale.

Raúl chuckled. "Hey, amigo, your face is red. Maybe there is a senorita in your past." He leaned closer, a sly grin playing at the corners of his mouth. "Just between us two viejos--."

"Oh, so we're old men now?"

Raúl grinned. "Who was she, Slim? Inquiring minds like me want to know."

Slim forced himself to look at Raúl. "I don't mean to talk about it, so your might as well let it go."

Leaning back against the rock, Raúl grinned. "So there was someone. All us kids wondered about that, and after we were grown, we asked Mamá. She said she thought you carried the torch for someone. Maybe a woman you met in the war."

Slim groused, "I never knew my love life was a topic that would interest a bunch of kids."

"Oh yes, my sisters especially, Raul replied," They all wanted to marry you, you know."

The idea of Raúl's five pig-tailed sisters pining away for an old man like him made Slim chuckle. "Now if I hadda known that…"

"See how well I keep a secret. You can trust me."

Raúl had always been this way. He'd peck away like a chicken after a kernel of grain until Slim told him something. The Martínez kids had always been a nosy bunch. An irritating quality they'd inherited from Luis, no doubt.

"Once upon a time there was a lady, but it wasn't meant to be. 'Nuff said."

"Was she pretty, Slim? As pretty as my María?"

In an effort to take the spotlight off his love life, Slim winked at Raúl. "I'll tell you this, abuelito, if I'da found a woman who cooks like your María, looks would've only been a minor consideration."

Raúl sighed. "María is a rare jewel. Without her, life for me would be unbearably lonely. Do you ever get lonely, old friend?"

"Sometimes, but I figger things usually turn out the way they're supposed to. I guess having a woman wasn't in the cards for me."

"I thank the Virgin each day for María. She is the heart of my life, the reason I open my eyes each day for almost forty years."

Raúl's deep love for his wife enflamed the old longing deep in Slim's gut. He had always wanted the special companionship only true love and a marriage could bring. It was just his luck to fall in love with his best friend's wife.

It was almost like Raúl could read his thoughts. "Marshal Slim, are you still angry with my father?"

Slim choked on his tamale. When he cleared his throat, he asked, "Who said I was mad at your daddy?"

Raúl shrugged. "You do not hide your anger well, old friend. We all knew how you felt when Papá married so soon after our mother passed."

"Well, now that you bring it up, that did chap me pretty good. Luis didn't even have the decency to wait a year. And then he picked a girl half his age--."

Laughter erupted from Raúl's mouth along with a half-chewed tamale. "Conchita is no girl! It is true she is much younger than Papá, but not half his age. Papá is eighty, a hale and hearty eighty, like you, and Conchita is already sixty."

Surprised, Slim stopped chewing.   Conchita seemed so young.

"Marshal Slim, maybe I should tell you something Mamá said a few days before she had the stroke. Then you will understand why my sisters and me accepted Papá's new wife so quietly."

Slim wanted to yell, "Don't tell me anymore about your mother," but as much as he knew it would hurt him, the old man still hungered to hear anything his darling Dolores might have said. Woven in and out like ugly black thread in a cloth of pure gold, pain had always been part and particle of Slim's love for Dolores,

"Mamá said that when she left this earth we should encourage Papá to marry again…soon. She said Papá could never survive this life without a woman by his side."

Slim's gut churned. The boy didn't know it, but his old man couldn't survive a walk down the street without a woman…any woman… by his side.

"Marshal Slim, Papá is your oldest friend and you know he is no saint, but Mamá also knew."

Slim blurted out, "Dolores knew?"

"<u>Sí.</u>"

"Why would she live with that?"

"She accepted the fact that Papá found monogamy…well… difficult. It was the way of her old Spanish family, you know? She told me her own father and grandfather had mistresses. But she raised us different. She said no child of hers would ever inflict or have to endure such pain." The younger man stopped talking and unwrapped another tamale.

Slim stared out across the desert. He'd never minded Luis's roving eye before Dolores died. The more time that old dog spent away from home meant more time for Slim to spend with Dolores…Dolores and her ever-increasing passel of kids. He tried to remember if she'd ever shown any sign that she might be worried or hurt about anything Luis might be up to when he wasn't at home. Slim didn't think so, but he wasn't sure. Maybe he'd always been so busy adoring her, he hadn't noticed she carried so heavy a burden.

Grieved, Slim hung his head. What kind of friend had he been to the woman he loved more than life itself?

When he finished his last tamale, Raúl continued. "So, you see, when Papá said he wanted to marry again so soon, we knew Mamá had given her permission, so we tried to smile and go along with what he wanted. Please, old friend, I would like for you to also honor Mamá's final wish. She would be unhappy if she knew her death caused this terrible rift between her husband and their dearest friend."

Slim wasn't sure how he felt about any of this. He mumbled, "I'll have to think on this some."

The younger man smiled. "That is all I ask." Raúl put the tamale container away and looked at Slim expectantly. "Now, tell me your plan."

"It's simple. I'm going in alone to find the baby--."

"Alone?"

"That's what I said, ain't it?"

"Marshal Slim--."

"Don't argue, we're going to do this my way or you, my young friend, can hit the highway. Like I said, I'm going to hide down there, and when all those perverts have arrived and it's good and dark, I'll glide in like a ghost and find the baby. Before they know what's going on, I'll grab her and disappear into the night."

"What is my part in this plan?"

"You'll wait up here with the horses. If anything goes wrong you'll have to be the one who calls the police."

"But--," Raul objected.

Slim held up his hand. "I said don't argue with me. I'm the head honcho here. You got that?"

He waited for a moment to see if Raúl would continue to disagree, but the younger man was quiet. Slim said, "Once I have the baby, I'll bring her back up here, and we'll ride out under the cover of night. Wham, bam, we're in. We're out. Now, if there is trouble, and I ain't planning on any, you hightail it home and call…"

That Detective's name had been right on the tip of his tongue and now it was gone. Why did his mind always fail him when he needed it most?

"Who do I call?" Raúl asked.

"Give me a minute. Detective…Detective…. I know his first name started with a 'M'. Mickey, maybe." He rolled the name over his tongue to test it. Mic-keyyy. That was it, Mickey. Now what was the rest of it?

Slim hated these spells of forgetfulness. They made him feel old and worthless, especially when Raúl just sat and stared at him.

"It's coming. Detective Mickey…Mickey…Rourke! That's it Detective Mickey Rourke at the Desert Valley Police Station!"

Raúl looked puzzled. "Mickey Rourke? Like the actor?"

"Are you questioning me?"

The look of puzzlement remained, but Raúl said, "Whatever you say, Marshal Slim. I'll call Detective Mickey Rourke."

"I want to make one thing perfectly clear. Under no circumstances are you to follow me down there. Somebody has to call in the cavalry if I can't control the situation. Comprende?"

Raúl shrugged. "I understand, but I do not like it."

"Don't make no never-mind to me if you like it or not. That's the way it's gonna be." Slim checked his pocket watch. "We got us a few hours, and it's only going to get hotter. I'll take the first watch. Try to get some rest."

It didn't take long for Raúl to doze off. His light raspy snore joined the trill of a nearby grasshopper and produced an unusual harmony. Combined with the oppressing heat, the sound lulled Slim. Fighting sleep, he watched a lean hare venture out into the clearing below and go about the business of finding food in the desert. The saguaros' shadows slowly stretched out across the hare's domain as the sun rolled across a brilliant blue sky following the same path it had for millions of years. In a place of such serene beauty, who would have thought they were up here to prevent a murder?

Slim sipped the tepid water from his old canteen. The afternoon dragged by as he pondered Raúl's request. Slim wasn't sure he wanted to forgive Luis. If he did, he would have no excuse to stay away from the Martínez tribe and being around them was too blamed hard, stirring up too many old buried feelings, confirming how empty his life was.

He thought of the first time he ever saw Dolores. It had been during World War Two. He'd come to Tucson on his last leave before the Marines shipped him to the Pacific and ran into an old movie friend, Luis Martínez. After a few beers, Luis asked him to come out to his ranch.

Slim didn't even know his old running buddy Luis had married until Dolores came out of the house to greet them. Like a Latin Madonna, she'd stood there in the sunlight, her belly big with child, her hand on her hip, her long auburn hair blowing in the hot afternoon wind.

The moment Slim saw her, the earth stopped moving, the songbirds lost their voice, and Tucson Slim gave away his heart. Mesmerized, he was captured by her silvery laugh, her dark eyes flashing inner light, her radiant smile, the tiny hand she ran carelessly through her auburn hair. That enchanting picture of Dolores standing in the sun stayed with him all through the war until it became permanently etched in his mind.

By the time the war ended, he knew he would love her forever. Hating himself for coveting another man's wife, he swore to God he would never see her again. But on the set of his very first post-war movie, there stood Luis and Dolores with their daughters, three of the prettiest little girls he'd ever seen, each one the image of their mama. And from that moment on, he was completely lost. Slim would never steal his friend's wife, but he had to see her, talk to her. He had to be near her or life had no meaning.

His eyes stinging with tears, Slim gulped down more water. He'd never wanted anything in his whole life the way he wanted Dolores, but she never knew. Thank God, she never knew.

Slowly screwing the lid back onto his canteen, weariness settled in on Slim like a great weight. He laid the canteen down, stretched out his long legs, and after a moment, gave up fighting sleep and joined Raúl in an afternoon siesta.

# # #

Running through the dark, dodging cactus and rocks, hearing the grunts and squeals of the demons behind him, Slim yelled, "Call Detective Mark O'Brien! Call him now!"

Drenched in sweat, Slim jerked awake and saw Raúl crouched on the edge of the cliff, staring at him.

"What did you say?" Raúl asked.

Shaking his shaggy head, Slim tried to clear his mind. The demons' cries grew faint; his pounding heart slowed. He pulled his bandana off his neck and mopped his sweaty face.

"Are you okay, Marshal Slim? Who is Mark O'Brien?"

Disheartened, Slim stood, walked to the edge of the cliff, and spat on the rocks below. Mickey Rourke! How could the memory of something that happened over fifty years ago be as sharp and clear as glass, and he couldn't remember the name of the man he met yesterday? It was plum disgusting.

"I told you wrong, Raúl. That Detective's name is Mark O'Brien, not Mickey Rourke. I can't even keep anybody's gol-durned name straight anymore."

Raúl smiled. "Don't worry so, amigo. Sometimes I have that problem too."

Slim stared at the clearing below where the setting sun washed the boulders and brush with an eerie blood-red light that was soon absorbed by the black desert night. The evening wind blew cool against his damp skin. His mind cleared.

"When do you think they'll come, Marshal Slim, the devil-worshippers?"

"I expect when it gets closer to midnight we'll see them scurry out like a horde of cockroaches. Pests like that always do their dirty business under the cover of night."

"I'll be glad when the moon rises," Raúl said. "I do not like the dark so much up here in this evil place."

Slim heard the nervous tremor in his friend's voice and decided a colorful story might help pass the time and keep Raúl focused on something besides why they were here. "You know, this reminds me of a picture me and your daddy did back in the early 70's. Duel in Darkwater Draw." He paused and scratched his head. "Duel at Darkwater Draw? Maybe it was Death at Darkwater…."

When Raúl didn't help him out, Slim shrugged. "Anyway, we played wild, hell-raising <u>banditos</u> in that one. Real bad guys hiding in a canyon, waiting to ambush the posse that was chasin' us. But the Sheriff, played by my good friend Ben Johnson, was smarter than we thought. He turned the tables on us, and those the posse didn't kill, was hung from a tree at the end of the film."

He paused. Once more, Raúl remained silent. Slim didn't understand. Raúl liked to talk about Slim's old movie days almost as much as Slim did.

Deciding his friend was too nervous to make small talk, Slim rattled on. "Yep, those were the days. The good guys always won, and the bad guys always paid for their evil doings. Not the same today, I'm sad to say. It's getting so you can hardly tell the good guys from the bad guys anymore, with all those anti-heroes."

Slim was on a roll and climbed up on his soapbox. "What-the-Sam-Hill is an anti-hero, anyway? Sounds like one of them oxy-mo-rons to me. In my opinion, most of them oxy-mo-rons are more mo-ron than oxy. Kids today are confused and who can blame them. There ain't no clear definition of right and wrong anymore--not in the movies, not on TV, and certainly not in that awful music they listen to. Shoot-fire! And I used to think disco was bad. That rap music makes me as jumpy as a cat with a long tail trapped in a room full of rockin' chairs. When they turn that noise up loud enough to vibrate their cars, somebody ought to arrest them." He paused again, waiting for Raúl to put in his two cents.

The younger man just stared at the unholy playing field below them.

"Got something on your mind, abuelito?"

"I am thinking maybe we have come on the wrong night."

Instantly ticked off, Slim blustered, "Tonight's the full moon, ain't it? Look, Raúl, if you got something else to do, just go on home and do it. Don't think you got to baby-sit me."

Raúl took a lightweight-hunting jacket out of his pack and put it on. He settled back against a rock. "I have nothing else to do, so if you think they will come, we will wait...together."

Before long, the warmth of the day dissipated replaced by the nip of the dark night. One thing about the desert, no matter how hot the day was you could count on the night to be cold enough to chill an Eskimo. Slim pulled on his duster.

The moon rose, full and luminous. Glacial moonlight illuminated the altar below. Slim remembered his theory on how the moonlight softened everything. Didn't work on that altar. Just made it look all the more stark and ominous...like a monster waiting for its next victim.

If circumstances had been different, Slim would have built a campfire, made a pot of coffee, and been content to sit with his good friend and discuss the world's problems, but not tonight. Tonight he spent his time mentally rehearsing his part in the upcoming drama, checking his guns, wishing someone would show up with the baby. But it continued to worry him that Raúl seldom spoke and moved only when he crept down to check on the horses.

Doubts began to spring up in Slim's mind like weeds. Maybe he had made a mistake. Maybe it was a coincidence that Dagger-girl wore that insignia. Maybe he didn't actually see what he thought he had on her wrist. Maybe he'd hauled Raúl all the up here for nothing.

Slim's pride refused to let him back down and admit he might have made a mistake. No matter if the night dragged on forever, he would stay here until dawn. No one could ever accuse Tucson Slim of being a quitter.

Chapter 4

Worn-out from another long night without sleep and more than ready to quit this evil place, Slim watched the golden fingers of dawn stretch out and lighten the cobalt blue of the eastern sky. When the day was more light than dark, he picked up his gear. "Looks like I wasted your time, Raúl. They ain't gonna do nothing up here in broad daylight. We might as well go."

The flicker of pity in Raúl's eyes blazed into a bright flame. "Don't feel so bad, <u>amigo</u>. Maybe the <u>abuelo</u> and the marshal will not return as heroes, but at least we tried. That is more than some people do."

The younger man's attempts to placate him infuriated Slim. "Dag-blame-it, Raúl. Have you forgotten there's still a baby out there who's needing her mama, and it's all my fault?"

Putting his beefy hand on Slim's shoulder, Raúl's voice was quiet and soothing. "Marshal Slim, you have told me what happened and how you reacted. Maybe you are taking too much on your shoulders. The police will find the baby. There are not too many chiquitas running around Tucson with eyebrows made of daggers. She will be easy to find, no?"

Slim couldn't think of anything else to say, and obviously, Raúl did not understand. He turned and started down the mountainside.

Good naturedly, Raúl called after him. "When we get home, María will prepare for us a big breakfast. We will talk, and you will feel better, eh amigo? Huevos rancheros sound good to you? María has made the salsa using Mamá's recipe."

Heading down the mountain to get the horses, the old man tried to ignore Raúl following behind him, chattering about breakfast. Tucson Slim was not a child to be consoled with the promise of food. Besides, nothing Raúl could say would change the fact that Slim had made a huge and humiliating mistake.

The roar of an automobile engine echoed up the mountain road. The vehicle ground to a rock-crushing stop just around the bend from where they stood. Car doors slammed and the muffled sounds of men's voices and boots on gravel destroyed the morning quiet.

Slim motioned to Raúl, and hid behind a large boulder. The old man hadn't expected to be caught out in the open in broad daylight. Preparing for the worst, he drew the Twins. Raúl crossed himself, his mouth moving in silent prayer.

"Slim Stevens, are you out there?"

Raúl grabbed Slim's arm. "They know your name!"

The voice came again. "Slim! It's Detective Mark O'Brien. Can you hear me?"

Raúl softly exhaled. "<u>Gracias</u>, Holy Mother."

As happy as Slim would have been to see the police the night before, he certainly wasn't thrilled this morning. He jerked free of Raúl's clutch and quickly holstered the Twins.

After a moment of quiet, O'Brien yelled again. "Raúl Martínez, are you out there?"

Before Slim could stop him, Raúl answered, "We are here." About to reveal himself, he moved toward the road, his rifle gripped in one hand.

"Raúl!" Slim whispered tersely. "You wanna get your fool head blown off?"

The younger man stopped and stared at him with wide eyes. "What do you mean? We have done nothing wrong."

"You go out there carrying that gun, and they won't wait to ask what we been doin'. You'll be going home in a box! Give it here."

Without a word, Raúl handed him the rifle.

"Now, you go on out there. I'll hide these."

Raúl walked toward the road with his hands in the air. "Sir, please do not shoot. I am coming out, and I am unarmed."

After stashing their rifles under a clump of sagebrush, Slim unstrapped his Buscadero rig and stuffed it into his saddlebag, pistols and all. The hideout pistol remained an uncomfortable lump under his duster.

He draped the saddlebag casually over his shoulder, steadied it with one hand, and walked out to the road. The detective, dressed in a suit and wearing police-issue oxfords, this time with socks, trotted around the bend with two uniformed police officers right behind him. "Well, if it isn't the infamous Tucson Slim?"

He looked at Raúl who was still had his arms raised high in the air. "This must be your sidekick Raúl Martínez. Put your arms down, Raúl. Y'all aren't in trouble, you know. You two okay?"

"Do we look like we're not okay?" Slim growled.

O'Brien turned to his men. "Why don't you both go have a look-see at that altar down there? Check for any signs of recent activity."

The two officers disappeared down the road. O'Brien looked Slim straight in the eyes and cleared his throat.

The old man prepared himself for an angry lecture, but was surprised when Mark spoke in a sympathetic voice.

"Slim, I know this has been especially hard for you, what with the baby and all, but you have got to let me run this investigation. I don't have the time or energy to go out on any wild goose chase." He wiped away the sweat running down his forehead and looked up at the blazing blue sky. "Man, it's getting hot. Slim, the sun's up now. How can you stand wearing that old black coat?"

Knowing if O'Brien saw him with a concealed weapon he'd be arrested, Slim clamped his arm down over his hideout pistol. "What I want to know is if you're so short on time, why are you here now?" Slim tried to make his voice cold and edgy. "You didn't seem all that interested yesterday."

"Well, my day began with two hysterical phone calls. The first was from Sam Turnbow who called early this morning telling me his old friend Tucson Slim has gone up on Mount Thunderbolt on a matter of life and death. Said he'd been out of town and didn't check his machine until this morning. You really upset him, Slim."

Slim thought about when he called for the Sizzlin' Shooters to help him out and having to endure that silly message on Sam's machine. "Well, yee haw, ain't that just too bad."

The detective continued, "Then, right after that I got a call from a Senora Raúl Martínez who's crying because her husband and the very same Tucson Slim went up on Thunderbolt yesterday and never came home. She said she and her priest believe there're evil things afoot on Thunderbolt, and you might never return unless I came up here to save you."

Raúl sighed. "María is a woman who carries the burden of much worry for her loved ones."

Mark O'Brien lifted an eyebrow and frowned at Slim. "So we dropped everything and hurried out here to find you. You know, Slim, Mount Thunderbolt's pretty easy to find when you have the right name."

Slim shifted his saddlebag and tried to ignore the remark concerning his memory. "As you can see, we're fine."

The detective's blue eyes darted from Slim to Raúl and back to Slim. "Can either of you tell me what in the world you planned to do if you found the baby? Any group who would sacrifice an infant wouldn't think twice about killing someone who tried to interfere."

Slim's always shallow reservoir of patience ran dry and he lashed out in anger. "If the police would've done what they're supposed to do and followed up on my information, maybe I would'na felt like I had to come up here."

"We did check up on your lead. Right after you blew up and reamed out Officer Diaz. He's the night duty clerk you met."

Slim's face suddenly felt hot, and he knew it wasn't from the sun. For a man who never blushed, he'd been doing it a lot the last couple of days.

The detective continued, "He decided maybe he should follow up on what you told him and called a retired officer, Sergeant Rob Cummings who used be on the force with Diaz's father. You remember Rob?"

Frantically trying to resurrect the memory of this Rob fellow, Slim bluffed, "Sure, I remember him."

"So, you remember that Rob was the local police expert on the occult back in the 70s. He worked undercover, had long hair, and wore beads."

Suddenly Slim could see Rob's face. Fellow had a beard and spoke all that hippie lingo; cool...groovy...far out...man...dude. He had irritated the fire out of Slim. Undercover or not, it was shameful to see a fellow officer acting like such a twit. "He's the one I gave all my information to, ain't he."

"The very one." O'Brien pulled a handkerchief out of his jacket pocket and wiped his face. "Whew! I'll make this short so I can get back into my air-conditioned cruiser which, by the way, barely made it up this crummy road."

Slim couldn't control the smirk forming on his face. Anybody could tell that was a jeep trail. Maybe old city-boy Mark O'Brien wasn't as smart as he thought.

"Slim, Cummings said you were right. A cult had been coming up here to conduct their services or rituals or whatever they call what they do. The thing is back in 1989, Serge something or another…he was their leader…was killed up here when the car he was driving lost its brakes and plunged over edge. He died at the scene. It was several days before they found him. Cummings said the scavengers got to him and it was a real mess."

"Marshal Slim, you remember that accident," Raúl said. "My two boys helped with the search."

Slim had no memory of the accident, but he nodded his shaggy head anyway. "Who took over after he died? What happened to the people who belonged to this cult?"

"No one took over. The cult disbanded. Hasn't been any recorded activity of this group in years, and just to ease your mind, Slim, their m.o. wasn't baby stealing or murdering children. They stuck to sacrificing chickens and goats and such as that. If you would've stayed home and rested like I told you to do, you would've heard all this at eight a.m. yesterday morning and saved everyone a lot of trouble."

Slim glared at the detective. "Then why did that girl have their emblem tattooed on her wrist?"

O'Brien shrugged. "You said yourself she pulled away so fast you could barely see it. Maybe it wasn't exactly the same. Maybe it simply triggered the memory of the one you saw up here, and you got confused."

Slim pulled himself up to his full height. "I am not confused," he roared.

Raúl, who had been standing there quietly listening, said, "Detective O'Brien, since you have come all the way up here, can we not go look at the altar?"

O'Brien wiped his face again and let out an exasperated groan. "Okay. What's a sunstroke or two between friends?"

Slim led the way, but Raúl stopped at the edge of the clearing. "I will wait here."

"I'll be back in a minute." Slim gazed at his loyal friend, standing alone, nervously shaking one knee, looking as if he might bolt at any minute. Slim knew the boy was reacting to the evil in this place. "Hang in there, <u>abuelito</u>. We'll be off this mountain before you know it."

Raúl smiled weakly.

Slim and O'Brien walked into the clearing, which Slim estimated to be about the size of a small corral. The two uniforms, hands encased in latex, were working their way through the litter. In the center of the clearing stood the grisly centerpiece of the cult's activities, the old stained altar.

Slim approached three flat pieces of sandstone stacked together like a single section of Stonehenge, The air felt heavy, laden with evil, and the hair stood up on the back of his neck. He glanced back at Raúl.

His friend's eyebrows lifted as if to ask, "Do you feel it?"

Slim nodded. Trying to shake off this unnerving, oppressive feeling, he assessed the altar with a practiced eye. Three feet high, six feet long. Erected on a fourth larger slab of sandstone covered with drifted desert sand, the altar base had four iron rings embedded in it, one at each compass point-north, east, south, west.

The old man had forgotten about those rings, and just as he had the first time he saw them, he wondered what they were for.

"I don't see any insignias or anything else carved on this ugly thing," O'Brien said.

"That's because it's down here." Slim put his saddlebag on the ground and squatted in front of the altar, his duster pooling around his body. Beneath his duster, sweat ran down an down his back as he brushed the sand away with several brisk swipes, revealing the distinctive carving, a goat's head in the center of an upside-down star, surrounded by some kind of wreath. Filled with relief, Slim stood. "See, just like I said."

"I know you saw this carving, Slim. It's all documented. Only I'm not too sure what you saw on that girl's wrist." O'Brien turned to his men and yelled, "You two find anything?"

The shorter policeman held up a crumpled beer can. "Nothing but the remains of one heck of a party," he said.

The other cop pointed to several burned-down candle stubs stuck around the base of the cliff. "Candles, empty beer cans, used condoms, and what's left of who-knows-how-many joints. Typical party remains."

O'Brien squatted down to examine the carving. "What do you think, Slim?"

"I think you should have the lab test these stains."

"They were tested. Back when Cummings ordered it, and I told you, it was all animal blood."

"That was a long time ago, O'Brien. Maybe you should have it done again."

The detective stood and closely examined the top of the altar. "Doesn't appear to be fresh."

Trying hard not to tell this young man what he thought about his sloppy investigation tactics, Slim walked around the clearing, stopping occasionally to move a piece of trash with his foot. "You have to admit something has been going on up here. Candles, drugs, booze; could add up to the black arts. Maybe you ought to have the C.S.I. team up here."

The short cop laughed. "Yeah, Boss, but be sure to get Marg Helgenberger from that television show to come out here. She's a lot better looking than Orville Bishop from our division."

The uniforms guffawed.

The old man stiffened. Why would O'Brien put up with such insolence? An Arizona marshal certainly wouldn't.

O'Brien stood and dusted off his pant legs. "All I see is a bunch of kids came out here and had a party."

Ever the law officer, Slim fought to control his temper. "I still say you ought to have these stains analyzed. While they're working on that, you should go check out the occult shops in town."

Now the taller cop was laughing. "And since we think it was a party, maybe we better check out all the convenience stores in town too, oh, and the liquor stores. Can't forget those liquor stores, can we?"

The shorter cop laughed and slapped his knee. "And while we're at it, don't our schools pass out condoms, and don't all gas stations sell 'em. We oughta go run down those leads too."

The uniforms cracked themselves up, their mocking laughter echoing against the boulders.

Shaking his head, O'Brien turned to his men. "All right, guys. No need to be nasty."

Raúl called to Slim from the edge of the clearing. "Come on, Marshal Slim. You and me, we will go home and let these police do things in their own way."

His friend's innocent words affected Slim in much the same way it would have if Raúl had lobbed an incendiary device into the situation. Slim yelled, "O'Brien, I'm making a formal complaint. I want these stains analyzed again."

O'Brien whirled around. "That's enough! I've got to get back to work. Too much time has been wasted as it is."

Slim glared at the detective. If he backed down now, the whole investigation would end right here. "I'm giving you fair warning. I'll keep pursuing this case even if I have to go over your head."

The redheaded detective's face formerly flushed from the heat turned deep purple. He exploded. "Don't you get it, Slim? Where this altar is concerned there is no case. Nobody trusts the information you provide!"

The detective's angry words ground into Slim's wounded ego like salt into a gaping wound. The old man faltered a moment and glanced at Raúl, who stared at him with great hangdog eyes.

"Mr. Martínez!" O'Brien's voice was tight with anger. "I want Mr. Stevens to ride with me in the cruiser. Can you get your horses home without him?"

"Sí, I can."

"My car's at the Martínez place," Slim roared. "I'll go home the way I came."

"Well, sorry about that! You don't get to!" O'Brien locked eyes with Slim and said each word crisp with authority. "We can take you to your car or we can take you to jail. You choose. Even if I have to arrest you for interfering with a police investigation, you will ride with me. We have a thing or two to discuss."

Slim held O'Brien's gaze with fierce intensity, but when the two uniforms snapped to attention and moved toward him, he knew he'd lost the battle. Still glaring at the detective, he spoke to Raúl. "You best go on. When you go back down the trail, pick up that that gear I stashed behind that boulder."

A blank look on his face, Raúl said, "Gear?"

Slim nodded. "That gear we left down there. Remember?"

Raúl continued to look at Slim, his dark brown eyes wide and questioning, then he understood what Slim was telling him. "Sí! The gear. I will take care of it. And you can get your rif…." He glanced at the detective, but O'Brien was talking to his men and apparently hadn't heard what Raúl said.

Slim shook his head. Just like his mama, that boy didn't have a deceitful bone in his body. He couldn't even bluff at poker. Everything he felt, everything he thought, was written across that broad brown face like a lighted up billboard.

Raúl dragged his hand across his mouth. "I-I mean your gear, Marshal Slim. You can get it when I get back to the house. Tell María to make us a big lunch."

Slim didn't respond to Raúl's invitation. He had no intention of hanging around and listening to Raúl's futile attempts to make everything better.

"Come on, Stevens!" O'Brien barked. "Officer Jeffreys, get down to that cruiser and turn on the air-conditioner. This sun's killing me."

The tall skinny cop took off down the road, and the short cop fell in behind Slim who followed the detective. As they were walking down the rutted narrow road, something near Slim's foot glinted in the bright sunlight. Apparently O'Brien hadn't noticed it.

The old man knelt down where he saw the tiny flash and pretended to tie the leather strings on his moccasin. O'Brien walked on, but the uniform stopped next to Slim and looked out over the edge of the high road at the vast desert vista shimmering in the morning sun.

Squinting, Slim saw the glint originated from some sort of silver doo-dad almost buried in the sand. Around it, looping in and out of the sand like a black snake was a long narrow piece of dusty leather.

Had he found an important clue?

It took him about a minute to decide once again he would break the law he'd vowed to serve. What was that old saying? Finders keepers, losers weepers.

When he saw his chance, Slim picked up something that looked like an old necklace and stuffed it in his pocket. If this was a clue, he had no intention of sharing it with the detective or his officers. Besides, didn't O'Brien just say the police were busy with other things and that they didn't trust anything Slim had to offer?

His find energized the old man. He stood and hurried to the cruiser. The sooner they got back to Raúl's place, the sooner Slim could take a good look at what he'd found.

# # #

When they got to the highway and turned south toward the Martínez ranch, O'Brien called María on his cell phone. The red-faced detective gave her a brief update, snapped the phone shut, and started yelling at Slim, speaking so fast and with such fury, he spattered the air with minute spit balls.

Blasting away mile after mile, in a tirade that seemed would never end, the more the detective fussed, the more Slim regained his composure and strength. It was like he was a well-used piece of steel, all worn and nicked, and this situation was the fire. O'Brien's angry words became a hammer pounding away at the super-heated steel, beating out the imperfections, shaping the very core of who Slim was into a sword, sharp and deadly, ready for war. With that image, Slim had an epiphany.

He had been chosen.

That girl hadn't accidentally stumbled into his life. She had been placed there for a reason. Maybe the Good Lord in Heaven…although Slim had to admit, he and the Man Upstairs hadn't been on such good terms since Dolores died…maybe God wanted to use Slim one last time. Didn't God know things about Slim no one else remembered? Like once Tucson Slim set his mind to do something, he was a regular bulldog…sinking his teeth like a spring trap, hanging on, never giving up…until he saw his mission to completion.

O'Brien intruded into his moment of insight with a loud, irritated, "Slim!"

Startled, the old man snapped, "What?"

"I said it's been a long time since Arizona allowed cowboy justice to rule."

"I know that."

"Then quit acting like you're Wyatt Earp or somebody. Look, I don't want to have this conversation again. Stay out of police business. If you don't, I'll slap you with an indictment so fast it'll make your head spin." He stared at Slim a moment and then, his voice filled with frustration, yelled, "Damn it, Slim, what do you have to say for yourself?"

Slim inspected his nails. "Don't appear to be a reason for me to say anything., seems you got it all figgered out."

O'Brien laughed sarcastically and shook his head. "You know, for an old man, you got a real arrogant attitude. It's beyond me why I ever felt sorry for you in the first place."

Insulted, Slim shot back, "Well, this is one old man who don't need you or anybody else feelin' sorry for him!"

O'Brien sighed and turned away. Now silent, he spent the rest of the trip staring out of the car window at the desert speeding by.

When they finally skimmed over the cattle guard and entered Rancho del Sol, Slim glanced at the clock on the car's dashboard. A trip around Thunderbolt by car takes forty-five minutes. He and Raúl had spent hours riding the horses up the backside of the mountain in the hot sun and the journey seemed much shorter.

It seemed odd to Slim that when you measured miles in angry words instead of feet, it took a lot longer to get where you're going.

When they pulled up next to his Pinto, the old man figured if he could convince O'Brien his reprimand had been successful, the sooner Slim would be shed of this detective and his two wise-cracking uniforms. Assuming an actor's face, the one that said, "I'm a whipped puppy," Slim got out of the vehicle.

O'Brien rolled down his window. "What are your plans?"

The old man hung his head and said in a quiet, subdued voice, "To live my life and stay out of your hair, sir."

The twist was Slim meant exactly what he said, only not in the same way he hoped O'Brien took it. Tucson Slim would now live his life doing the job the Good Lord saw fit to give him. He would find that baby before it was too late. And while he moved about his task as wary as a snake and as secretive as a spy, he would definitely stay out of O'Brien's thinning red hair.

The hard line of the detective's mouth softened. "You know old fella, when I look at you, I see myself in fifty years. Once a cop, always a cop. I hope when I reach your time in life, someone has the nerve to tell me what I'm gonna tell you. You're day is over, Slim. I'm on the job now, so get out of my way and let me do it. Now, you go have a nice breakfast with your friends. When I have something worth telling, I'll give you a call." O'Brien rolled up the window, and the cruiser roared away, disappearing in a cloud of desert dust.

Jerking open his car door, Slim placed his saddlebag on the floorboard behind the driver's seat and mimicked the detective. "Run on, you helpless old fart. Have a little breakfast, and make sure they grind it up real good because you're so decrepit you might choke on regular food. Oh, and don't call me, I'll call you...as soon as Hell freezes over." He spat on the ground. "Nice try, O'Brien, but you ain't stopping me."

Slim took what he'd found in the sand out of his pocket. He held a long strip of crumbling leather, ends knotted together. Hanging from the leather was a tarnished silver charm with a flat wedge-shaped piece of turquoise about three inches long attached to it.

Slipping on his reading glasses, Slim studied his find. The discolored charm was actually a bird's foot of finely wrought silver. The narrow end of the dusty turquoise was clasped in its claws, the wide end had been engraved. The old man rubbed the turquoise wedge on his sleeve, angled the stone to obtain the best possible light, and squinted. There was an engraving, the same design Slim saw at the altar and tattooed on the girl's wrist.

Holding up the necklace against a sky-blue backdrop, Slim watched it spin in the bright morning sun. A shiver danced along his spine. The silver thing wasn't a bird's foot at all. It was a dragon's...or maybe even a demon's claw grasping the turquoise in its talons...long, sharp, shredding talons. The longer he stared at the necklace, the less he liked it, sensing that what he held in his hand was a thing of pure evil, a deadly harbinger of things to come.

Around him, the sunlight dimmed, the morning took on a vague, uncharacteristic pall. Glancing up at the seamless bowl of blue over his head, the old man's skin crawled, the desert seemed filled with watching eyes.

Feeling vulnerable and anxious, fighting the urge to fling the necklace as far from him as possible, Slim jammed it deep in his pants pocket where he couldn't see it. He ripped off his duster, shed the hideout pistol, and jumped into his car. The necklace, a hard malevolent lump, lay cold against his thigh. Slim gripped the steering wheel with both hands. As much as he wanted to walk away from this strange situation, he could not let anything, not this premonition of danger, not the threat of jail, not his frailties or his fears, keep him from his mission.

Slim started his car, and by the time he drove by the house, he'd managed to reign in his fears, reassign the necklace to a proper perception, and focus on the plan forming in his mind. Feeling more like his old self, he slowed the car when he saw María waiting on the side of the driveway waving. Before she could ask any questions, he told her when to expect Raúl and sped away. Today he'd let the boy do his own explaining.

This old man had important things to do, secret plans to put into action. Tucson Slim would show the world a person his age should not be discarded like an old newspaper, an expired coupon, an empty roll of toilet paper. His jaw set, his heart filled with resolve, the lone vigilante and crusader for the elderly zipped over the cattle guard, careened on to the highway, and sped towards Tucson.

Chapter 5

Slim was up before dawn, his plan locked firmly in his mind, set in concrete as it were. At least the old man hoped his plan was set in concrete. Today would be the wrong day for his brain to turn to mush. Today he would begin his under-cover work. Today he would visit the occult shops listed in the telephone book. Twelve of them scattered across Tucson.

He set aside his usual black western duds and donned a white dress shirt, brown slacks and his only sport coat, a baby-blue polyester fashion faux-pax from the late 70s. He tugged on some faded black soaks and winced as he crammed his twisted old feet into a pair of white tennis shoes. After combing back his long silver hair, Slim put on a hat he'd been given several years back, a hat with Desert Grove Golf Club emblazoned across the front, and took a long, nit-picky look in the mirror.

Success!   Staring back at him was Harvey Hanson, concerned great-grandfather, another one of the many snowbirds who spent their retirement winters in Tucson.

With the claw necklace in one pocket, a sketch of the girl's tattoo in another, and the Thunderer strapped safely under his arm, Slim tucked his old marshal's badge into his wallet. Just because he was retired, he thought, and had no authority, didn't mean he couldn't flash it if he thought it might open a door or garner some information.

He glanced at the clock. He didn't have to be at work until five that afternoon. He had all day. Slim grabbed his list of occult shops--the list he'd painstakingly searched out on the city map and arranged in a time-efficient grid--opened the door and dodged the Tucson Daily News as it sailed past him.

"Sorry, Slim," the newspaper boy yelled as he pedaled away.

Slim shot the boy's back a hard look, kicked his newspaper into the hall, and hurried to his car.

At his first stop, A Little Shoppe of Witchcraft, a bored young woman behind the counter was more interested in playing with her nose ring than talking to an old man in a sport coat. When he tried to show her the drawing, the telephone rang, and she left him standing there, paper in hand, and answered it.

His patience slipping away, Slim fought to stay in character, desperately hanging on to his long-suffering great-grandfather face, as he listened to the girl complain about her boyfriend. Then she complained about her seats at the latest Ozzfest—whatever the heck that was. When she told a dirty joke…the nastiest joke Slim had ever heard pass through a woman's lips, and one he was sure she'd told for his benefit…he resisted the urge to drag the girl into the bathroom and wash her mouth out with soap. Instead, the old marshal proudly stalked out of the shop and slammed the glass door behind him.

Reining in his anger, he went to the next store on his list, Mystics and More, and then on to the next, Bells, Spells, and Candles. Heavy into the New Age, aromatherapy, and tea, these two shops were more kitsch than cult and no help at all. His next stop, The Shaman's Medicine Bag, was a burned out shell, so it was on to The Crystal Orb. There, a woman with long blond hair told him she knew nothing about the drawing or the necklace, but for a mere seventy-five dollars, she would channel her spirit guide, someone she called Angelique, and they could ask her. It seemed Angelique was a voo-doo priestess from turn-of-century New Orleans. Slim declined the offer.

When he left the Crystal Orb, the old man's energy level was dropping fast. He stopped at a corner grocery and bought a candy bar and a soda pop. After his sugar and caffeine fix, it was on to The Unicorn's Horn, a tiny shop in a rundown part of town.

The minute he opened the door, Slim could see The Unicorn's Horn was a place the serious witch might frequent. On three sides of the small space, the floor-to-ceiling shelves were stacked with dusty tins, small boxes and glass jars, all shapes and sizes of jars containing floating things, sludgy things, and things…well, things that were probably classified as God-only-knew-what.

On the fourth wall, the shelves held books. Slim stopped and read a few of the titles: Witches, Itches, and Herbs, Conversations from the Great Beyond, Voo-Doo for Dummys, A View from the Third Eye, and a massive tome entitled Spells and Incantations for the Experienced Conjuror.

A woman's disembodied voice came from behind a curtain on the back wall. "I'll be right out, but we're out of spell candles, you know, having just had the full moon and all."

Slim's pulse quickened. She'd mentioned the full moon. He picked up a jar sitting on the counter and held it up to the light. Small, gelatinous orbs, suspiciously eyelike, stared back at him through thick, amber liquid. Trying not to gag, he fought to keep his candy bar in his stomach.

A short, round elderly woman with a sweet smile suddenly stood next to him. She wore a bright red dress and red tennis shoes with gold shoelaces. When she fluffed her hair…lavender hair, all curly like a poodle…her many gold charm bracelets jingled merrily. "Sorry to keep you waiting. Did'ya need something special, darlin'?"

Slim stood there, staring down at her, completely at a loss for words. He'd prepared himself for one of the child-eating witches from that movie Hocus-Pocus, or maybe a wizened old crone, but not this friendly, perky little woman who could pass for Santa's sister.

The woman glanced at the jar in his hand. She lifted a knowing eyebrow. "If you're looking to make a little aphrodisiac, this wouldn't be what you want."

Slim's stomach heaved again, and he almost dropped the eyeballs.

She took the jar from his hand and set it back on the counter. With one finger tapping her chin, the woman looked him up and down. "Well, I know a good-looking man such as yourself couldn't be looking for a love potion."

Slim was flattered, but lavender hair? No, he'd have to pass on that. He went for the dark-haired beauties like Dolores…. He caught himself drifting and forced himself to stay focused. "Nope, don't need that."

Before he could tell her what he did need, she said, "How about some dried frogs or spiders? Or stump water, cobwebs, lizard tongues, bat wings, eye of newt? You know you what they say…." Cackling, she hunched over and stirred an imaginary cauldron, saying, "Bubble, bubble, toil and trouble."

Slim frowned and took a step backwards.

The woman burst out in a trill of high-pitched laughter. "You should see your face. I love acting like I actually made my business that way. The Horn is more of a…."

She hesitated. Her brows knitted, her eyes narrowed. "Say, Mister, you okay? You want something to drink. Water? Tea? I have some bourbon in the back room."

Slim pictured her running into the back room, scooping a cup of something vile out of a rotting stump or a steaming black caldron, scraping off any floating eyeballs, and bringing it to him. He vigorously shook his head, so vigorously he made himself dizzy, and he staggered a bit.

She took his arm. "Are you sure? Won't take me a minute."

When she touched him, Slim's head cleared. He had to focus on extracting the information he needed. He could handle one small woman. He could handle any woman....

His instincts kicked in. Time to turn on the charm. Before the old master was through, little Miss Claus would tell him all she knew.

Slim smiled. "I don't need anything to drink, ma'am. It's just that I've never been in a shop like this before, and when I came through the door...."

He gave her a bashful smile and ducked his head. "I didn't expect to find a such lovely woman running the place. Kinda took my breath away."

The woman's round face blazed with color. She giggled like a girl. "You probably thought I'd be wearing a black pointed hat and riding a broom, didn't you? Don't feel bad, the uninitiated usually make that mistake, but I'm here to tell you, real witches would never fall into that degrading stereotype."

Real witches? Right there and then, Slim decided to handle this lady with care, because she obviously needed one of those head doctors. He'd best ask his questions, and then get the heck out of Dodge. Turning the corners of his mouth down and wrinkling his forehead, Slim said, "I have problem, ma'am. A problem I was hopin' maybe you could help me solve."

"Honey, have you ever come to right place. Did you know they call me Opal Oliver, the problem-solver?"

"No ma'am, but that's good to hear." He held the necklace up. "Do you know anything about this? Where it came from? What it means??"

She studied it for a moment. "Honey, you can buy this claw charm anywhere. It's so common I won't even carry'em here at the Horn, but I've never seen one holding a chunk of turquoise like that. Too bad it's not a little smaller and made of gold." She rattled her bracelets. "I do like the gold stuff."

Stuffing the necklace back into his pocket, Slim took out the drawing. "How about this? You see, my great-granddaughter came home with that necklace and an ugly tattoo on her wrist that looks like this drawing, and the next thing we knew she'd run off. I'm trying to find her. We're afraid she'd gotten herself mixed up with a cult or something."

Opal squinted. "Wait a minute, honey, I got to get my eyes."

Unwilling to think what her "eyes" might be, Slim fought the urge to run the other way, right out the door.

The woman pulled a pair of red half glasses out from under the counter. "You know how it is when you get older. You either wear glasses or get longer arms. Personally, although I am a witch--." She smiled impishly. "I find glasses easier."

She put on her eyes and took the paper out of his hand. The instant she saw what he'd drawn, Opal's smile vanished. Trembling from head to foot, she pushed the paper back into his hand. "You'll have to go now. I got work to do."

Slim could see the design obviously upset the woman. "You can trust me, Opal. No one will ever know we talked."

"Mister, you get out of here right now." Opal reached for something under the counter.

Slim's hands shot into the air. Nothing scared him more than an untrained novice with a gun, unless it was an untrained female with a gun. "Don't get nervous. I don't mean you no harm."

To his surprise, instead of a gun, Opal took out an odd-looking mass of feathers and clutched it to her chest.

Slim slowly lowered his arms. "What is that thing?"

Opening her hand, Opal showed him something that looked like dried cat puke, kind of bird and mouse and string all scrambled together with a bone or two thrown in for good measure.

"This is my guardian fetish. When I hold this, I have nothing to fear."

"Opal, you don't have a reason in the world to be afraid of me," Slim said, keeping his voice gentle and reassuring. "I'm just an old man trying to help his family." Then he threw in the plea no woman could resist. "I need your help, ma'am. If I can't save my darling little Susie, I'll never forgive myself."

"Susie your great-grandchild?"

"Yes ma'am, she's a teenager."

The woman gradually relaxed her white-knuckled grip on the fetish. "I never had kids, but I was a girl once myself. The teen years are a real hard."

"Opal, you're the first person I've talked to that seems to recognize this emblem. Can't you tell me what it means and why it bothers you so much?

Once more, she gripped the fetish tightly to her chest. "I'll tell you this and only this. If your Susie is wearing that mark, find her and get her out of Tucson. Hide her away--some place as far from here as possible and have that evil insignia removed from her skin."

"But what does the design mean?"

Opal looked at him with wide, staring eyes and whispered, "It means death, that's what it means."

# # #

Unable to convince Opal to tell him anything more, Slim returned to his car. As he pulled away from the curb, she ran out of the store, waving something in her hand. "Wait, Mister!"

He rolled down the car window. "You callin' me?"

"Yes, when you walked out the door, my psychic vibe said I should give you this." She held up her guardian fetish.

It still looked like a mass of regurgitated feathers, string, and bone, and he wasn't sure he wanted the ugly thing. "But it means so much to you."

"That's okay. I have another one."

The one thing Slim did know was he didn't want to hurt Opal's feelings. Stashed away in the back of his mind somewhere, he had another plan concerning her. If he failed to get enough information from anyone else, he would come back to Opal and charm her into telling him everything she knew. "Dear lady, I thank you, but I can't take your charm. It wouldn't be right."

Opal came closer to the car. "You don't realize what kind of hornet's nest you're stirring up asking all these questions." She pressed the fetish into his hand. "You take this and keep it on your person. When that vibe hit me, I saw you and those close to you are in great danger."

"If you think I should."

"I do, and please be careful. My vibe said you are a marked man." She turned and ran back into the store.

Slim sat there a minute staring at the thing she's given him. Still looked like a product of cat puke. He shook his head, tossed the fetish into the passenger seat, and continued on his quest. He didn't believe a word that woman said about her psychic vibe, but he did wonder, if he continued his search, and he would, what "others" might be put in danger.

He pulled into the slow-moving traffic and headed for the next shop. He knew one thing. No group that disbanded over twenty years ago could still cause the kind of fear he saw in Opal's face. Something was going on, and, no matter if it was dangerous or not, he would get to the bottom of this mystery one way or another.

# # #

The rest of the day dragged by, and by the time Slim set out for the last shop on his list, he was positive the world was losing its collective mind. He'd met more nutty people in one day than he'd met in the last thirty years. Slim had always considered the chaos of the 60's and 70s an aberration and had been thrilled when a sense of normalcy returned in the 80s with the Reagan years. But today...today he found out some of those people he'd found so irritating all those years ago, those draft-card burning, drug-taking, peace-loving hippies weren't really gone. Some of them had simply hidden themselves away in odd little shops and had no information to share with an old man.

At his last stop, Slim parked and stared at the sign on the side of the old stucco building. The Gypsy's Curse. What kind of strange person would he encounter here?

He got out of his car and hobbled into the shop, his poor feet complaining about those uncomfortable tennis shoes with every step. Slim's blue sports jacket, damp with perspiration, had wilted and hung loose on his spare old frame. His eyes bleary with fatigue, Harvey Hanson, concerned great-grandfather, was tired and ready to go home. So was Slim. He only hoped whoever ran the Gypsy's Curse was forthcoming and provided him with the information he needed.

Each passing minute of the long hot day had only served to inflame his anger towards Detective O'Brien and his two uniforms. If they'd been doing what they were supposed to do, an old man wouldn't have to. But Slim knew, for him, anger could be a good thing, fortifying his resolve, reinforcing his determination, giving him the final burst of energy he might need to finish a task. Slim would show those three cops. Just because he was old didn't mean he'd lost his edge.

When he was inside the shop, Slim stopped let his eyes adjust to the dim lighting. Cool, moist air scented with lavender and desert sage blew through a vent into his sweaty face. Above his head, countless bundles of dried herbs and flowers hung blossom-down from the rafters. All around the shop, candles in mirrored containers reflected soft diffused light. Rock and terra cotta fountains of varying sizes lined one wall, their happy bubbling waters stirring the air, moving tiny wind chimes suspended over them. Celtic music playing in the background pleasantly mixed with the tinkling chimes.

The old man suddenly relaxed. For some reason he felt peaceful, like he'd come home, and this shop was nothing like any home he'd ever lived in. Then he remembered. Sage and lavender. The hacienda at Rancho del Sol. Sometimes Dolores burned sage when she did her curandera healings. Thinking of the woman he loved encouraged Slim. Through the years he'd learned a lot about what Dolores believed even if he didn't buy into all of it. Maybe that knowledge would help him here, and if it did, it would be like he and Dolores were working together.

Slim limped to the counter. Off to the side, crystal blue beads hung motionless in a narrow doorway, an exotic entryway to the dark room behind it.

A stunning woman, steel-gray hair cut in a blunt old-fashioned bob, slipped through the whispering beads and stood behind the counter. She was tall…tall and bone thin…and her dress was a black Chinese silk with a deep red trim. Even in the dim lighting, Slim could see her pale skin was flawless, her eyes the color of wheat, and there was a beauty mark between her pencil-thin brows.

The woman stood there silently staring at him, the tip of her long elegant, diamond-studded nose slightly lifted, her expression aloof, aristocratic. Although the shop was cool, the temperature seemed to drop when she spoke in a voice, purring with an exotic accent Slim did not recognize. "May I help you find something, sir? Something for your painful feet, perhaps?"

The peace he felt when he entered the shop vanished. Slim shivered. This woman wasn't anything like Dolores, and how did she know his feet bothered him? He hadn't moved since she came through that beaded curtain. Unless…unless…she'd been watching him when he didn't know it.

The longer she stared at him with those bold unblinking eyes, the more the woman reminded him of a rattlesnake preparing to strike. He decided to sidestep this viper and go straight to the top. "I ain't here for my feet. I came to see the owner of this establishment."

"I am Mrs. Sonya Szymanski. I am the owner of The Gypsy's Curse."

His dodge had failed. The old man's strength was flagging, but it was either leave or deal with this...this...Serpent-woman.

The woman smiled, a smile as cold and flat as her reptile yellow eyes. "And your name, sir?"

For some reason, Slim was reluctant to tell her any name, even his alias, but he said it any way. "Harvey Hanson. Have you ever seen this before?" He gave her the sketch.

She quietly studied his drawing. Her lifeless smile never changed. "And if I have?"

"Then I hope you'll tell me about it."

Serpent-woman looked up at him, pinning him with those steady, unfeeling eyes. "Why are you interested?"

"My great-granddaughter gets herself a tattoo like this on her wrist, and then she ups and runs away. I'm thinking she's gotten mixed up with some kind of cult or something."

She returned the sketch, and Slim noticed her hands. She wore silver rings on each of her long fingers, but her nails were ragged, inflamed, chewed down to the quick. One thumb had a severe hangnail crusted with dried blood. At least Slim hoped the blood was from the hangnail.

However, seeing her mangled nails bolstered Slim's courage. Maybe Sonya Szymanski, Serpent-woman, wasn't all she appeared to be. "You've seen that before, haven't you, ma'am?"

"Maybe I have. A very long time ago, Mister.... What was your name again?"

"Stone." Slim hesitated. Was that right? He tried to ignore the unsettling feeling in his gut that he had royally screwed up.

She leaned across the counter and hissed, "Did you say Stone?"

Slim's old mind frazzled in a dozen different directions. What had he told her the first time she asked him what his name was? Hanson or Stone? When he couldn't be sure, he went with an old adage: the best defense is an offense. And Tucson Slim could be pretty offensive if he set his mind to it.

Pulling himself together, Slim stood straight and tall, and in a loud, firm voice, said, "That's right, ma'am. Hank Stone, General Hank Stone, United States Marines, retired! Hoo-yaw!"

All right, maybe the hoo-yaw was a little over the top, but he was determined to salvage this visit.

"Should I call you General?" Mrs. Szymanski asked in a mocking tone, the words sliding slowly through her thin lips.

The hair on the back of Slim's neck prickled. It was almost as if she could see right through his skull into his brain and knew he was lying. He mumbled, "No, Mr. Stone is fine."

Tilting her head, she smiled that wintry smile again. "Somehow the name Stone does not fit your aura."

The prickle on the back of Slim's neck turned into a raging case of the heebie-jeebies. What the heck was an aura and how could she see it? Afraid the woman had tapped into some kind of cosmic lie detector, Slim blustered, "I don't give a hoot what fits my aura. Stone's my name, and I think you know exactly what this design means."

"Yes, I do, but it hardly seems relevant now."

Slim compared her reaction to Opal's. Cold admission to stark fear. This woman not only knew something, but was probably somehow involved. "Can you tell me what you know about the group?"

"Mr. Stone, I only know that this emblem once was used by a group who called themselves the Scarlet Host."

Hoping his mind wouldn't erase it before he needed it, Slim made a mental note, while she continued in a dry, distracted way.

"They disbanded many years ago. So you see, Mr. Stone, it is not possible for your great-grandchild to be involved with them."

"Disbanded, huh?"

"Yes, a very long time ago, Mr. Stone."

Did she have to keep hissing out, "Mr. Stone," like that? Now his heebie-jeebies had heebie-jeebies. "Then how do you suppose she got this insignia?"

She shrugged. "The goat's head and pentagram are not unusual symbols. You see them everywhere, on rock albums, tee shirts, also tattoos. It's the wreath that makes this design unique. Perhaps you should go bother the tattoo artists. Or simply find your granddaughter and ask her what it means. What is her name again?"

"Didn't say."

"Why the child wears this emblem is probably harmless. Perhaps you should allow her to be free, to try her wings."

"She's too young to have that kind of freedom."

Her eyes still as warm as an irritated rattler, Mrs. Szymanski leaned forward again. "But the young are so resilient. What might not harm a young one could destroy an older person. Take care, Mr. Stone. If the Scarlet Host were still a dynamic gathering of disciples, they would not like you delving into their business."

"Is there any possibility this group's gone active again? Do you know any of the old members? I'd like to talk to them. To find out if anyone has seen my great granddaughter."

Mrs. Szymanski's smile faded. "I was not personally acquainted with any of the Host." She glanced at her watch. "I am sorry. It is time for me to close the store."

As she herded him toward the door, Slim reached into his pocket and gripped the necklace's crumbling leather cord tightly in his hand. "Before I go, Mrs. Szymanski, could I show you one more thing I think might be connected to the Scarlet Host?"

She frowned, her thin brows almost meeting the beauty mark between her eyes. "More sketches?"

Slim played his trump card and revealed the old necklace.

Almost imperceptibly, Mrs. Szymanski's strange eyes widened. Her trembling right hand jerked as if she wanted to reach for the spinning bauble, but she pulled back and curled her wounded fingertips into a tight fist. "Where did you find this?"

"Have you seen it before?"

"No, Mr. Stone. I have not."

As she spoke, the woman glanced away for only an instant, but Slim caught it. She was lying. He took a step toward her. "Are you positive?"

"Mr. Stone, I know nothing that would help you, but if you would like to sell that small, unattractive trinket--."

"Ain't for sale!"

Mrs. Szymanski tore her eyes away from the dangling pendant and smiled the serpent's smile again. Slim half expected to see a forked tongue dart in and out of her mouth. "Mr. Stone, I must have that necklace. Name your price."

Slim's old mind raced. He wasn't about to sell Sonya Szymanski anything, but if he could trick her into helping him by letting her think this strange piece of jewelry would be her reward…. "You know, for some reason, I don't think I can sell this thing."

"Why not? It would be a simple cash transaction."

"I dunno. Feels like bad luck for me to sell it, but I might be willing to trade."

"For what?"

"Information. Find out if there're any of those Scarlet Host people still around. Ask if they have a young girl hiding out with them. A young girl with a baby."

"Ah, a baby. You did not mention a baby before."

Hoping he looked like she'd offended him, Slim glared at her. "Bandying my family's disgrace around in front of strangers ain't the way I do things."

She nodded. "I understand. If I were to find out this information how would I reach you?"

"You can call me at--."

"Wait. I will write this down." She picked up a pen and looked at him expectantly, her hand poised over a pink pad.

Slim suddenly realized he'd almost given this strange woman his home phone number. What a blunder that would have been. "On second thought, I'll just call you."

"But, if I discover something--."

"Nope, I said I'd call you."

"But, Mr. Stone--." She grabbed his wrist. Her fingers were warm and soft against his skin, but there was something about Sonya Szymanski's touch…something unclean…something evil.

He pulled away and fumbled for the doorknob. "Like I said, I'll call you."

The woman's eyes flattened. In a quick movement, she reached past him and jerked down the shade on the shop's front door. "Before you go, come into my back room for a moment, and my assistant will prepare a special oil to help the pain in your feet."

Slim thought he would rather dance naked in a rattler's den than go into this woman's back room. Hoping his aura didn't show how spooked he was, he slipped his hand into his jacket front and held it over his small hideout pistol…in case he needed it. "Can't take the time right now."

Before she could say or do anything else, Slim opened the door with his free hand and stepped out into the searing Arizona sunlight. He stood there a moment, soaking up the intense heat, hoping to cleanse himself of the evil coldness he'd picked up in that shop, but he could feel the woman's icy eyes boring a hole into his back.

Hurrying away from The Gypsy's Curse, his hand firmly on his pistol, Slim lapsed into the embarrassing little skip/hop trot he'd fallen into using when flat-out running would have killed his crippled feet.

When he was safely in his car and driving away, the old man glanced into his rear-view mirror, but the road behind him was empty. He kept watch all the way home.

He sure didn't need that woman or her "assistant" tailing him. Serpent-woman wanted his necklace. No doubt about that, and if she wanted it that bad, Slim meant to keep it. He wondered why she'd been so calm, cool, and collected when she saw the drawing, but got all bothered when she saw the necklace. What did she know? And why was Opal so afraid, and Sonya wasn't?

He glanced at Opal's ugly fetish laying there on the car seat. Could this doo-dad actually have some kind of protecting power? With a slight shrug, the old man picked it up and put it in his jacket pocket. Right now, with his heebie-jeebies still raging, he would accept any help he could get.

The farther away Slim got from The Gypsy's Curse and Sonya Szymanski, the better he felt. He allowed his mind to catalogue the information he'd gleaned that day, but when you added up one very strange woman, one very fearful woman, one kidnapped baby, a group called the Scarlet Host, one horrible altar, and one ugly necklace, the sum total didn't amount to anything. Something was missing, and until he found it, Tucson Slim wouldn't rest.

Chapter 6

The old man hobbled into the dark house and stumbled over the morning newspaper. With a deep complaining sigh, he picked it up, tossed it on the hall table, and cranked up the central air. He was hot. Hot and tired and more than ready to shed his Harvey Hanson persona and return to being plain old Tucson Slim. Shuffling down the hall toward his bedroom, he realized a whole lot more of his body hurt than just his feet. His head, his arms, his neck, even his bones ached.

Maybe he was getting too darned old to go undercover, and then there was that monumental name slip-up with Serpent-woman. Thank the good Lord, he'd managed to cover his backside on that one.

Or had he?

With a weary shake of his shaggy head, he threw his golf hat on the dresser and emptied his pockets into the ceramic dish. Wallet, coins, parking tickets, gas receipts, a candy wrapper. Then his searching fingertips encountered a feathery--.

"What the heck?" His heart pounding, the old man snatched his hand out of his pocket and then remembered. Opal's gift. He removed the fetish with two fingers and dropped it into the dish with everything else. Every time he saw that black magic gris-gris, that nasty-looking feather, string, and bone mass of yuk, he could only think of one word. Hairball.

After shedding his damp polyester jacket, Slim unbuckled his hideout pistol holster and gingerly touched where it had pressed against his ribs. Bruised. It had been a long time since he'd worn that particular pistol three days in a row. How he missed the Twins, their weight perfectly balanced on each hip, their familiar presence so comforting, the protection they provided.

The colorful little cuckoo bird in his Black Forest clock popped out four times and reminded Slim he had to be at work in an hour. He quickly dressed in his beloved cowboy attire, stuffed his wallet into his back pocket, and carried the pile of sweaty clothes he'd just taken off out to his small laundry room. The mundane routine of doing the wash, punching all the right buttons on his stacked unit, pouring the detergent, closing the lid, and listening to the tub fill, settled Slim. Now, if only he had time to fill a big pan with hot water and soak his feet, but sore feet and wet clothes be damned, he had to go to work.

Thinking about his feet reminded Slim of that snake-like Sonya Szymanski. Harvey Hanson or Hank Stone? The idea he couldn't remember exactly what he'd told her still bothered him.

A nagging fear wormed its way back into his day.

The old man hurried back to the bedroom and retrieved Opal's fetish. With a pitying shake of his head that Tucson Slim, Arizona Marshal, could be so superstitious, so illogical, as to believe that ugly thing could actually protect him, Slim tucked it into his vest pocket. Donning his Stetson, he picked up his heavy saddlebag. He was so tired, for a brief moment, he toyed with the idea of leaving the Twins at home.

Nope, he thought. I might not be able to wear them, but I'll sure feel a lot better if they're with me.

Slinging the bag over his shoulder, he grabbed his newspaper and walked to his car. If he hit the traffic lights right, he'd have enough time to get a cup of coffee at Pinnacle Peak Perk and read his newspaper before his shift started.

# # #

His keys in one hand, a grande cup of steaming African/Kona blend in the other, his newspaper tucked under his arm, and his saddlebag draped over his shoulder, Slim saw a strange man, dressed in wrinkled khaki pants, a bold red tie, and a faded denim shirt walking toward him. When the man smiled, his unnaturally tanned face seemed to crack, revealing a set of unnaturally white teeth. He reminded Slim of some actor, a too-tan ladies' man that'd once starred in a movie about the great country singer, Hank Williams Senior. What was his name? George something.

"Mr. Stevens?" the man called out. "I'm Gary Mason from the Daily Star. I'd like to ask you some questions."

A reporter! Slim never cared much for reporters out on the snoop. Especially those that slanted the story they were working on to fit their own personal agenda.

The old man jammed his key into the keyhole and ignored the man.

"Mr. Stevens, don't you have a minute for the press?"

"No!" Juggling his coffee and newspaper, Slim turned the key and pushed open the office door with his hip.

"I won't keep you long," the reporter. "I'm following up on the kidnapping that happened here the other night."

Slim jerked around to confront the man. "What part of 'No' don't you understand?" The saddlebag, which had been precariously balanced on Slim's slumping shoulder, shifted and crashed to the ground. Its leather tie popped open, and Slim's precious Colts slid out on the pavement.

Slopping hot coffee everywhere, Slim scooped up one of his guns, pinching his fingers firmly on the grip as the barrel swung down toward the ground.

The reporter's eyes widened. He raised his hands. "Hold on there, old timer." Babbling something about the rights and responsibilities of the press, the reporter backed away in mincing, hesitant steps. When he reached the edge of the building, he ducked into the alleyway and disappeared.

Slim stood there, listening to the man's dress shoes slip and slide on the round landscaping rocks that covered the narrow space between the main part of the Square and the Security office. What on earth was wrong with that guy? You'd think he'd seen a ghost or something.

He went into the office, put his coffee down, and wiped his dripping hand on his pant leg. Taking out his reading glasses, he put them on and carefully checked the reddening skin between his fingers. No blisters. One thing about getting older, his hands weren't as sensitive to heat as they used to be. That was a good thing today. Scalding hot coffee would have hurt.

Stepping back outside, the old man picked up the other Twin and his saddlebag. After a quick look up and down the walk, he limped back inside his office, closed the door, and laid his six-shooters on the desk.

Seeing his prized pistols shining in the sunlight streaming through his one office window, Slim thought about the reporter and how he'd acted when Slim picked up his pistol. White faced. Hands held high in the air. That fellow thought Slim was going to shoot him. It was almost laughable. People today didn't know a thing about guns. You can't shoot a gun holding it with two fingers on the bottom of the grip.

Besides, was he waving his six-shooter around and acting like he wanted to shoot somebody? No.

Did he even have his finger on the trigger? Certainly not.

Did he ever do anything that could make that man think Tucson Slim might shoot him? Then he remembered the incident with the New York tourist and decided the reporter had most likely leapt to one very stupid, very unfortunate conclusion. Greenhorns! He was doomed to live in a world filled with fools and greenhorns.

Sitting in his chair, Slim groaned as he stretched out his toes and rotated his ankles. His feet hurt like blazes. When he got back home, he was going to throw those dad-blamed tennis shoes in the trash and soak his feet. With that decided, he read the headline on the front page of his newspaper.

ANOTHER COLLEGE STUDENT MISSING
FOUL PLAY SUSPECTED

Disheartened, Slim shook his head. What was Tucson coming to? How many did that make now?

He sipped what was left of his rapidly cooling coffee and skimmed the article. Six male college students had disappeared in as many months. The only thing the boys had in common, besides the school they attended, was the fact they went to a rave on the wrong night.

Slim tried to remember what he'd heard about raves. They were illegal dance parties usually held in vacant warehouses. The kids paid to get in, and a variety of drugs were always available. Sounded like a bad mix to this old man. What were kids today thinking? Stealing babies, doing drugs, putting themselves in dangerous situations.

He turned the page. A few seconds passed before it clicked. The elderly cowboy staring back at him from the printed page was him, Tucson Slim. The marshal's mouth gaped.

But that couldn't be him. He wasn't that old, that feeble looking. And he looked so confused, so lost. Squinting, Slim inspected the fuzzy shapes behind the disheveled old man. The baby's mother, and she was hanging on Detective Mark O'Brien.

The header read:

POLICE RESCUE LOCAL ECCENTRIC
LOST ON MOUNT THUNDERBOLT

The article began with short recap of the kidnapping followed by a long, distorted account of how the former Arizona Marshal had gone up on the mountain all by himself, looking for a cult that didn't exist anymore, gotten lost, and had to be rescued by the police. The reporter had dug up a lot of Slim's personal history and thrown that in for good measure. Writing about things the old man was proud of, his time in the service, the drug busts he'd made along the border in the 60s and 70s. Things he'd rather not see lumped together with the biggest mistake of his life, the incident with the tourist and his car door.

"Dag-nabbed meddlin' bunch of busybodies, anyway. Who wrote this?"

The byline read Gary Mason. Why, that was that same tanned fellow he'd just scared off. Slim flung the first section of newspaper across the room and watched the pages flutter to the floor. He should have shot that reporter while he had the chance. Lying like that, and coming back for more dirt. That yellow-rag journalist obviously wanted everyone to think Tucson Slim was some kind of escapee from a rest home, a pathetic old nincompoop doddering around in the middle of the night looking for spooks, ready to shoot anything that moved. How in the Sam-hill did the Daily News find out about his night on Thunderbolt anyway?

The redheaded detective came to mind.

Yep, Mark O'Brien was right there in that picture. As the man in charge, he was the one to blame, and he would soon regret he'd decided to talk to the press about this old fellow. Slim had known cops like that in the past. Happy to be in the limelight. Always ready to preen for the cameras.

He faltered for a moment. There were those who might say that about Slim himself. He'd never minded having his picture made or having people know he'd been the one who'd brought the bad guy in.

But this different.

Tucson Slim had never in his whole life deliberately tried to make a fool out of a Brother Cop. Didn't matter one smidge to Slim that the detective hadn't been quoted and his picture was only in the background. He was mad!

The old marshal picked up the telephone receiver and punched in the number for the department. A woman answered. Her soft voice sounded sleepy…somehow familiar. "Hullo."

"Hullo?" Slim ranted, "Did you say hullo? Is that the way a professional answers the telephone?"

"A professional what, Tío Slim?"

Slim jerked the receiver away from his ear and stared it. Since when did the cops call him Tío?

He could hear the woman say, "Tío, this is María. Are you all right? We have been worried."

A tremor shot though Slim's body. He'd dialed the wrong number. What was wrong with him? Now he couldn't remember a simple telephone number.

"Tío, are you okay? Should we come?"

Putting the receiver to his mouth, he said, "Sorry, María. I musta dialed the wrong number."

"But are you okay?"

"I'm fine, Marícita. Just in a hurry. I'll talk to you later." Before she could respond, he cleared the line and carefully dialed the number to the police station.

When the duty officer answered, Slim demanded to speak to O'Brien. After a few rings, he heard, "You have reached Detective--."

"I know who I've reached."

"Mark O'Brien's voice mail. Please leave a message--."

Voice mail again! Was that cop ever in his office?

With a disgusted grunt, Slim slammed the receiver down into its cradle. After taking several deep breaths to calm himself, the old man picked up one of the Twins, took out his well-used polishing rag, and slowly rubbed the gun's bright nickel finish with such tender care it was almost a caress.

Slim could be very patient when he had to. He knew how to bank his anger like a campfire and wait. When the time was right, he'd let it flare and settle this thing with O'Brien. That cop wouldn't get away with plastering Slim's face all over the newspaper....

The old man stopped polishing the Colt.

That rag of a newspaper had blown his cover. Everyone he'd met today probably knew he wasn't Harvey Hanson, concerned great-grandfather, or Hank Stone, retired Marine General. They all knew he was Harold Stevens, also known as Tucson Slim, former marshal, inept security guard, old fool.

An icy finger of fear unexpectedly lodged itself in Slim's gut. Serpent-woman. It didn't matter what he'd said his name was. Sonya Szymanski had known he was lying, and all that aura stuff she kept talking about was a load of horse hockey. But, if she'd known he was lying, why had she told him anything about the cult at all?

Or had she told him anything?

He carefully went over what he could remember of their conversation.

Dag-nab-it!

She hadn't given him a thing except the name of the group, the Scarlet Host, and she'd probably known he'd find that out sooner or later anyway. The only time she hadn't been running the show was when he showed her the necklace. That tripped her up for darned sure. Maybe only a little bit, he'd admit that, but it was enough for Slim to see she knew more than she was telling.

Narrowing his eyes, he slugged back the last of his cold coffee and dragged his hand across his mouth. "You haven't told me everything you know, Serpent-woman, but you will. Consider yourself warned. Tucson Slim, Arizona Marshal is on the case."

He traded the polished Twin for the dusty one on the desk. As he buffed that gun and tried to decide what he should do next, someone tapped on the office door. "Harold, are you in there? It's me, Carter Winslow."

Great! Now his boss was here, calling him Harold. That always meant trouble. This day was just getting better and better.

Slim spread the remainder of the newspaper over his saddlebag and the one pistol on the desk. He laid the other Twin, still clutched in his hand, in his lap. "Come on in, Carter. Since when do you knock?"

His pallid face streaming sweat, Carter peeked in and looked warily around the room. "Everything all right?"

"Why are you slinking around like there're are rattlesnakes in here?" Slim barked. "Come on in."

"Tell me where they are first?"

"Who you looking for?"

"Don't try that 'butter wouldn't melt in your mouth' routine with me, Harold. You know darn good and well why I'm here. You nearly scared that reporter half to death."

"Scared him? How in the Sam Hill did I do that? I barely had time to say anything before he took off like a scalded yellow dog."

"What did you expect him to do when you pulled your guns?"

"He said I pulled my guns on him? I never did no such thing. I dropped my saddlebag. The Twins slid out and I picked 'em up. If he said I drew down on him, he's nothing but a stinkin' liar."

Head lowered like a pit bull ready to fight, Carter snarled, "Harold, I can't have some maniac working here." He jerked a pink termination slip out of his shirt pocket and threw it on the desk. "Get your things and get out. You're fired."

The last two words reverberated through Slim's mind like gunshots in a cavern. Fired! Now he was fired?

Forgetting about the gun he still held, the old man stood. "Wait a minute."

Carter stared at the gun. Gaping like a fish out of water, his mouth opened and closed several times, as he slowly backed away from the desk. When he bumped into the wall, he found the knob, yanked open the door, and took off down the sidewalk screaming something about calling the police.

Dazed, Slim stood there a minute trying to comprehend what had happened. He noticed the pistol tightly gripped in his hand.

Reality hit him like a plunge in an icy mountain creek. Now he'd never be able to convince anyone he hadn't intentionally drawn his guns and threatened people.

Almost in a panic, Slim stuffed his guns back into his saddlebag. He dumped the contents of his wastebasket on the floor, grabbed his desk calendar, and dropped it in the bottom of the plastic can. He turned in a tight circle, running his hands through his hair, looking for things he should take with him, knowing whatever he left behind would be lost forever.

He opened the bottom desk drawer and took out his gun oil, rags, foot powder, and a few odds and ends of personal items and dropped them in the can.

His manuscript. He jerked open the middle desk drawer, and hoping he'd remembered to save the last time he worked on his novel, retrieved his only floppy disc. The one labeled HANK STONE.

The last thing he did was strip the wall of his prized photographs and stack them precariously on top of his things. Somehow, his own eight by ten glossy wound up on top. Seeing the young, handsome Slim staring back at him enraged the old man. What shame he'd brought to the proud name of Stevens. What a mess he'd made of his life.

Tucson Slim picked up the glass-framed photograph, and with a stifled curse, sailed it across the room. Storming out of the office, he barely heard his picture hit the wall and crash to the floor.

# # #

Carrying the heavy wastebasket into his house, Slim placed it on the floor, closed the drapes, and unplugged the telephone. He didn't want to be disturbed while he waited for the police to come and arrest him. And they would come. He'd been a burr under Mark O'Brien's saddle for days now. If the redheaded detective were any kind of cop at all, he would jump at the chance to rid himself of his own personal nemesis.

After a quick trip to the kitchen, Slim settled in his Lazy Boy chair and popped the tab on a cold Coors beer. The last cold beer he'd have before he went to the gray-walled hoosegow. Staring at the front door, he slowly emptied the can and chose to think about the other shameful thing that happened that day.

He'd been fired.

He couldn't believe it. In all his long years and many jobs, he'd never been fired before. Oh, it wasn't like he needed the money from this part-time rent-a-cop gig. With his Social Security, his G.I. benefits, his retirement from the State, and his savings, financially he'd be fine. He led a spare life, as lean and mean as Slim kept himself. What he would miss were his time with the tourists. Signing autographs, posing for pictures, being somebody, playing the role he'd been destined to live—Arizona Marshal—strong, silent, upholding the law.

Upholding the law…. Well, these last few days he'd certainly failed in that respect.

Slim wondered where was it he stepped off the path of truth and honor. He was no longer the person he'd always been, a man of strong moral fiber, a man who'd never been exactly humble about his ability to live a clean, upright life.

And that was pride, wasn't it?

Maybe that was where he'd gone wrong. Mama always said he was too proud. What was it the Good Book said? Pride goeth before the fall? Shoot, with eighty years of arrogance under his belt, his would be an epic crash. A lawman in jail. How much more monumental could it be?

For the first time since Dolores passed away, Slim was almost glad she was gone. For her to see what he had come to….

He hung his head. Even if the entire world knew he was an old fool, it would have been more than he could bear if Dolores had lived to think that.

Maybe that was where he'd gone wrong. Had his all-consuming secret love for another's man wife been his downfall? But surely the fates-that-be knew he couldn't help himself. He had tried to fight, but his love for Dolores, that sweet, sweet bondage, had always been a silken web holding him captive, never allowing him to follow the natural course of a man to marry and have children. Maybe if he'd been a husband and a father he would have had more than his career and his celebrity to bolster him in his old age. Maybe he wouldn't have become this caricature of the man he'd once been.

Slim slugged down the last of his beer, crushed the aluminum can with one hand, and placed it on the table next to him. Drifting off to sleep, his dreams were filled with the desert. Vast vistas of sand and volcanic rock. Prickly cactus mixed with fragrant sagebrush. Tumbleweed and rattlesnake. Blazing days and fiery sunsets. Bitter nights and frost-glazed dawns. And then in the serenity of his dream, the desert floor shuddered. Slim turned and saw a herd of mustang thunder over a ridge and bear down on him.

As the lead stallion, a foam-flecked black with red-glowing eyes, raced by, Slim grabbed the horse's mane, and just as he had in the movies, the old cowboy swung up on the horse's broad back. He clamped his knees and hunkered down over the mustang's muscular neck, his silver hair blowing in the wind, mingling with the black's streaming midnight mane, as he urged the horse through the cactus and rock-studded sand. The rest of the herd fanned out on each side of Slim and the mustang, and together, they rode across the desert, a thundering dust storm. Around him, the horses' hooves flashed, manes and tails billowed, eyes shone with joy.

They went on and on, riding fast and hard, chasing the setting sun, or were they running from the coming night? Terror seized Slim's heart, and he spurred the horse on, faster and faster, until they raced over the rim of the Grande Canyon. For a second or two they flew, free, unfettered, and then gravity caught up. The mustang screamed as they plummeted down, falling toward the Colorado River lying in the canyon below like a narrow glistening ribbon.

Covered with sweat, Slim jerked awake. The room was dark. All he could hear was the sharp tick, tick of his old mantle clock. He'd never put much stock in analyzing his or anybody else's dreams, but he knew those mustangs were a symbol of what he'd always had and would have no more. The police would lock him up. He would never escape.

As much as he wanted to leave behind the nightmare his life had become, he was too old and too tired to run. He would wait for his destiny right there in his leather Lazy Boy.

Slim shifted his weight and tried to ignore the demand his body was suddenly making. He slammed his fist on the arm of his chair.

Couldn't anything ever go the way he wanted it to?

With a disgusted sigh, he quickly altered his plan. He would get up and go to the john. Then he would come back and wait in this chair for his destiny. Wait until the authorities came to take him away.

After attending to the needs of nature, he settled back in his chair, and between fitful catnaps where he was always running, he waited. Mid-morning, he was still waiting. Now his stomach complained with low rumblings. Nature called again. And a spark of anger smoldered deep within his heart.

How long was it going to take the Department to do their duty, anyway? They knew where he lived. If the police moved this slow in all their cases, no wonder the crime rate soared. No wonder they couldn't find that baby. The longer Slim waited, the madder he got.

Finally, when he was unable to disregard his body any longer, Slim stalked to the bathroom. After he took care of his most pressing need, he glanced in the mirror and saw his wild tangled hair and grizzled cheeks. His mouth tasted like a barroom floor. Remembering the time he'd actually tasted one, face down in a fight back in Nogales many years ago, the old man almost smiled and decided he'd better make himself a little more presentable.

When the newspapers got a hold of this story, they would grind Tucson Slim like grist, and he would not have his face plastered all over the Daily Star looking like Nick Nolte's older brother. The next picture they took of Tucson Slim, Arizona Marshal, he'd be standing tall, steely eyed and proud.

With determined firm strokes, the old man combed his hair into place and brushed his teeth, most of which were his own personal, still-in-his-mouth teeth, thank you very much.

He picked up his old shaving mug and stared at the faded logo. U.S.M.C. He and that stoneware cup had been around the world together, all the way from the Arizona desert to the Philippines and back again. They'd never let him take this to prison. Break it, and you've got yourself a nice sharp weapon.

Blinking back a shameful rush of tears, Slim worked the soap into a rich foam, held his mustache out of the way, and furiously lathered his face. He picked up his straight razor.

One more thing he'd have to give up. They'd never let him keep his razor. They'd relegate him to one of those cheap plastic things, and a shave just wasn't a shave without thick lather and the smooth strokes of real tempered steel.

Blocking the thoughts that led him closer and closer to tears, he quickly shaved and after thoroughly rinsing his face, he dashed a stinging splash of Old Spice on his cheeks and neck. Feeling a little more presentable, Slim quickly straightened up the bathroom, took his towels to the laundry room, and remembered his wet laundry was still in the washing machine from the day before. He threw his wet, slightly sour clothing into the dryer and tossed in a softener sheet. Tucson Slim might be going to jail, but the cops who came to take him away would never say he lived like a pig!

Railing about the ineptitudes of the Desert Valley Police Department and all the extra work they were making for him by being so late, the old man slammed into the kitchen. He washed his hands and made a peanut butter and banana sandwich. After melting a pat of butter in his old cast iron skillet, Slim plopped the sandwich in and mumbled, "Here's to you, Big El."

While his sandwich grilled, Slim gazed out his kitchen window at his neglected back yard. There had been a time when America couldn't imagine life without Elvis Presley, the King of Rock and Roll. But here they were, years later, still motoring on, having to live with the Prince of Pop because the King was dead.

Slim wondered who'd take his place when the oldest living Arizona Marshal was in jail. Jail. A cop in behind bars. He was no fool. He knew what happened to ex-cops in lockup. Cops rated right up there on the prison social register with baby rapers. Baby rapers!

A sizzling noise brought the old man back to Tucson, and he picked up his skillet, and with a well-practiced move, flipped his sandwich to the uncooked side. When it was all butter-browned and crispy on the outside and gooey inside, he put it on a plate and poured himself a big glass of whole milk. No fat-free for this old man. His mouth watering, his stomach growling, he carried his lunch to the kitchen table and sat down.

The doorbell rang.

The old man slammed his plate down. "Wouldn't you know it? I sit up all stinking night waiting for the police, and as soon as I decide to eat a bite, here they come. It's a gol-durned conspiracy."

The doorbell rang again.

Slim stood and stomped to the front door, but before he got there, the bell rang three more times. As he prepared to ream out whatever policeman had the audacity to sit on his doorbell like that, the bell rang again.

Slim yanked open the door and roared, "Keep your britches on, you impatient insolent pup!"

The only person on his front step was a teenaged girl, her hand poised to ring the bell again. When he yelled, she jerked away and almost stumbled down the front steps. "Crickey, do you always scream at people when you open your door?"

Finding one small girl and not the entire Tucson police force on his porch robbed Slim of any response. He stood there and stared at the girl. She was a petite little thing, swathed in an oversized orange tee shirt with silver glittered words proclaiming "Girl Power" that almost covered her baggy, fraying denim shorts. She had extremely short, spiky bleached blonde hair and shaved eyebrows.

Groaning under his breath, Slim wondered if today's youth had an aversion to regular eyebrows, but he would admit, except for the shaved brows, she looked somewhat familiar and could have been any of the countless kids who roamed his neighborhood. Even down to the prerequisite backpack she wore. Next to her sandaled feet was a large yellow canvas duffel bag, its zipper not quiet closed.

Well, one thing he did know, he didn't need this right now. He had more important things on his mind.

His intense stare apparently made her uneasy. Shuffling her feet, she nervously glanced over her shoulder at a passing car.

Anxious to get rid of her so he could continue to wait for his fate in peace, Slim said, "Look, kid, if you're selling something, don't matter if it's religion or band candy, I ain't interested."

She said, "That's good 'cause I ain't selling nothing. I'm here, because, like, I need your help."

Slim looked for a disabled car parked somewhere on his street. Finding none, he focused on her face and tried to remember where he'd seen her before. "Do I know you?"

"Sorta." She picked up her duffle, and catching him by surprise, pushed her way through the doorway, and hurried into his living room.

"Hey," Slim blustered. "Who invited you in?"

"Like, if you had any manners, you would have." The girl dropped her backpack on the floor and carefully placed her duffle bag on his sofa. After a quick peek inside, she wandered through the room. "Man, it's dark in here. Why don't you, like, turn on your lights or open some curtains, sheriff?"

"I ain't no sheriff. I used to be a marshal…an Arizona Marshal."

"Sheriff, marshal, cop, schmop, whatever. They're all the same to me."

Slim bristled as she brazenly inspected his bookshelf and picked up his quick-draw trophy. "Put that down."

"Gosh, I guess you used'ta be a pretty good shot."

"Still am."

"Cool!" She set the trophy aside and ran her index finger across his books, wrinkling her nose. "Louise Lamour? Why does an old guy like you read romance novels?"

"For your information, young woman, it's Louis not Louise, and the man was a great writer."

"Oh, yeah, what did he write?"

"Western novels. Like Zane Grey and Elmer Kelton."

"Right, like those are titles I ever heard of. Don't you have any sci-fi or horror? I love Stephen King."

The idea came to Slim that maybe the only reason this girl was here to get a good look at the "Local Eccentric." Time for her to go. "My reading material is none of your business, so why don't you run along and pester somebody else?"

"Hey, what's this?" She pointed to the glass jug he thought he'd hidden behind two large American History books, a glass jug filled with silver dollars Slim had been saving for years. "Wow, I've never seen so many Lady Libertys. My grandma used to save 'em too. Must be an old person thing."

He decided right then and there he'd have to keep a close eye on this girl or his silver dollars would probably vanish. "Leave those alone," Slim snapped. "And tell me what you want."

She jerked her head around, stared at him for a moment, and shrugged. "Don't get your panties in a twist. I ain't gonna steal 'em."

Slim jaw dropped. No child had ever talked to him like that before.

She noticed an old magazine photograph Slim had framed and hung on his wall and walked across the room away from his jar of silver. "Who are these guys?"

"You mean to tell me you don't recognize General Douglas MacArthur when he reclaimed the Philippines? What're they teaching in school these days?"

She glared at him. "For your information, I don't go to school. I never got to take history."

Slim wanted to yell at the kid for quitting school and being so disrespectful, but he decided if he answered her questions, maybe she would go away. "Okay, that photo was taken back in World War Two the day the General returned to Philippine Islands and reclaimed them from the Japanese."

"Like, what was his name again?"

"Douglas MacArthur."

"Why do you have this picture all framed and everything?"

"Because it was a great day in American history, and I'm in it. That's me right there behind the General."

Squinting, she moved closer to the picture. Then she turned and looked Slim up and down. "Man, if that's you, this picture musta been taken a long, long, <u>long</u> time ago."

"Thanks for remindin' me."

"Like, why did this General guy let the Japanese have the Philippines in the first place if he was gonna come take 'em back? And why was he wading in the ocean? Wasn't there like a boat or something?" She looked at Slim again. "And why were you with him? Were you, like, important or something?"

Hungry and tired, the old man fumed. Be a little bit nice, and it was like he'd opened some kind of floodgate to hell. Besides, since the police would be here any minute, he didn't have time to answer all these questions. "Don't matter. You gotta leave. I'm expectin' someone."

She ignored him and pointed to his wastebasket of photographs. "Hey, why are you throwing John Wayne away?"

"That ain't none of your business." Slim picked up his office trash can and stowed it in the hall closet. When he returned, the girl had kicked off her sandals and flopped down on the sofa next to her bag.

After making sure his silver dollars were still where he'd left them, Slim said, "Miss, I said you had to go, not sit down and make yourself to home."

"Don't it matter that I said I need your help? You sure didn't hesitate to help that fat cow. Why won't you help me?"

Each time this girl opened her mouth, Slim aged another decade. The rapid twists and turns of her conversation confused him. "What on earth are you talking about? No, no, I don't care what you're talking about. I want you to go."

"Man, do you always have such a short fuse?"

"Only with the rudest girl I've ever met. Now, shoo. I said I'm waiting for someone."

The girl grinned. "Wow, you must be expecting one hot date."

Her bold insinuations shocked Slim, but before he could say anything, she jumped up, grabbed her duffle and her backpack, and took off down the hall. "Man, like, I gotta go to the john."

Before he could stop her, she was in the bathroom, slamming the door and clicking the lock.

Standing there, completely at a loss for what he should do next, Slim heard her murmuring something. He yelled, "If you're talking to me, I can't hear you."

"I ain't talking to you!" The murmuring continued.

Slim froze. What if she'd opened the window and was letting some lunatic in to rob him? What if there were guns in that duffle she kept hanging on to?

Keeping to one side…just in case she decided to shoot him through the door…Slim crept closer, but could only hear the soft rise and fall of her girlish voice.

Hurrying to his bedroom, Slim opened the window as quietly as he could and poked his head outside. No one by the bathroom window. The screen was still up. No bushes broken or moving. Nothing. What the heck was going on?

He closed the window and returned to the bathroom door.

She was still murmuring, but then he heard her squeak, "Ouch."

Unless she was a complete psycho who talked nonstop to herself, there was someone in there with that girl.

Slim pounded on the door. "I said I was waiting for someone. You've got to leave--right now."

No response.

"Young woman, I want you out of my bathroom right this minute."

"I'll come out when you promise to help me."

His first thought was to call the police. Why bother? He could be dead and gone, and that girl plum grown up by the time they arrived. Maybe he could call the fire department and tell them he had a stray cat trapped in his bathroom.

Almost as if she could read his mind, she said, "Marshal, if you're thinking about calling the police, you'd better not. I'll tell them I locked myself in here because, you like...like...you lured me into your house, and then tried to molest me. Now, are you going to help me or not?"

"Do you think the police will believe that ridiculous story?" Even as he said it, Slim knew that today, the police would believe her and he'd have one more strike against his record. If he could only figure out what she was up to.

Staring at the glass doorknob, Slim slapped his hand against his forehead. He had another key in the kitchen junk drawer.

"Hey, marshal, can you hear me? Are you still out there?"

"I can hear you just fine. I guess if you're gonna tell a bunch of lies about me, I'll have to help you."

"Ha," she crowed triumphantly. "I knew if I said the word molest, you'd crumble like a cookie. Man, can I call'em or what?"

Chapter 7

Slim stood in the hall, staring at the girl cowering like a cornered bobcat in his bathroom. He imagined if he tried to touch her, she'd hiss, and he'd draw back a bloody stump.

She hugged the baby tightly to her chest and watched him with eyes spilling tears. "You got to help me. If they find me, they're gonna kill me."

"Now, Miss, regardless of what you've seen on TV, the police don't kill people they're looking for. Their main goal is to return that baby to her mama."

She scrunched further back into the corner. "I ain't talking about the police, and you don't understand. This is my baby. I'm her real mama."

The girl looked so young, so wounded, so desperate, cringing against his aqua blue ceramic tile wall, Slim's heart softened a little. "Come on, girlie, let's go in the kitchen and have us a sodie pop. Then you can tell me what this is all about."

She didn't move, just stared at him with those haunted eyes.

Slim remembered a little filly he'd once had. Some jerk had beaten her real bad and left her out in the desert to die, only she didn't. When Slim found her, covered with oozing welts and stinging flies, she was half-crazed and so afraid that every time he came near her, she'd bolt and run away. He'd gotten the bag of oats he carried for his own horse out of his pack, found himself a comfortable rock to sit on, and spent an afternoon talking to her all sugary and soft. Finally, the little thing either overcame her fear or got so hungry she decided to trust him. Taking the time to win her over worked like a charm.

Hoping this tactic would serve him as well this time, Slim said, "Okay, we don't have to go anywhere. I'll sit out here, and when you're ready, you can talk to me."

He sat with his back to the wall, his long, thin legs stretched out in front of him. This was another time he could be patient. When he could see his redemption just over the horizon.

All he had to do was gain her confidence, call O'Brien, and the baby would be back in its mother's arms before dark. His reputation would be restored. He'd be a hero again. Maybe he wouldn't have to go to jail, and he could get his job back. "What's your name, girl?"

"Vamp."

"Vamp? What kind of name is that?"

"One I chose myself, and one everyone calls me."

"I didn't ask what everyone calls you. If you expect me to help you, I need to know your given name."

"But I hate my real name."

"Too bad. Maybe you can change it later, but right now I need to know your legal name."

"Oh, all right. My name is Katy."

"Katy--."

"I told you I'd rather be called Vamp."

"And I ain't calling you no silly made-up name, so get used to it."

The places where her eyebrows should have been peaked in surprise. "Hey, don't they call you Tucson Slim? Ain't that a made-up name?"

Slim glared at her. "When people been calling you Vamp for sixty years, I will too, but for now I'm calling you Katy, and you better tell me your last name."

She chewed her lip for a moment, then blurted out, "My name's Katy Ann Cleary. How's that for boring?"

"Katy ain't such a bad name. Is it short for Katherine?"

"Nope, just plain ol' Katy Ann, a name that says you're a weak little red neck. Vamp's short for vampire and says you're cool and smart and mean…real mean." She sighed, and still cradling the baby in her arms, leaned back against the wall. "You have to be smart and mean if you're gonna live on the streets."

"Been on the streets long?"

"Long enough."

Slim decided it was time to ask about the baby. "How's little...." He did a quick mental search for the infant's name. He could almost see it right next to his in the newspaper, and it started with an "F". "How's little...Frances? That's her name, ain't it? Frances?"

She shot him such a look that Slim thought if he'd been made of rock, he'd now be blasted into a million grains of sand. "Don't call her that. I named her Jasmine Skye."

"Is she as pretty as her name? Can I see her?"

"No."

"Come on, Katy, why did you come here if you don't trust me?"

"I came here because I read all about you in the newspaper. I knew you couldn't be a crazy old coot like they made you out to be. Only a truly righteous dude would risk his life to save someone else's kid."

Slim wasn't sure how righteous he was, but he wasn't going to debate the issue and destroy this child's illusions. "Well, I guess I ain't changed much since you got here."

"No, I guess you haven't." She put her hand up under the blanket, wiggled around, and then revealed the child, a rosy-cheeked angel with a halo of golden fuzz and a translucent trickle of milk running out of the corner of her rosebud mouth. The sleeping infant suckled the air. The house was so quiet Slim could hear her breathing, soft panting baby huffs.

His heart swelled. No doubt, this little doll was the baby from the Square, and before long, he would be out of this mess, smelling sweet with plenty to eat.

Katy's face beamed as she gently stroked the infant's downy cheek. "She's three weeks old. Chuchi said she weighed right around six pounds, but she's sure chubbing out now that I'm nursing her again."

When Katy talked about the baby, her face opened up like a flower in bloom, and the rebellious teenager disappeared. If it hadn't been for that ring in her nose, the spiky peroxide hair, and the fact she had no eyebrows, she might have looked like any new mother.

Slim caught himself. Except this kid wasn't the real mother. Katy was the kidnapper, but if she was the kidnapper, how did she know how much the baby weighed? Unless she was making it all up. Maybe she was crazier than he thought. Or maybe she was clever...really clever.

The girl murmured, "She's so pretty."

"Yep, she's a real peach, but don't you think it would be best for everyone, especially the baby, if you returned her to her mother? She's mighty worried about--"

The girl clutched the infant tightly to her chest again. The baby squealed, balled up her tiny fists, and screamed her face purple. "I told you she's my baby, not hers."

Trying to make himself heard over the complaining child, Slim spoke in a loud voice. "Last I heard that other woman was still claiming she's the mother, and since I don't possess the wisdom of Solomon, can you prove she's yours?"

Katy's face closed, and Vamp returned. She jerked up her tee shirt, and before Slim could look away, exposed a rather large, distended breast.

His face blazing hot, Slim clamped his eyes shut. "Girl, what do you think you're doing?"

"Breastfeeding <u>my</u> baby." Katy shifted around, and then groaned, "God that hurts." There was some more shifting and she said, "Okay, you can look now. I'm covered."

Slim scratched his head. He didn't know much about the habits and instincts of a nursing child. Maybe Katy had lost her own baby, and this one was so hungry she'd suckle at any breast.

Katy's accusing voice cut into his thoughts. "You don't believe me, do you?"

"Don't you have any other proof? A birth certificate--something?"

She reached into the unzipped duffle, pulled out a photograph, and threw it at him.

A Polaroid snapshot landed on the floor next to Slim's leg. He picked it up and slipped on his glasses. Someone had taken a picture of Katy and a baby covered in a blood-streaked waxy substance, umbilical cord still attached.

"This could be any newborn," Slim said.

Katy gave a disgusted look and uncovered Jasmine's chubby legs. She pointed at a rather large strawberry birthmark on the child's upper thigh. "Now, look at the picture. Like, can't you see it's the same?"

Slim compared the child's leg to the photo. As best as he could tell, the bright red birthmark was in the same place and had the exact shape as the one in the snapshot. "Okay, let's say you've convinced me, but you'll still need real proof to convince the authorities. Don't you have a birth certificate? That would have her footprint on it, and if I remember correctly, it would also have your fingerprint."

"No, I had her at home, and duh, Marshal, I don't need any of that. Haven't you ever heard of DNA?"

DNA? Of course he'd heard of DNA. Embarrassed, Slim shot back, "Girl, if you got it all figured out, then why are you here? And if you haven't done anything wrong, why don't you go on to the police? But wait, if you're afraid of the police, maybe you did do something wrong."

"I haven't done anything wrong, and the police are the least of my problems."

"Then what is your biggest problem?"

She turned away. "I don't want to talk about it. Look, all I need is a place to stay until I can find Chuchi."

"Who's that?"

"Chuchi? She's my friend. She drove the van the night we took Jasmine back."

"Where is she?"

"I don't want to talk about it."

Slim fought his rising anger. "Then tell me how that other woman wound up with your baby?"

"That'll take too long."

"Katy, if you want me to help you, you've got to give me something to work with or this conversation is over, and I'm calling the police."

Katy glanced down at the baby's exposed foot and touched each tiny toe. "Okay, I'll talk, but I need some water. I feel like I'm thirsting to death. And I don't want to nurse Jasmine in your john if I don't have to."

Lurching to his feet, Slim said, "No problem. Let's go into the living room, and you can tell me everything."

# # #

Slim tossed out his stone-cold Elvis Special sandwich, and got a large glass of iced water, and went into his living room where he found the girl curled up in his Lazy Boy, nursing her child. When he gave her the water, she said, "You know, me and Chuchi would have gotten clean away if you hadn't blabbed to the papers about my tattoo. But we fixed that little problem." She showed him her wrists, her pale, unmarked wrists.

Scolding himself for not remembering her tattoo sooner, Slim sputtered, "Where is it? Did you have it removed?"

Katy scrubbed her arm against her shorts and revealed the now all-too-familiar mark. "After you snitched on me, Chuchi showed me how to cover it up with some kind of stage make-up."

Slim slowly sat down. A good lawman would have immediately looked at her wrists. Unsettled by his sloppy observations, the old man had a sneaking suspicion he'd forgotten to ask about something else, too…something important.

"Marshal, I think they must've found Chuchi."

"Who found her?"

"I don't want to talk about it."

"Katy, the people who probably found your friend, are they who you're running from?"

"I said I don't want to talk about it."

"Well it's like I said, Katy. If you don't tell me anything, I can't help you."

She mumbled, "I'm running from Alastair Light."

"What's Alastair Light?"

"It's who, not what."

There she went twisting and turning the conversation again. "Katy, I don't understand."

"Alastair Light is my baby's father, okay?"

Fishing out the small pencil stub and notebook out of his shirt pocket, Slim wrote the name down so he wouldn't forget it. "Light's his last name?"

She snuffled. "Yeah."

Slim looked up as Katy scrubbed away her tears. "Can you believe it, Marshal? Her very own daddy sold her for twenty-five grand. And I thought my dad was a loser."

She looked so vulnerable, so hurt, Slim wanted with all his heart to believe her, but his lawman reserve continued to hold his emotions in check. "Why would the baby's father sell her?"

"Well, duh again, Marshal. For the money."

"How did you get mixed up with this Alastair?"

More tears sprang her eyes and rolled down her pale cheeks. "Like, I met him at a rave."

Again with the raves. With all those college kids disappearing, the girl was lucky to be alive.

"We hit it off so I went home with him."

Slim tried to keep his expression from registering how he felt about her bold announcement, but apparently he wasn't very successful.

Katy said, "Don't you look at me like that. I was living on the streets, and Al seemed like a real nice guy. He said he worked in computers and owned his own house. I couldn't believe how lucky I was to have found someone who could take care of me. Someone older--."

"How old is he?"

"Twenty-seven. He bought me some really cool clothes and a stack of my own CD's. We were just like the happy little married couple. I kept up the house. He brought home take-out 'cause I can't cook. The only time we ever fought was when he went out with his weird friends, but that was only once or twice a month. But he changed as soon as he found out I was expecting…."

She paused, chewed her lip a second or two, and then said, "No, that's wrong, Al didn't actually start acting funny until after he took me to the parlor."

"The parlor?"

"The tattoo parlor. Fantasy, Feathers, and Frills down on Pecos. He said if I was going to be a part of his family, I had to wear his family crest." She gestured to the tattoo on her wrist.

"Said that was his family crest, did he?"

"Yeah, some family man he is. I only got this ugly thing to please him." Her eyes filled with tears again. "That's when he started pressuring me to let him sell our baby, and that's when I found out he didn't even have a job. He gets all his money from his mother and selling babies."

"He's sold other babies?"

"Oh, yeah. Lots. He has his own little production line going. When he realized I wasn't gonna just hand over my kid like his other hos, he tried to buy me off. He said if I'd stay with him and keep having babies, he'd take care of me, and give me anything I wanted."

"What'd you do then? Give him the baby and then change your mind again?"

"No," Katy wailed.

The girl's cry startled Jasmine.

I'm sorry," Katy murmured to the baby. She shot Slim a hard look. "I told Al this was my baby and if he didn't want it, that was fine. We'd leave, but he freaked out. Said the baby was already sold. Then he took me to the house where all his other girls live and dumped me. That's when I met Chuchi. She's twenty-five and like the leader in that house. She's the one who told me this tat ain't no family crest at all. It's the mark of that bunch she and Al belong too. The Scarlet Host."

Slim jumped to his feet. "The Scarlet Host? I knew they weren't dead and gone away, only I thought they were gonna sacrifice this baby, not sell her."

"Sacrifice?" Katy shook her head. "I never heard nothing about no sacrifices. Chuchi said the Host has rituals every month, and that was where Al was always going when he left me, but Chuchi's a nice person. She wouldn't have nothing to do with no baby sacrifice. Besides, Al wouldn't let them kill some baby he could sell."

Opening his wallet, Slim took out the necklace. The turquoise spun as he held it up. "Have you ever seen anything like this before?"

"Bring it over here so I can see it up close. I ain't got telescopic vision, you know."

When Slim gave her the necklace, he scrutinized her every move. Unlike that Szymanski woman, Katy's face lit up like Christmas morning. "Wow, a claw with turquoise. This is so cool, but it ain't exactly your style." She turned the stone over and saw the engraving. "Hey, where'd you get this?"

Slim grabbed the necklace. "Don't matter where I got it."

The girl's face fell. "Gosh, you don't have to get so jazzed. I thought we were gonna be friends."

Slightly embarrassed, Slim tried to make up. "We are friends, but the necklace is part of my investigation."

"Oh, I get it." The girl narrowed her eyes and frowned. "You don't trust me, do you?"

"I don't know you, Katy."

Katy looked away and mumbled, "Well, I don't know you either."

"Then, I guess only time will tell if we placed our trust in the right person, won't it?"

She stared at him a moment. "Yeah, like, I guess it will."

"Do all people in the Scarlet Host wear that tattoo?"

She hesitated a moment before answering. "I've already told you enough to get me killed, so I guess I don't have nothing left to lose. I might as well tell you everything. These wrist tattoos are only for Al's girls." She flicked another renegade tear from her cheek. "It shows you're a bearer for the Host."

"A bearer? What the Sam-Hill does that mean?"

"It means these girls get pregnant and have the babies so the Al can sell'em for the Scarlet Host."

Slim shook his head. This was all so unbelievable. "Katy, why did you stay with those people after Al left you at that house?"

"Because when I tried to run away, they locked me up."

"Locked you up?"

"Shoved me in a room with a half bath and burglar bars and padlocked the door on the outside. Presto-chango, instant jail."

"What happened when you had the baby?"

"Nothing until she was about two weeks old. Chuchi thought maybe Al decided to let me keep her, because all the other babies left when they were only a couple of days old. Then he shows up like the Lord and Master of Everyone, and says he's taking Jasmine. Says he got an extra five grand for keeping her so long. And do you know why we had to keep her? Because her new parents wanted to go to Europe before they took her. Europe! I told Al he wasn't getting my kid. When I tried to stop him, the bastard knocked me down and choked me. I passed out. When I came to Jasmine was gone."

Katy turned her head toward the light and rubbed the side of her throat. "If you look real close, you can still see the bruises."

She was right. Slim could see greenish yellow mottling on her lower neck. He fought the protective feeling welling up inside him. There were too many questions left to ask.

One in particular kept bugging him. He didn't know much about human babies, but he knew calves. If the calf didn't nurse on a regular basis, the mother would lose her milk. "If Jasmine's been gone a week, how'd you keep your milk?"

"After Al left with Jasmine, Chuchi told me he said I was too much trouble, and he was sending some guy named Roadkill to take me out to the desert and get rid of me once and for all."

Slim's old head was absolutely swimming. This girl's story got more bizarre by the minute. How much of this was he supposed to believe? "But you don't seem to be dead."

She lifted an eyebrow. "Observant for an old guy, aren't you?"

"Well, what the-Sam-Hill happened? And you still ain't told me how you kept your milk."

"I'm getting there."

"This is taking a long time, Katy."

"Well, I told you it's a long story, Marshal."

Slim glanced at the clock. Still no police and now it was lunchtime. "You hungry?"

The girl's face lit up. "Man, am I ever."

"How about I rustle us up a couple of cheese sandwiches and some chips."

"As long as it's on white bread with lots of mayo, sounds great."

"Be right back." Slim smiled as he walked to the kitchen. White bread and mayo. Katy was his kind of girl.

"Quit your bragging and tell me what you want." He backed down the hall toward the kitchen. With key in hand he returned to hear her say, "So you see, you got it all wrong, Dude. I'm the innocent victim here, not that fat cow at Centennial Square."

He hesitated. Why did she keep referring to a cow? There were no cattle at the Square.

"So, like you gonna help me or wh--"

He turned the key and opened the door.

Sitting on the floor Indian style with a cloth thrown over her shoulder, the girl held a bundle of rags or something in her arms. The duffle was open next to her. Her cocky attitude gone, her eyes widened, her mouth formed a prefect "O".

Slim suddenly knew those wide, dark eyes. Only the tattoos were missing.

Crablike, Dagger-girl scrambled into the corner, clutching the bundle to her chest. A tiny bare foot poked out the end and flexed its toes.

The frightened girl cried, "You're not taking my baby. You'll have to kill me first."

Chapter 8

The old man watched the girl wolf down her sandwich like a starving animal, daintily wipe her mouth on a paper napkin, and smile. "Thanks, Marshal. I needed that. Since I been nursing Jasmine I'm hungry all the time."

When she grabbed a handful of chips and munched away like she had all the time in the world, Slim decided to get her back on track. "Tell me how you missed your appointment in the desert with the killer your boyfriend sent."

"Oh, yeah, Roadkill. Turns out the creep's a major tweaker."

"Tweaker?"

"A meth head. A person who uses methamphetamines." Katy spoke slowly like she thought Slim couldn't understand her.

"I read the papers, girl," Slim protested. "I know what meth is. I just never heard of the tweaker part before."

"A tweaker is a meth user, Marshal. Tweakers live for the high, so Chuchi hooked Roadkill up with a new supplier and promised him a butt-load of meth, so he went away."

"He left the Host?"

"Naw, they don't allow druggies in the Host. Chuchi said dope messes with their auras or something woo-woo like that."

When the girl said aura, Sonya Szymanski's face popped into Slim's mind. The old man shivered. He wasn't sure he liked where this was leading.

"After he left, Chuchi said if I'd keep my mouth shut about the house, she'd help me get Jasmine back."

"How could she trust you? Why wouldn't you get the baby and go straight to the police?

"Why would I? I don't care what those crazies do as long as me and my baby don't get mixed up in it."

Resisting the urge to lecture her on social responsibility, Slim sighed. No wonder the world was going to Hell-in-a-hand-basket. Young people today didn't care a fig for anybody but themselves. He wasn't surprised drugs, illegal guns, kidnappings, rape, organized crime were on the rise. Why, when he was young--.

"Earth to Marshal Slim," Katy called out. "Do you wanna hear the rest of this or what?"

His face hot, his voice indignant, Slim snapped, "I heard every word you said. What happened after Chuchi dealt with Roadkill?"

"She told me to go to her godmother's house and wait, and while I was waiting, I should pump."

"Pump what?"

Katy rolled her eyes. "If breast milk's the very best food for a baby, and I had to keep my milk, what would I pump? Gosh, do I have to spell it out? She gave me a breast pump."

Slim's old mind reeled at the picture in his head. Women lined up, bare breasts attached to black hoses, like so many cows in a dairy. "They have milking machines for humans?"

"Not milking machines, breast pumps. Didn't they have'em when your kids were little?"

"Never married. Don't have kids."

Gently jiggling Jasmine, Katy nodded. "Like, no wonder your house looks like this. You oughta watch some of those decorating shows on the tube. Hey, where is your TV anyway?"

"Don't you worry about my TV or my house, tell me what happened next."

"I did what she said. I went to her godmother's and pumped. It was hard, but I did it, and while I was pumping my brains out, Chuchi hacked into the Host's computer files and found out where Jasmine was." She stopped and ate another chip.

"And…?"

"And then Chuchi came to get me. We staked out that baby buyer's house and followed her everywhere. When she went to the Square, she got sloppy. The minute her back was turned, I moved in and…well…you know the rest. Me and the baby were supposed to disappear forever, but you pretty much wrecked that plan."

Slim ignored her last remark. She wasn't going to make him feel guilty for doing his dad-blamed job. "Why would a girl like Chuchi, a faithful devotee of the Host, go against Alastair?"

"'Cause she said he was wrong to involve an outsider, especially a kid. She said the group used'ta have vision and principals, but then the leader died."

"How would she know that? He died years ago."

"Her parents were like founding fathers or something. You know, going against the Host was real hard for her."

"Then why would she do it?"

"She told me what Al did to me proved he ain't a good leader. She said all she was waiting for was the day the Host finally accomplished their great mystic purpose, then she and Booth—that's her boyfriend--are going to an island off the coast of Washington State and start a colony based on the way the Host used to be."

Slim's ears perked up. There was a reason behind all this madness. "What's their mystic purpose?"

"Didn't ask, don't care. All I wanted was to find Jasmine and get away." Katy shifted the baby to her other arm and fanned the blanket. "Did you know babies are like little pot-bellied stoves?"

The front doorbell rang.

Picturing the entire Tucson police department standing on his front step ready to arrest him, Slim mumbled, "Now they come."

"Who?" Her baby clutched tightly in her arms, Katy scampered into a shadowy corner where she couldn't be seen from the front hall.

Dread rose in Slim's chest like a flood. The moment she saw the cops, she'd run out the back door and head for parts unknown. If that happened, he would never see her or that sweet little baby again. The idea of losing those two suddenly seemed unbearable.

Slim shook his head as if to clear it. What was he thinking? That girl and the baby were his ticket to freedom, nothing more.

"Marshal, don't open the door if it's a guy with bleached hair and a ring in his right eyebrow. That would be Al."

Creeping into the dark hallway, Slim hoped whoever it was would give up and go away, but the insistent caller only changed his tactics, going from ringing the bell to pounding on the door.

He glanced at Katy peeking out from her hiding place. "Who is it?" She mouthed silently.

Slim shrugged and waved her back out of sight.

Much to his horror, the front lock clicked and the door slowly opened to the tune of jingling keys. Slim shuffled backwards into the living room. He'd locked that door. He knew he had. He always locked his front door. Those policemen better have a search warrant.

A hand reached in, flipped on the light, and Raúl, carrying Slim's rifle, stepped into the hall. "Marshal Slim, are you here?"

His heart pounding, Slim whispered, "You alone?"

The younger man whirled around. "Aye carumba, you scared me."

"I asked you if you're alone."

Raúl's thick black eyebrows knitted together. "<u>Sí</u>. I came to see if you were all right. You did not answer your phone all day yesterday and this morning. I even telephoned the Square. Senor Winslow said you do not work there any longer. What happened, old friend? You okay?"

"Can't you see I'm alive and kickin'?"

"What I see is you have been fired from your job. You didn't answer when I knocked, and the house, she is dark." Raúl walked to the gun cabinet Slim had in the entry hall, opened the glass doors, and placed the rifle in its proper bracket. He turned to Slim and put his hands on his broad hips. "Now you must tell me, are you in trouble, Marshal Slim?"

"Let me ask one. How'd you open a locked door anyway?'

"The key you gave me. In case there is an emergency." Raúl moved closer. "You must tell me, old friend. What is wrong? Why are you acting so strange?"

Torn between appreciating Raúl's thoughtfulness and defending an old man's right to be independent, Slim struggled to find the appropriate way to respond. "Raúl, you can see I'm perfectly fine. You go on back home and tell Marícita I said thanks for the concern, but it ain't necessary."

Raúl stared at him for a moment. "No, Marshal Slim. I do not think I will leave until you tell me why you are hiding in this house. Why did you not answer your telephone?" Raúl walked toward the living room. "Why are the curtains drawn like someone has died?"

Slim stepped out in front of him. "Look, I don't want to be rude, but you got to go now. I'm too busy to visit."

Sidestepping the old man, Raúl continued into the living room. The girl bolted for the kitchen door.

"Hey!" Raúl yelled.

"Katy, don't run off!" Slim pushed the younger man out of his way. "This here is my friend, Raúl. He went up on Thunderbolt with me to look for your baby."

Katy stopped and slowly turned around. The knowing scowl had returned. "Who are you trying to kid, Marshal? The paper didn't say nothing about anybody else being with you."

"That's probably because they were only interested in making me look like an old fool. But he was up there with me, weren't you, Raúl?"

Raúl stared at the girl. "Is this the baby, Marshal Slim? The one from the Square?"

Katy backed toward the kitchen. "I gotta go."

Slim rushed to her side. "No, no. We can trust this man. He's my friend. One of the good guys." Slim gently took her by the arm and led her back to his Lazy Boy chair. "You sit down and hear me out. It might be good to have Raúl's help. He ain't had his face plastered all over the newspaper."

Slim turned to Raúl. "Ain't that right, amigo? You'll help us, won't you?" He hated it when the eagerness in his voice overplayed his lawman's composure.

Raúl looked from Slim to Katy and back again. "Who is this girl?"

"I'll explain all that in a minute. What Katy needs to hear is that she can trust you. Then we can sit down and fill in all the details."

Slim quickly turned back to the girl. "That's okay, ain't it, Katy? We can tell Raúl what you've told me. He's a real smart man. He can help us figger all this out."

Katy continued to glare at Raúl, but she sat back down in Slim's chair. "If you say he's okay."

Slim gave Raúl a quick run-down on what the girl had told him so far, but instead of jumping in and promising to help, the younger man frowned and said, "Marshal Slim, the girl who took the baby. Didn't you say she had tatuaje de la daga, you know, dagger tattoos, for eyebrows."

The old man's faith in himself weakened even more. The dagger tattoos. That's what he'd forgotten about. A wave of disgust washed over Slim. What else had he overlooked? Was he losing his edge? Had a devious female and that pretty baby clouded his judgment?

"I did have daggers," Katy said. "That was Chuchi's idea. She got me the wig too."

"Tattoos do not come off," Raúl growled.

"They do when you draw them on with washable marker," Katy said. "With Alastair thinking I was dead, nobody was supposed to be able to figger out it was me who took Jasmine." She suddenly glowered at Slim. "And they wouldn't have if the marshal here hadn't shot off his big mouth to the newspaper."

Slim grimaced. He wished she'd quit saying that.

"You leave the Marshal alone, he was doing his job." Raúl turned to Slim. "I think we must take this girl to the policia."

"Hey," Katy yelled. "I ain't going to no police. They ain't gonna let no fifteen year old street rat raise a baby all by herself."

"You are fifteen?" Raúl said.

Slim was stunned right down to the core. He would have bet his savings that Katy was at least eighteen or nineteen. There wasn't a shred of innocence about her. Her dark eyes were wise with the ways of a world he never even knew existed.

Slim remembered Celestina, Raúl's youngest, at her Quincenera, the scared rite of passage for Hispanic girls. Fifteen-years-old, dressed in her first formal gown, Celestina had been surrounded by loving family and supportive friends. Giggling behind a tiny lace fan, she'd blushed when the boys came around. Celestina had been so pure, so innocent, so like her grandmother Dolores. How sad Katy's rite of passage had been marked with tattoos, lies, and pregnancy.

Slim's heart stirred in response. Someone had stolen this girl's innocence, tried to steal her baby, and now wanted to steal her life. "And we're gonna help Katy, ain't we, Raúl?"

Raúl answered with a stubborn thrust of his chin.

Slim looked anxiously from the girl to his friend. Raúl not agreeing with him made Slim question his judgment even more. If only they weren't rushing him so. "Hold on a minute. Let me think on this a bit."

Wrapping the blanket snugly around her sleeping child, Katy stood. "Don't bother, Marshal, I don't want your help anymore."

Why?" Raúl demanded. "Why do you change your mind now that I am here?"

She looked at Slim. "Because when I read about some old guy who risked his life to save my baby, I thought he had to be the bravest man in Tucson. Guess I was wrong. So, things being the way they are, I ain't gonna hang around here, until Alastair shows up looking to kill me."

Slim suddenly felt like a piece of meat caught between two pit bulls. "Wait just a dog-gone minute. This is my house. And last I heard I could still make my own decisions. Raúl, like it or not, I'm helpin' Katy, and we ain't callin' the authorities until we get to the bottom of this thing."

"There is much danger here. I feel it. You must call the police." When Slim didn't respond, Raúl ran his hand down the side of his jaw and sighed. "I am trying only to be a good friend."

Jasmine whimpered, and Katy gently shushed the baby's cries.

Slim glanced over his shoulder at the two females in his Lazy Boy. Her guard down, Katy's gaze darted from Slim to Raúl and back again, anxiously watching the two men decide her fate. In those dark eyes Slim saw the real Katy Ann Cleary, a fifteen-year-old child, frightened, alone, trusting no one. The child tough, street-wise Vamp kept hidden.

The old man laid his hand on Raúl's arm. "Then be a good friend by helping me, and I promise the first time things look any different from what she's sayin', we'll call Mark O'Brien."

Raúl thought a moment. "Before I agree, she must answer a question. If there are girls willing to bear children for this hombre to sell, why did he bother to trick her?"

They both turned to Katy.

Katy gulped nervously. "Well, Chuchi said Alastair thinks if he brings in more money for the Host than his big brother does, he'll be made the next leader. She said Al is getting desperate, 'cause the drug business moves a lot faster than the baby-selling business."

"So Al sells babies and his brother…." Slim paused. "What's the brother's name anyway?"

"Jude Light."

"And Jude sells drugs. Nice pair that mama raised, ain't they?"

Raúl shifted restlessly from one foot to the other and lifted his chin toward Katy. "This Chuchi sure told this one a lot of secrets."

Slim had just thought the same thing. "Why would that be, Katy?"

"I think she wanted me to understand how dangerous Alastair is so when I got the baby I would go far, far away and stay there."

"Why is Chuchi not helping you now?" Raúl asked.

Katy shrugged. "I wish I knew. She drove me and the baby to her godmother's and said she was going back to the house so she'd be there when the news hit about the kidnapping. She was gonna act all outraged and stuff, so nobody would suspect she had anything to do with it. When it was safe she was gonna buy me a bus ticket someplace."

Her eyes glimmering with tears, Katy paused and took a ragged breath. "Then that newspaper article came out. She never called or came back. Her godmother got scared and threw me out. Said I was bad luck."

"Maybe your friend's still bidin' her time," Slim said. "It's only been a couple of days."

Katy shook her head. "No, you don't know Chuchi. She would never make her godmother worry like this. I think they've found out Chuchi helped me and got rid of her." She pressed the back of her hand to her mouth and stifled a sob.

Slim sank down in a nearby chair, rested his elbows on his knees, and laid his head in his hands. Even though Katy was obviously upset, her story was getting harder and harder to believe. Maybe Raúl was right. Maybe Katy was a kidnapping con artist drawing them into a clever web of lies. Right now that scenario seemed more plausible than a shadowy cult trafficking in drugs and babies and killing errant members.

Slim wanted to see how Raúl was digesting this latest news, but Katy's eyes pinned him and the scared, lost, little girl spoke. "You got to believe me. If Al finds me, I'm dead, and Jasmine will go back to that cow who bought her."

"Why do you not go to your parents for help?" Raúl asked.

Slim stiffened. He should have asked that right off. What was the matter with him?

Her expression hardened. "Mom's a drunk with lots of boyfriends. After a couple of them decided my little body came with the package, I left. I was thirteen. Been on my own ever since."

Raúl continued to press her. "What about your father?"

"Well, since my dear old daddy's doing time.... He won't be out until Jasmine's grown, but I guess I could always go to Texas and live with my stoner stepmom. That's a great idea."

As Katy explained how her life had been, Slim's stomach churned. He knew lots of kids grew up in awful situations, situations even worse that Katy's, only difference was he'd never had one land on his doorstep before.

"Oh, crap!" Katy jerked the baby out from under the blanket, flopped the groggy infant up on her shoulder, and banged so hard on the baby's back, Jasmine sounded like a tiny drum. "I forgot to burp her. She'll be pukin' all over everything. Sure is a lot to remember when you have a baby."

"It is not necessary to beat the air bubbles out of one so small," Raúl said.

Katy made a sour face and beat Jasmine's back faster. "Hey, you don't know my kid. She happens to be a cranky burper."

Raúl held his arms out. "I will show you a trick of my mamá's. It is especially for burpers <u>irritables</u>."

Katy stopped banging the Jasmine drum, tightened her grip on the child, and glared at Raúl. "You ain't getting her."

Slim intervened. "Katy, my <u>amigo</u> here is one of six kids, father to four and is grandfather to…to…. How many is it now, Raúl?"

"Six. Three boys and three beautiful girls. And I do not have to hold the child. I can tell this girl how it is done."

"You see Katy," Slim said. "Raúl's gonna tell you what to do, not steal your baby."

She mumbled, "Whatever," and continued to press the child tightly to her chest. Jasmine whimpered and squirmed.

Slim leaned back in his chair and sighed. "If you ain't gonna trust us, how can we help you?"

Chewing on the side of her mouth, Katy seemed to consider his remark. "Okay, what's the big secret?"

"You hold the baby like this." Raúl held an imaginary infant to his shoulder. "Starting low and working up, you rub with the flat of your hand in small circles, firm but not hard."

Katy followed his instructions. Still no burp. "Fat lot of good that did."

"Please, may I show you?" Raúl asked.

The girl's inner struggle was plainly written on her face.

"I will not trick you," Raúl said in the voice he used with his own children. "I give you my word."

Katy, her eyes icy cold, handed Raúl the child. "You better not try anything. I may be little, but I'm fast and I'm mean as hell."

Raúl rolled his eyes as he took the baby and placed her on his shoulder. Following his own instructions, he rubbed and rubbed, but Jasmine held on to her burp.

"Yeah, like, that really works like a charm, dude."

"Now I will do the second part." Raúl placed the baby tummy down on his forearm, her feet toward his elbow, her head cradled in his palm, the child's pale complexion a sharp contrast to the sun-baked brown of Raúl's skin. Humming softly, he bounced his arm and rubbed the child's back.

Through the years, Slim had seen Dolores and Raúl burp many a baby using that technique, but never had he seen any baby that stole his heart like Katy's golden haired angel. Trying to keep his emotions from becoming even more entangled with this girl and her baby, he stood, limped to the window, and looked out. Still no sign of the cops.

Finally a soft belch escaped the sleeping infant's lips.

Slim turned and stared at the baby. No use fighting it, he was hooked.

Katy grinned. "Hey, that was a good one."

Raúl gently flipped the child over and returned her to Katy. "My mamá knew many things to help the little ones."

"You said knew. She's dead?" Katy asked.

"<u>Sí</u>." Raúl sighed. "She was truly an angel who has returned to God. We miss her, eh, Marshal Slim?"

Slim's heart twisted. "Yep, that we do."

"That's the kind of mama I want to be. One Jasmine can be proud of after I'm gone." Katy cuddled Jasmine close and stroked the baby's head. "You know, I don't even care if she was born for all the wrong reasons. It wasn't her fault. She's an innocent little baby, and it's my job to protect her. If her own mama won't do it, who will? This is a cruddy, old world in case you haven't noticed."

An unexpected rush of concern for the two females sitting in his Lazy Boy surprised Slim. If the girl was being honest with him, and he'd about decided she was, her parents never protected her. Shoot, no one had.

As Slim considered his epiphany and the task he felt God had assigned him, the old man remembered something he'd heard one of those T.V. preachers say. God always had the bigger picture in mind, and sometimes humans missed the opportunity to do something important because they didn't take time to consider the bigger picture.

If the Good Lord put him in this girl's path, maybe his mission was bigger than just saving this baby. Maybe he was supposed to save Jasmine and Katy, and in the process, bring down, that baby-selling, drug-dealing cult. Seeing Alastair, that exploiter of young flesh, behind bars, his knees clacking together because he was terrified he would wind up some hulking fiend's bitch, would make Slim's day…shoot…it would make his year, maybe even his life, to. Picturing Alastair in that awful scenario, instead of himself pleased Slim. Without another moment's hesitation, he blurted out, "I decided. I'm in. What about you, Raúl? Will you help Katy and Jasmine?"

Glancing at the sleeping child in Katy's arms, Raúl rubbed his jaw, again. "For the child, I will also help, but if things do not line up as this one said…."

Slim wasn't about to let his friend finish that sentence. The girl didn't need to be spooked again. "Katy, I want to see the house where Alastair took you. The one with the girls. Who knows, maybe we'll see Chuchi."

"I don't want to go back there," Katy said, her voice trembling. "But...but, I guess if we can find Chuchi I'll do it."

Raúl said. "I do not think this will be a wise thing to do."

Slim held his hand up. "Raúl, I didn't ask you what you thought. I'm the one with the most experience here, and I say the most obvious place to start is where Katy says Alistair's girls live. We'll go in your van. My Pinto's too small."

"His van better have a car seat for Jasmine," Katy said.

"Well, it don't," Raúl snapped.

"Then my baby ain't riding in that van. Chuchi said--."

"Do not quote from the Chuchi book for raising kids to me again," Raúl countered, his jaw tight, his voice low. "I am a father four times, a grandfather--."

"I know, I know" Katy yelled. "You're the father of all Mexico--,"

Raúl bristled. "I am born American."

"Okay, you're the father of all America and you know more about babies than any female ever born."

"That's enough!" Slim roared. Raúl and Katy jerked their heads around and stared at him. "You two knock it off. That gol-durned squabblin' is wearin' on my last nerve, and when that's gone, I won't be held responsible for what I do."

"What about the car seat?" Katy asked in a small voice. "It is the law, you know."

"Yes, I know the law," Slim said. "And, thanks to you, I been breaking it plenty these last few days. Besides, Katy, a car seat won't work in Raúl's van."

"Why?" The girl demanded.

"You'll see," Slim muttered. He thought for a moment. "Now, I promise we'll get Jasmine a car seat ASAP, and the next time we go out, it'll be in a car that'll hold it. You got any problem with that?"

"I guess not, but you better hope this guy can drive, because--."

"I can drive," Raúl said.

Slim sighed and ran his hands through his hair. Maybe when they got on the road these two would quit arguing. "Katy, you tell Raúl how to get to the house, okay?"

"Yeah."

"Good, then you and me'll sit in the back of the van so one can see us. Let's go."

"Gotta change Jasmine's diaper first." Katy pulled a tiny disposable diaper, a plastic bottle of baby power, and a box of wipes out of her backpack.

While she stripped the sleeping child, Raúl whispered to Slim. "We will soon know if this chiquita is truthful or not."

Katy looked over her shoulder. "If I'm telling the truth? Give me a break! Why would I lie?"

Slim held up his hand again. "Enough arguing!" Now he remembered why he never had kids.

# # #

The instant Katy saw Raúl's '69 Volkswagen van, she burst into a gale of loud hooting laughter.

Great, just when he thought those two were going get along. "Katy, you best hush that up now."

But the girl continued to laugh, tears spilling down her cheeks. "Raúl drives a hippie van?"

Slim would admit the old classic, modeled after Ken Kesey's Magic Bus with wild psychedelic splashes of color and dated hippie slogans scattered across the sides, looked like it had been painted by some demented Van Gogh flying high on acid, but this was Raúl's pride and joy, and the girl shouldn't be laughing like that.

Slim glanced over his shoulder as he opened the van's side door, but thankfully, Raúl was still inside locking up. "Come on, girl, you're gonna make him mad all over again."

She clamped her free hand over her mouth, but couldn't quit giggling. Now snorting through her nose, she placed Jasmine in his arms, climbed into the back of the van, and plopped down in one of the four beanbags Raúl kept for passengers.

Gently cradling the tiny baby, Slim ignored her rude mother and found himself mesmerized when Jasmine yawned and opened her eyes. Like a newly-hatched bird, she smacked her lips and searched Slim's face with big slate blue eyes that captured an old man's heart. Then she yawned again, a huge yawn that ended in a body-shaking shudder. Completely at loss for words, Slim stroked the back her tiny hand and smiled when she curled her pudgy fingers around his thumb.

Interrupting his moment sublime pleasure, Katy whooped. "Man, I ain't never seen fluorescent orange shag before. This van's like a big ol' fuzzy cocoon."

Slim reluctantly gave the girl her baby and crawled in after her, choosing to sit on the floor instead of a beanbag. He'd learned a long time ago once he got in one of those things he had a hard time getting out. Flopped around like a fish out of water until he rolled off and landed face down in the orange carpet Katy was so enthralled with.

While he got his old legs arranged and leaned back against the passenger seat, Katy continued to cast aspersions and cackle like a setting hen. Slim warned, "You better quit that infernal laughing. It ain't polite to insult a man's ride, 'specially one he's so darn proud of."

"You know, when I saw your friend wearing that silly straw cowboy hat and that western shirt, I thought he was in the Mexican Mafia. They all dress like that."

"Don't let Raúl hear you say that. He has no truck with that bunch of criminals."

"You mean then, he's like a real cowboy? The kind that ropes cows and stuff? Does he live on a ranch?" Her eyes lit up. "Does he have horses, riding horses?"

"Yes, he has horses."

She grinned impishly. "But this van looks like something an old hippie would drive."

"An old hippie does drive it."

"Naw."

"Yep, he bought this van when he came home from 'Nam and decided he wanted to be a Dead Head. Followed the band for a whole year. Can't say I cotton to that kind of music myself, but Raúl likes it, so since I got some manners, I keep my mouth shut."

"He sure don't look any Dead-Head I've ever seen. What happened to him? Where's his long hair and tie-dye? How did he go from cool to corn?"

"Not that it's any of your business, Miss Nosy, but when Raúl was needed at home, he cut his hair and went to work on the family ranch with his papa like the good son he is."

"Or maybe he was just too chicken to make a complete break and live the life he really wanted."

"Seems to me, coming back to take care of his parents and the ranch would make him a hero, not a coward."

Raúl opened the driver's door and climbed inside. The old captain's chair groaned as he twisted around and looked at Slim. "The house, she is locked, and I checked all the windows." He jerked his head toward Katy. "And I heard this one laughing. She don't have to ride in my van if she thinks it's so funny-looking."

Slim closed the side door. "Don't pay her no never mind, <u>amigo</u>. She's a kid. What does she know about classic vehicles?"

"Hey, I know what's funny-looking," Katy shot back.

Slim gave her a hard look. He suddenly remembered what MacArthur had endured in Japan after W.W.II. Finding a way to keep the peace between these two warring factions would take all Slim's persuasion, wit, and charm. He could almost understand Katy's problem. A kid living on the streets, fighting for whatever she got, being taken advantage of. Her natural instinct would be to cause offense before you're offended.

He glanced at the back of Raúl's head, red neckerchief tied around his thick neck, straw cowboy firmly in place. But Raúl he didn't understand. Why would a grown man argue with a kid like that? He'd known Raúl since the day he was born and had never seen the man clash with anyone the way he did with Katy. Did his old friend sense something Slim had missed?

Well, whatever the reason, there wasn't time to worry about it now. "Katy, where is this house you were taken to?"

"Just north of Old Towne. You go down Midline Road and turn left on Eucalyptus Lane. Once we're on the Lane, you can't miss that gawd-awful house. It's a huge stucco painted a toothpaste mint-green. Oh, and there's a long string of red chili peppers hanging on the front door."

"Let's get this show on the road, Raúl. Maybe we can find Chuchi and get to the bottom of this thing."

Chapter 9

Raúl drove slowly past the shabby green house. "Are you sure this is the place, Katy? I don't see no ristas anywhere."

Katy peeked out of the window. "This is it. Man, if somebody stole Chuchi's chile peppers, she's gonna be mad."

"Marshal Slim, the house, she looks empty. No peppers, no cars, no people, <u>nada</u>."

"It can't be empty," Katy protested. "Six girls live here."

Once more, Slim intervened, "Relax, Katy, we'll go down to the corner, turn around, come back and park for awhile. Maybe we'll see somebody."

Raúl shot him a disapproving look. "You said we would drive by, not stop."

"Do what I ask, Raúl."

When they were parked, Slim slowly got to his knees and looked through the porthole window behind the passenger's seat. The bubble shaped Plexiglas gave the green house a slightly warped appearance. Warped, just like its owner.

Behind wrought iron burglar bars, the windows were closed, the curtains drawn. The swamp cooler on the roof was silent. "I say let's go in and check it out."

"I say let's go," Raúl argued.

"And I say let's do something besides sit here," Katy chimed in. "Like, what if Alastair comes back or something?"

Tired of the bickering, Slim opened the side door, "Well, I'm gonna have a look-see. Raúl, if you decide to come with me, leave the engine running, and the air on."

"Leave her alone in my van? No, I will not do that."

Katy swelled up like a stomped on toad frog. "Like I'd risk goin' to jail and losin' my baby by stealing this piece of junk."

Raúl shot the girl a withering look and unscrewed his chrome floor shifter with a skull knob. "You will not have the chance, chica."

Katy's lower lip popped out. She turned and glared at the orange shag carpeting.

Taking advantage of the momentary quiet, Slim asked, "Or you goin' or not, Raúl?"

"I will go." He opened his door and jumped out, his shifter in his hand. "I will not sit here and listen to this one run her boca grande."

"Hey," Katy cried, "I heard that, and I don't have I big mouth...you...you pendejo!"

"You dare to call me that? You must learn respect, muchacha." Raúl slammed his door and stormed around the van, spattering Spanish like a machine gun.

Although she needed her mouth washed out with soap for calling Raúl a pubic hair, Slim hoped Katy didn't understand the gist of his friend's tirade. Something about the girl having the tongue of an adder, and being raised by the sons of wolves and the daughters of witches.

Determined not to let these two start the mother of all word wars, Slim spoke over Raúl's ranting. "Katy, you wait here with Jasmine. Lock the doors and stay out of sight. If anyone bothers you, hit the horn and let her rip."

Raúl helped Slim inch his way out onto the hot pavement. With great flourish, the younger man slammed the door behind him, swore softly in Spanish, and stalked across the street.

Slim waited until he heard the door lock click and then followed Raúl. "We'll try the bell first. Just in case anyone's to home."

"What if someone is here?"

"Let me do the talking, okay?"

Despite the heat, Raúl shivered like he had on the mountain.

The old man slowed his pace. "You picking up on something? Like you did on Thunderbolt?"

Raúl shrugged. "Maybe."

Trying to encourage him, Slim patted Raúl on the back. "Press in, <u>amigo</u>. Better we see what's been going on here, then to turn tail and run."

When they reached the front door, Slim hesitated before he pushed the glowing doorbell button marked "No Solicitors." For a brief instant, he wished he'd brought the Twins, but before he left the house, he'd made an important decision. As long as Katy and the baby were in his home, he'd keep his firearms locked up tight. He'd admit he'd struggled when he actually had to turn the key and lock the Twins and his hideout pistol in with his rifles. But it had been the right thing to do. He'd been a cop long enough to know you didn't leave firearms out where kids could get their hands on them. Kids and guns don't mix.

He'd put the key to his gun cabinet in his wallet, right next to the necklace. Later, he'd find someplace else to hide them, someplace at home, someplace handy, but not too easy to find.

Straightening his shoulders, he pushed the button with his knuckle. Through the door came a chirpy little bell-like snatch of music he recognized.

Raúl's eyes widened. "I know that song."

"Me too." Slim rang the bell again. Both men cocked their ears toward the door and listened to the tune.

"I was right," Raúl said. "Santana. <u>Black Magic Woman.</u>"

"Yep," Slim agreed, "But how did they manage to get <u>Black Magic Woman</u> on their doorbell?"

"Programmable," was all Raúl said.

Slim snorted and rang the bell again. He was right. Computers <u>were</u> taking over the world.

They waited for a moment, but when no one answered the bell, Slim said, "Get over to the side of the door. We're going in."

Slim did the same, leaned his back against the wall, and pulled his handkerchief out of his pocket. Reaching around, he used it to turn the doorknob. "Ain't locked. Watch out now."

He winked at Raúl, opened the door, and yelled, "Tucson Police Department. Anyone home?"

No answer.

Slim swung the door wide open. After a moment when no gunshots were fired, Slim leaned around the jamb, peeked in, and saw only an empty room. "Looks like they hightailed it out of here."

Slim noticed the younger man's ashen face. Raúl wasn't a fearful man as a rule. "The atmosphere still botherin' you?"

Raúl nodded.

"Why don't you go wait with the girl? I can look around by myself. Ain't nobody here."

"No, better I stay here and fight the sensaciones malvadas, you know, this evil I feel, than go back to the van and strangle that chica with the big mouth."

"Raúl, what is it with you and that kid?"

"Something about her I do not trust."

Slim stared at him a moment. "I can spot a liar at forty feet, boy, and I don't think she's lyin'."

His friend shrugged. "But as much as you believe she is not lying, I believe there is something not right with her. For me, until she proves herself trustworthy, I will watch her every move."

Slim sighed. "Just remember she's a kid, so try not to argue with her all the time, okay? You two are drivin' me crazy."

Raúl shrugged again. "We should hurry, Marshal Slim. The people might return."

Slim looked up and down the street. No movement. No cars that weren't there a moment ago. "Come on."

Inside the large stucco, the dim light quivered with floating dust motes, the air smelled faintly of bleach. Eerily quiet, the house echoed with the men's footsteps as they walked through empty rooms painted bright fiesta colors. The floor, a burnt orange Mexican tile, was littered with dust bunnies, food crumbs, and trash.

"Messy bunch," Slim mumbled. "Wonder why would they clean up with bleach, and then leave trash all over the floor?"

"Maybe they didn't finish. Maybe they will return. We must hurry."

The two men searched the house, all five bedrooms, three baths, a kitchen, and a large living area. Being careful to use their handkerchiefs, they looked in every closet, opened drawers and cabinets, finding nothing that could prove Katy's story except one of the bedrooms had a padlock hasp on the outside of the door and a private bath. The bleach smell came from this bathroom.

In the rear of the house, they found a small, carpeted room where shredded paper littered the floor.

Raúl kicked some of the trash aside and pointed with his shifter to an indention in the carpet. "There are more. Four deep ones. A desk, maybe. Look over there." He pointed to a cluster of phone boxes on the baseboard.

"This had to be an office," Slim said. "But why would they need that many phones in one room?"

"Modems."

"Modems?"

"Computers must have modems to do the email. You know, to call the Internet."

"Makes sense. Katy said Chuchi hacked into their computers to find Jasmine."

Using his shifter again, Raúl brushed more of the paper out of the way, and revealed another set of carpet markings. "File cabinets maybe."

Picking up some of the paper shreds, Slim tried to discern what had been destroyed, but all he saw on the narrow strips of paper were snippets of words that made no sense. He tossed the paper on the floor. "Let's look out back."

# # #

Raúl waited in the shade on the covered patio as Slim walked across the flagstones to the edge of a small kidney-shaped pool. The motionless water was littered with leaves, and a rock fountain stood dry and silent at one end. "Well, looks like they're gone all right. Too bad. I'd sure like to get my hands on that Alastair, or at least find Chuchi."

The hot wind kicked up, and the air was filled with dusty sand and tinkling music. Slim squinted and followed the sound, walking through dry, crackling grass to a spindly tree standing in the corner of the yard. From its sad, crooked branches hung wind chimes, spinning merrily in the breeze. All kinds of wind chimes made of copper, brass, bone, and shell. Beneath the tree, almost hidden by native desert bushes, stood another altar, identical to the one on Thunderbolt only smaller.

Fountains and wind chimes reminded Slim of Sonya Szymanski and the Gypsy's Curse. The old man shuddered and walked to the altar. Except for puddles of black wax that had hardened around the goat's head carving at its base, the sandstone was unstained.

"Marshal Slim." Raúl called, his voice guarded and low.

Slim turned. His friend had left the shaded patio and was squatting next to a door Slim surmised led into the garage. "What'cha got, amigo?"

"Flies."

"Flies?" Slim hurried to Raúl's side.

Right below the door, in the middle of a large patch of crystal-flecked gravel, a swarm of iridescent blowflies crawled and churned. Some would lift, then settle looking for a more opportune spot to get at whatever had called forth the growing mass of insects. Raúl waved his hand. In protest, the flies flew in mad circles, buzzing furiously, but Raúl refused to let them land in the viscous black substance covering the gravel.

Slim awkwardly squatted next to his friend, his stiff, old legs popping and complaining all the way down. The black stuff had dried on the top of the gravel pieces, but between the rocks, it glistened. Slim poked a twig into the moist part and caught the faint, but unmistakable smell of copper. "Blood."

"There's more at the edge of the patio."

Slim glanced over his shoulder. "A lot, like here?"

"No, <u>un poco</u>, not so much."

The old man noticed the garage door was slightly ajar. "Let's see what's in there."

Raúl stood and reached for the knob.

"Wait!" Slim cried as he struggled to his feet. "We might be dealing with a murder scene here."

Raúl froze.

"Use the gear shift, amigo."

Nodding, Raúl pushed the door open to the tune of a loud complaining squeak. The garage was empty except for more flies.

The outside flies swarmed around him and joined their brothers on a black drag smear that ran from the doorjamb across the oil-spotted concrete floor, to where a car would be parked.

Raúl whispered, "Maybe someone has been killed."

Slim nodded. Deep down in his gut, he had the horrible feeling they might have found out what happened to Chuchi.

A long shrill blast of a car horn shredded the quiet afternoon. The two men locked eyes. Raúl said, "My van!"

"Katy!" Slim took off across the patio and into the house, Raúl following close behind. When they bolted through the front door, the horn stuttered to life again.

Raúl loped by the old man, crossed the street, and ran to the side of the van. He banged on the window and when the horn finally stopped, Slim heard him yell, "Are you trying to kill him?"

"Who?" Slim panted. "Who's she killing?"

Raúl turned, his face red with fury. "You!"

"Me? How's she killin' me? What's wrong?"

Raúl unlocked the side door and jerked it open. "Nothing is wrong, that is what is wrong."

Slim's heart was pounding so hard, his words poured out chunky and disjointed. "What the Sam-Hill are you talkin' about, Raúl?"

"I was worried," Katy yelled from inside the van. "You guys were taking so long."

Slim stopped and tried to calm his ragged breathing. "No one's bothering her?"

"No. This one doesn't listen, Marshal Slim. She is always trouble."

Slim's heart rate slowed. After a moment, he said, "She's a kid…a kid. You had kids. Lighten up."

The muscles in Raúl's jaw swelled, and Slim knew his old friend was mad, good and mad. "My kids did as they were told."

"Well, Katy didn't have you for a daddy, did she?" He patted Raúl's shoulder. "More's the pity, eh, old friend?"

Raúl slowly unclenched his jaw. "She is bringing danger to you, Marshal Slim. You saw what I saw back there."

Clutching the baby to her chest, Katy appeared in the open van door. "What did you see? Is Chuchi okay?"

Slim gave Raúl his hardest glare. "All we saw was an empty house. They've moved."

"Moved?" she wailed. "In two days?"

"It's been done," Slim said. "Now you get back before someone sees you."

The girl paled. She scurried backwards and sat in her beanbag. "Sorry, I wasn't thinking."

Raúl opened his mouth to speak, but Slim closed it with another glare. "Let's get back to the house."

# # #

On the way home, the unlikely trio stopped at Slim's favorite restaurant, a bar-b-que place called The Porcine Pig. Clara, the dour black waitress he'd known for years, smiled when he ordered a whole pie, one of her mother's famous homemade lemon meringue pies, to go with three pulled pork sandwiches with sides of French fries. Katy's sandwich sans sauce as per Raúl's instructions.

After he paid, Clara said, "You must have family visiting, Marshal Slim."

As the word "no" formed on the old man's lips, he hesitated. Family? That's kind of what it felt like. He returned Clara's wide grin with one of his own. "Yep. Family."

"They staying for a while?"

Slim considered the question before he answered. "I hope so."

Back at the house, the baby slept, and everyone else feasted on the Pig's delectable cuisine. Between great gulping bites, Raúl tried to convince Slim it would be safer for everyone, if the two girls went to a motel, but when Slim saw Katy's eyes widen to the size of dinner plates, and her lower lip tremble, he said no.

Raúl argued, but when he realized he wasn't going to win this battle either, he gave up. Then, in true Raúl style, he offered to come back early the next morning with María's Lincoln, so they could go to a nearby discount store to buy Jasmine a car seat.

When Katy heard that, she jumped out of her chair, did a little victory dance, and breathlessly plopped back down.

"Raúl," Katy panted, "you bringing another car so Jasmine can ride in a car seat is, like, really cool. Thanks, dude." She stuck out her hand.

Raúl stoically accepted her handshake, but Slim knew his friend wasn't ready to let bygones be bygones. Katy would have to prove herself, and from the looks of it, it might take a while to win Raúl over.

The girl forked up a large bite of pie, shoveled it into her mouth, chewed a couple of times, and said, "Hey, Marshal--."

Grimacing at the sight of meringue and lemon custard, Slim decided he might as well show her what his dad had always shown him. Tough love, they called it these days. Firm, but honest discipline is what Slim called it. "Mind your manners, Katy. At my table, people don't speak with their mouths full."

He expected the girl to blow up and defend herself, but she surprised him. She quietly finished chewing, swallowed, and took a long drink of water. "Sorry. I forget sometime. Ain't a lot of tables on the street."

Slim smiled. She'd taken correction without argument. They were making progress. "Did you want to ask me something?"

"Yeah, like, what are we gonna do after we get the car seat?"

Next he would work on her constant, improper use of the word "like." "I'd like to see where you lived with Alastair before he took you to the green house."

Raúl glanced away. Slim could see that once again, his old friend didn't agree, but now the almost minute-by-minute disagreement didn't bother him as much.

Katy said, "What if Al sees us checking him out?"

"Don't worry, Katy, I'll be there." Slim glanced away. What she didn't know was he'd already decided he'd take a bullet for these two girls.

# # #

Slim watched Raúl climb into his van and pull away from the curb, he suddenly remembered his own problems with the police and glanced at his watch. Twenty-four hours had passed, and they still hadn't come. Maybe that was a good sign. Maybe they weren't coming at all.

The old man's spirits lifted a little. Maybe Carter had managed to calm down that reporter. Oh, Slim wasn't kidding himself. He knew his former boss wouldn't have done a thing to help Tucson Slim, but Carter would do anything to protect the Square's reputation.

Before he went back into the house, the old man stopped on his front porch and took one last canvas of the street. No unusual activities, no strange vehicles.

He smiled as he went inside. O'Brien had been right about one thing. Once a cop, always a cop. Habits born from years of law enforcement died hard.

After refilling his favorite coffee mug, a heavy pottery tankard he'd purchased at the Arizona Renaissance Festival several years before, he returned to the living room where Katy sat in his Lazy Boy. She smiled. "Mr. Hot-head gone?"

"Raúl? Yep, he's headin' for the ranch."

"He don't like me very much, does he?"

"Don't take it personal. Raúl's worried about me, that's all. You see, we've been friends a long time, and he watches out for those he cares for."

She looked down at the baby and mumbled, "I wish somebody cared about us like that."

Slim's old heart broke. "Things are gonna be different from now on. You got me on your side, and Raúl's gonna come around. I guarantee it."

But it was too late. The girl's protective shell was back in place, and she cut him off. "Jasmine needs a bath. Can I use the kitchen sink?"

"Sure, there's a washcloth and towels in the bathroom. Soap and shampoo are in there too."

Juggling the baby in one arm, Katy stood and picked up her backpack. "Thanks, but all I need is a towel and the sink. Chuchi got Jasmine everything she'll need for awhile—everything except diapers. We're getting kind of low on those."

"Well, we'll pick up a bunch tomorrow when we buy the car seat. If you can think of anything else, let me know."

"You know, Marshal, for an old guy, you're pretty nice."

Slim smiled. "And even though you're only a little punk kid, you got some redeemin' qualities too, Katy Cleary."

The corners of her mouth turned down. She looked at her feet, dug her bare toes into the carpet, and said in a small voice, "Do you think Chuchi's okay?

Slim had wondered if he should tell her everything he'd seen, but decided not to. Katy was a kid who'd never had anyone to count on in times of trouble. He didn't want to be the one to tell her someone she cared for was most likely dead. Not until he was sure he had all the facts. "Let's hope she's hidin' out somewhere."

Her eyes, so old with the ways of the world, filled with youthful optimism "You think so? Can I call her boyfriend, Booth? He'll know where she is."

"No! No one knows you're here. Let's keep it that way."

"Oh, all right, but, tomorrow, can I call Booth from a payphone? That'd be okay, wouldn't it?"

"We'll see." Slim surprised himself. The voice and the words coming out of his mouth sounded so much like his own father, and just like with his dad, "we'll see" meant no.

The baby woke up and began to snuffle and complain. Katy said, "I better get her bathed. She needs to eat."

With all the paternal feelings he'd never had occasion to use welling up inside him, Slim smiled as he watched Katy quietly pad down the hall, whispering to her child. He couldn't explain it, but in less than twenty-four hours, those two girls had stolen his heart. What was left of his life might almost be worth living if they could be a part of it.

Feeling quite good about himself, Slim sat on the companion chair next to his couch, propped his feet up on the ottoman, and sipped his coffee, smiling all the while.

Wouldn't Dolores find this amusing? After all these years, a child had stolen Tucson Slim's heart. Oh, he loved all of the Martínez children--loved them from a safe distance--but he'd never been responsible for them. He'd always been their parents' over-indulgent friend, riding into their lives with his pockets filled with surprises and a head full of wild stories. He'd always been free to leave whenever he wanted to. Dolores and Luis did all the real work, keeping a roof over their heads, clothes on their backs, and food in their bellies.

Slim finished his coffee, enjoying the sound of the girl singing to her child as she bathed her. Even with all the mystery and murder whirling around in his head, for the first time in a long while, Slim's loneliness abated. He felt at peace with the world.

Tapping the side of his empty mug with his fingertips, he began to consider Katy's future. There were several ways to go. He sure didn't want the girl to be swept into the state foster care system and separated from her baby. That was completely unacceptable.

Maybe Katy and the baby could stay with him. He had plenty of room. Or maybe they could go out to the ranch. María would love having another baby around, and she knew how to rein Raúl in. But there was a strong element of risk in either of those solutions. What if he did bring down the cult and every one of them went to jail? What if one day they were set free and returned for Katy with revenge on their minds?

There were no other options. Katy would have to leave Tucson. That was the only safe choice.

The old man sighed and scratched his cheek. But how could he tell that child she had to go away? She had an infant to take care of. She didn't have a dime, or any place to go, or any one to take care of her when she got there.

Then a light snapped on in his head! This was what he'd been called to do. Get the girls out of Tucson and make a safe home for the two of them as long as he could. Katy would be glad for his help. After all, she'd come to him, hadn't she?

On the practical side, he had enough money, especially if he sold his house and all his junk. What stuff he couldn't bear to part with, he could store down at the Hide-A-Lot until he and Katy were settled. Of course, it would mean he'd have to leave Raúl and his family, but shoot, Slim hadn't seen them all that much since Dolores passed away. And they could stay in touch by mail and telephone.

He'd let Katy choose where she wanted to live, any place warm and dry. He'd lived in the desert too long to contend with ice and snow nine months of the year. But that left Texas, California, New Mexico, and Nevada. He'd feel right at home in any of the states in the Great Southwest, but they'd have to stay away from the big cities like L.A. and Houston.

Katy could go back to school. He could afford to pay for a good day care for Jasmine. No problem there. He'd watch the little doll himself, but that might be too hard while Jasmine was so young. Truth be told, he didn't know that much about babies. But when she was up and walking, more kid than baby, he could manage. He would protect them and provide for them. They would be a family. His family.

Suddenly the old man's life had purpose again. He leaned back, closed his eyes, and imagined how different his life would be if Katy and Jasmine stayed with him. He didn't know how much time he had left in this world, but he'd make every day count. Maybe he'd change his will. Leave everything in trust for his two girls. His two girls.

Something crashed in the kitchen.

Slim's eyes popped open. "Katy?"

When she didn't answer, he stood and walked down the hall, heavy mug in hand. "Girl, you okay?"

When she still didn't respond, Slim crept to the kitchen door and peeked in. One of his ladder-back chairs had been knocked over. No sign of Katy or the baby.

Slim's hand automatically went to his side. No gun. He'd forgotten. The Twins were locked up. If someone had the girl, he needed a weapon.

The old man crept to the front hall, placed his cup on the floor, and tried to open the gun cabinet's glass-front doors. The glass rattled, the cabinet wobbled slightly, but didn't open. He'd locked it, and the key was in his wallet.

Hands shaking like the leaves on a quaky aspen tree, Slim jerked his wallet out from his back pocket. As he fumbled through it, trying to find the key, the necklace fell to the floor. When he bent over to retrieve it, the air above his head whistled.

Slim glanced up and something hard smashed into the back of his head.

Fighting against the black tide threatening to sweep him away, Slim crashed into the gun cabinet. He leaned there, trying not to fall, cheek pressed against smooth wood, blood gushing down the side of his face. Someone stood behind him, so close he heard panting.

Barely able to stay conscious, the old man slid down the cabinet front to his knees and picked up his coffee mug. In a last ditch effort, he aimed for where he thought the intruder's nose might be and swung the mug over his shoulder. The heavily glazed earthenware connected with a solid crack, and someone screamed in pain. Another whoosh of air, and the room went black.

Chapter 10

Determined Tucson Slim would never enter the Great Spirit's realm, the Indian women screamed shrilly as they thrust their awls repeatedly into Slim's eardrums. He tried to fight, but they pulled the leather bands wrapped around his neck, choking him. The women would go for his eyes next, so the old man squinched them tightly shut. The pain in his head intensified. Everything around him rolled and pitched and shuddered. He wondered how the women had found him on this boat in such a bad storm. Slim didn't like boats, especially ones that were sinking. And this one was sinking. There was water on his nose.

Swiping his hand across his face, he hit a plastic mask. His hand fell against his neck and landed on a thick padded collar. Not leather bands. A neck brace. And the screams were sirens not women.

With great effort, Slim opened his eyes. Two men bent over him, identical twins whose arms threaded through countless wires and tubes and became one single unit pressing a stethoscope to Slim's naked chest.

The twins spoke, but Slim heard only one voice. "He's coming around."

The rocking vehicle collided with Slim's stomach. He yanked the mask away, and his supper spewed from his mouth, erupting like a volcano, spilling down the sides of his face, through his mustache, into his ears, onto his neck.

The EMTs yelled, "Aw, man." They grabbed a tube and suctioned Slim's mouth. After they were satisfied he was breathing okay, they took a handful of paper and tried to swab and blot away the mess. "Don't worry, old fellow. That happens all the time. They'll clean you up in the E.R."

Completely humiliated, Slim closed his eyes. Vomiting all over himself wasn't something he did on a regular basis. The sour smell of bile, regurgitated pulled pork bar-b-que and lemon pie permeated the van. Slim's stomach rolled again. The Indian women were back, irately driving their awls into his ears and eyes with sharp lightning strikes of burning pain. Slim wished he were dead.

"Do you think he can answer a few questions?"

A new voice.

Slim slitted his eyes and saw doppelganger police officers tilting toward him from the passenger seat in the front of the ambulance.

"Not a chance!" Pumping up the blood pressure cuff on Slim's arm, the double EMTs answered in their single voice. "He's taken a major hit in the head. He'd got at least a concussion, maybe a skull fracture. When we get to the hospital, why don't you talk to that Mexican guy following us in the hippie van? If he makes it to the hospital. He must think he's Mario Andretti or somebody."

Mexican guy...hippie van...Raúl. Raúl had come. Katy and the baby must be with him.

Feeling things were under control, somewhere between the screaming women, the throb in his head, and his churning stomach, Slim allowed himself to answer the call of nothingness begging him to return to the place pain didn't exist.

# # #

"B.P. eighty over sixty." A female voice this time. "Pulse sixty-one."

Even though the Indian women were gone, and the boat had quit spinning out of control, the excruciating pain in Slim's head remained. When he opened his eyes, the light pierced all the way to back of his brain. Around him, metal clanged, machines beeped, and far away a woman sobbed.

A young dark-haired girl dressed all in white peered down at him. She had a baby face, a bright smile pasted on her pink lips, and blue eyes that were too blue to be real. "Mr. Stevens, I see you're awake."

Knowing the effort it would take, Slim decided he'd forego telling her she'd blown him away with her sharp powers of observation. His mouth was as dry as desert sand, his tongue swollen and furry. His lips cracked when he asked, "Where am I?"

Her answer was as perky as her smile. "You're at County General, sweetie, and I'm your nurse, Darla Johnson. But you can call me Nurse Darla, everybody does."

Slim wasn't in the mood for perky, and he certainly didn't care what anybody called this child. "Water."

"No, sweetie, no water for you. You've been spitting up, you know. How about an ice chip?"

Spitting up? Slim definitely remembered something like Mount Vesuvius spewing out of his mouth. He could still smell it all around him. Shoot, he could taste it.

She put a small ice chip between his crusted lips. Its moist coolness brought a touch of blessed relief as it trickled down his parched throat. When it was gone, he croaked, "More."

The nurse patted his shoulder. "No, sweetie, not right now. Let's make sure the ice stays down, and then, we'll see."

When she said the words, "we'll see," it sounded so familiar, so recent, that Slim could almost remember saying those words himself, but then the nurse's face seemed to blur. For an instant, she looked like his father when he said, "We'll see."

"I'll be right back, sweetie. Doctor Doolittle wanted me to call him the minute you woke up."

Dr. Doolittle? His doctor talked to animals? Where did she say that fool ambulance took him? To a veterinary clinic?

Hoping to clear his mind, Slim tried to shake his head, but the room swam, and something poked his scalp. When the world corrected its orbit, he reached back and gingerly inspected his crown. A big mushy bump with small metal bands pinching his scalp together. They felt like...like.... Staples? They stapled his head?

The little brunette returned with a tall, hulking man in a white lab coat. He picked up Slim's chart and ran his index finger down the paper. "Hmm-hum, hmm-hum. Good!"

He looked at Slim. "You're doing much better, Mr. Stevens, and I'm happy to say the x-rays show no sign of a skull fracture. I'm Doctor Matthew Doolittle. And no, I don't talk to animals, and yes, I am totally aware of the fact I am neither suave like Rex Harrison nor funny like Eddie Murphy."

Not caring a whit about the man's movie reference, Slim moaned. "What kind of doctor are you, anyway? Stapling my head together like some kind of...of...office project?"

"Well, you had a pretty nasty gash, and--."

"But staples? Couldn't you take the time to use a needle and stitch it up right?"

The doctor stared at Slim a moment and his smile changed from salutation to sympathy. "Mr. Stevens, I don't know how long it has been since you've had stitches, but now, we always staple instead of stitch."

"What next?" Slim thundered. "Glue?"

Nurse Darla burst into a gale of high-pitched giggles. When she saw Dr. Doolittle's disapproving stare, she gulped them back and slapped her hand over mouth.

"We do that too."

Slim gaped at the man. "What kind of rinky-dink outfit is this?"

The doctor's nostrils flared. "We are a highly-rated medical facility. Look, Mr. Stevens, I know this is all little confusing."

"I'm not confused."

"But, we are a bit testy, aren't we?"

Everybody kept saying we. Slim wanted to yell if they were truly "we," they'd be laying here with him, thirsting to death, being treated like some kind of imbecile, but he was too tired to speak. Way too tired. All he wanted to do was sleep.

His eyelids collapsed, but someone immediately shook his arm. "Oh, no, Mr. Stevens." Dr. Doolittle's voice. "No nap for you. Not right now. I know you're tired, but you took a couple of pretty good hits on the old noggin, so right now, you have to wake up."

Nurse Darla chimed in, her perky voice grating on Slim's tortured ears. "That's right, and before you know it, you'll be your old sweet self again."

With that remark, Slim reached his full capacity for perky. His eyes snapped open. "Who in-the-Sam-hill told you I was sweet in the first place? Now get all this crap off me. I'm goin' home."

The room swam when he sat up, threw back the sheet, and stared at his skinny bare legs. They'd put him in one of those white hospital nightgowns. The kind with tiny blue squiggles all over it. The kind that showed your bare butt if you stood up.

Slim glared at the nurse. "Where are my consarned pants?"

The doctor, whose lantern-jawed face was now steeped in a wrinkled frown, stepped between Slim and the nurse. He held up a cautioning hand. "Now, Mr. Stevens, calm down. No one took your clothing. It's all right here in a plastic bag under your bed. You bled all over it. Now, if you don't lie back down, you'll force me to restrain you. You don't want that, do you?"

Dr. Doolittle spoke in the kind of voice people used to calm old fools and irate children. When Slim combined that with Nurse Goody-Two-Shoes' constant state of perkiness, the way she called him "sweetie" all the time, his pounding headache and stapled scalp, it was more than an old man could bear.

"Don't tell me to calm down! And if you try to restrain me, you'll find out I ain't so old I can't get out of this bed and whip your a--."

Raúl charged into the room. "Marshal Slim, you are awake! I could hear you yelling all the way down the hall."

Slim jerked the sheet back over his legs. "It's about time you showed up. I wanna go home. Now!"

Dr. Doolittle stepped between them. "You'll have to leave, Mr. Martínez. Mr. Stevens is very upset."

Raúl lifted his chin in Slim's direction. "This one is always grumpy and complaining, like the toe when the shoe is too tight and there is a corn."

"You mean he acts like this all the time?" Nurse Darla whined.

"Sí, unless he is muy enajado, you know, really mad. Then it is much worse."

"I may be an old man, but I can still hear you." Again the words Slim spoke sounded so familiar, and then he remembered. Katy had said that same thing when she and Raúl were fighting. Katy. Raúl hadn't said a word about her or the baby.

Because Slim didn't want anyone besides Raúl to know about the girls until he figured out a way help Katy, he said, "Doctor, could my friend and I have a moment alone, please?"

"No, Mr. Stevens," Dr. Doolittle answered. "You've had quite enough excite--."

Slim exploded. "Look, my head hurts like the dickens, and I'm sick and tired of everybody arguing with everything I say. I need a minute alone with my friend, so please get the heck out of here, like I asked."

Nurse Darla gasped and darted from the room, but Dr. Doolittle stood his ground. "I'll go, Mr. Stevens, but I'll be right back with that police officer who's waiting to see you." He pointed to Raúl. "And you better be gone. Visiting hours ended fifteen minutes ago."

When the angry squeak of Dr. Doolittle's athletic shoes marching down the hall faded, Slim asked, "Where're the girls?"

Raúl frowned and shrugged.

"You didn't leave them at the house, did you? All alone, with no protection?"

Again, the younger man refused to answer.

"You better tell me where she is, Raúl. I don't wanna think you did something as dumb as leaving them alone, when you know she's got people chasing her."

"Marshal Slim, when I came back--."

"Came back? I don't remember you leavin'."

"Sí, I left for the ranch after we ate the pig sandwiches."

Struggling not to crumble as the pounding in his head intensified, Slim tried to recall the events of the evening. "I recollect eating supper, but after that...well, that ain't so clear. I...I guess maybe that doctor was right." He touched the staples in his head. "How did you find out I was hurt? Did I fall? Did Katy call you?"

"No, after I left, I got the strong feeling you were in danger. You know, like Mamá used to get."

"A premonition?"

"Sí, sí, a premonicion that you needed help. When I got back to your house, the front door was open, and you were laying in the blood from your head. The glass in the gun case was broken, Marshal Slim. At first I thought you had fallen, and the glass cut you, but then I saw your shooting trophy on the floor. The metal was bent, and the wood was bloody."

When Raúl mentioned the trophy, Slim could almost feel something crack against his head. But then he remembered another sound, his pottery mug smashing against flesh and bone. He'd hit someone, someone who'd be carrying the mark. "Raúl, did you see Katy when you got back?"

The younger man's expression hardened. "No, she was gone, Marshal Slim. First she tried to smash your head. Then she robbed you."

"Robbed me?"

"Sí, all the guns from the cabinet."

Slim's heart sank. "Not the Twins?"

"Everything. She even emptied your wallet and threw it in your blood."

"She took the necklace?"

Raúl shrugged again. "I know nothing of a necklace."

"The one I found." Then Slim remembered. He'd never told Raúl what he found at the altar site.

"If you had a necklace, I am sure that lardrona, that thief, took it. I knew she was not to be trusted, Marshal Slim, and when we find her, baby or no, that one will pay for what she has done. After all you have done for her she left you to die. If I had not returned…."

Silently, the Indian women returned with their awls, striking hard and deep into Slim's skull. He could barely think. "Katy didn't do this, Raúl. She wouldn't have."

"You were there with only her and the child. If not the lying chica, who else would have hit you?"

Slim rubbed his temples with his fingertips, trying to reconstruct what had happened after supper. The pains in his head sharpened until they felt like lightning strikes in his brain. His vision dimmed. The nausea returning, the old man sank back against his pillow and closed his eyes to the hateful light. "I…I…I can't remember. The pain…. My head…."

"Sir, I'm afraid it's time for you to leave."

Slim opened one eye, and filling the doorway was one of the doppelganger cops from the ambulance. Doctor Doolittle pushed his way into the room and put his stethoscope on.

Raúl placed his broad hand on Slim's arm. "Do not worry, amigo. The police are at your house. They will prove to you the girl did as I have said. And I will track her down to get the Twins back for you. She will pay for what she has done. This I swear on my mother's eyes."

The doctor checked all the monitors and listened to Slim's heart. "Officer, I'm sorry, but it seems Mr. Stevens is in distress again. You'll have to wait until tomorrow to interview him." He looked at Raúl. "Didn't I tell you to leave? Shall I have this officer remove you?"

"No, I will go, but María and I will come tomorrow." Raúl said as he backed out of the door.

Squeezing his pounding head between his palms, Slim rolled over onto his side and tried to hide the tears leaking from his eyes. Katy wouldn't have done this. She couldn't have. She came to him for help, not to rob him. But Raúl seemed so sure, and he'd had that feeling about not trusting her.

What if Slim had been wrong about Katy? Nothing in his life seemed hard and fast anymore. The lines blurred more with each passing day, making it difficult for him to know what to do. Consequently, he'd made a few bad decisions...decisions that had adversely affected his life.

He pressed his knuckles into his temples. If he could only remember what happened. Maybe he saw who hit him. Maybe it wasn't Katy.

"There, there, Mr. Stevens, don't you cry." Nurse Darla patted his shoulder. "You'll feel better soon."

Tears flowing freely, Slim ignored her as he turned over and drew his knees up to his chest. More than anything, he wanted Raúl to be wrong, and the only way he'd know who was right and who was wrong, was to remember what had happened. If Katy hadn't done this, she and the baby were probably in deep trouble. What if they needed him, and after all his bold promises to help, he'd let them down?

# # #

Before she left him alone, Nurse Darla told Slim he was lucky his private room was adjacent to the third floor nurses' station, and he could just punch a handy button if he needed anything.

The thought depressed him. He knew the third floor well. Too well, in fact. The third floor housed the geriatric unit. He'd been there many times visiting friends as they slipped away into the next life.

Slim lay there in the dim light, trying not to hear the soft chatter of the night nurses right outside his door. His head was killing him. Every bone in his body ached. The staples in his scalp pinched and stung.

Trying not to give in to the pain, he stared at the blank wall at the end of his bed and struggled to reconstruct what had happened at home. Instead, the fact that his instincts, the ones he'd lived by his whole life, had failed him again, kept intruding.

The old man finally gave up, and like a dust devil in the desert, worry and fear swept him away. What if he was losing his mind? What if his judgment had become so clouded with age, he'd lost the ability to reason things out, to tell right from wrong, to know the bad guys from the good? What if the kind of life he'd always had was slipping away?

Why hadn't he trusted Raúl? He was a younger man and he had his mama's gift of second-sight. Maybe not as strong, but without a doubt, Raúl had it. If Slim had listened to his old friend's warnings, Katy would be in custody, and the baby would be back with her parents.

But no, he'd had to have his own way. He always thought he knew better, and this time, everything had gone to hell in a hand-basket.

And why was he this way?

Because Tucson Slim was too proud for his own good. And he was as hardheaded as one of those big-horned rams. That's why.

He'd always been that way, and look where it had gotten him. In a hospital with his brains almost knocked out, his head stapled like a stack of paperwork, and a nurse who chirped like a canary. It was a miracle he wasn't dead, and as old as he was, he probably should be. Almost everyone he'd ever admired and called friend was gone, and those that weren't, pitied him.

At this very moment, Slim decided he didn't much care if he lived to get out of the hospital. It would sure save him a lot of embarrassment and everyone else a lot of trouble if he gave up the ghost and died right here. Probably make a whole lot of people happy too. Mark O'Brien, Carter Winslow, Dr. Doolittle, Nurse Darla, Katy.

The idea that Katy would be happy if he was dead and gone, hurt Slim, and all his happy plans for the future fizzled like steam and disappeared.

The old man wiped away a tear. Maybe Bran Phillips was right. Maybe Slim did belong in a nursing home, but if he had to choose between an old folks' home or death, Slim would prefer to die while he still had a smidge of dignity.

By the time the sun lightened the window in his room and Nurse Darla had gone off duty, Slim had covered himself with a mantle made of doubt, recrimination, self-pity, and sorrow. He lay on his side, staring at the wall, and willed his heart to quit beating. If he had to live without respect, without someone to love, without trust or joy or confidence, he'd rather not live at all.

"Tío?"

Slim groaned when he heard María's voice. He didn't need this right now. He closed his eyes and wouldn't look at her. "Go away."

"Oh, Tío, I am sorry you are hurt."

"Why are you here?"

"I was worried, and Raúl cannot come until the cattle and horses are fed. I did not want to wait, so I came early with the things Raúl went back to your house for. I know you will feel better with the face shaved and the teeth brushed."

She lifted the hair on the back of his head and gasped. "Your cut is much worse than I thought. Oh, Tío, you are so fortunate to be still with us. It is muy peligroso, you know, so dangerous, for a man of your age to have such an injury."

Irritated, Slim looked at her over his shoulder. "I don't mean to be rude, María, but I don't want any sympathy or company."

As he returned to staring at the wall, she answered, "It's okay, Tío. You do not wound my feelings. I know your head hurts. The nurse, she told me there is still much pain."

She smoothed his sheet, and then Slim heard the soft leather soles of her moccasins pad away from his bed. Good! She was leaving, and he could get back to the business of dying.

"I will sit over here while you rest, and I will be very quiet. As quiet as the mouse that lives in the church. You will not know I am here."

Slim bit his lip to keep from ordering her out of his room, but he knew María meant well. She had always been a gentle, good-hearted girl, as sweet and kind as Dolores had been. He would never deliberately hurt her feelings. And if she kept quiet, he could die in peace.

"Tío, look what I brought to work on while I sit with you." She came back to the bed, leaned over Slim, and showed him a long, lacy, white infant's dress.

The dress reminded him of the first time he'd seen Jasmine at the Square, and he suddenly missed her so much it made him ache way down deep inside.

"See how pretty," María said. "It is for our Celestina's baby. You know, a gown for the christening. And while I embroider, I will pray you are out of here by Sunday. Celestina has asked for you to come to the ceremony. She is so proud of little Luis. Even Papa Luis is coming from Mexico to see his namesake baptized."

Slim was thrilled. Another christening out at the ranch. And that dog Luis was gonna be there, probably with that woman he married.

María patted his shoulder. "You sleep now. Mama Dolores always said, sleep for a man is a great healer. I am so happy to be here with you, Tío. Now, I will sit and work."

As María returned to her chair, Slim knew there was no way she was leaving any time soon. His only hope to achieve his goal was if she'd be quiet and let him focus all his energy on being dead by Sunday.

Any likelihood of a quick demise was immediately dashed when María began to hum. He'd forgotten she always hummed while she worked, just like Dolores had. At first, the sound annoyed him to no end, but he kept reminding himself María was a good girl. She meant well, and he didn't want her last memory of Tío Slim to be him yelling as he ordered her out of his room.

Her humming, as soft and melodic as it was, made it hard for Slim to focus on dying, so he finally gave up and lay there with his eyes closed. He hoped she would think he was asleep and shut up. If not, he'd put everything off until she left. She couldn't possibly stay forever, could she?

But María stayed and kept humming away, and all Slim could do was lie there and listen. After a while he found that her music didn't bother him so much. His head seemed better, and he almost smiled when María began to hum a lovely tune he'd heard before, Dolores' favorite, El Cielo Lindo, the beautiful sky.

Slim floated along on the familiar melody, and one by one, his muscles relaxed, his anxiety melted away. He could almost see Dolores standing barefoot in her kitchen. She always sang as she patted out countless tortillas for her family, her long auburn braid swinging as she moved her slender body matching the rhythm of the melody. With that image in his mind, Slim forgot about failure and dying, and sank into a pleasant, restful sleep.

Chapter 11

Slim opened his eyes and stretched, happy that all the monitor attachments and needles had been removed. The staples made his head itch, but his headache was almost gone. And he was hungry. Being hungry was always a good sign

"Tío, you are awake." María put down her handwork. "Good. Your lunch has come."

"And I'm ready to eat, so bring it on, Marícita."

Smiling broadly, María pushed a narrow rolling table over the bed and removed the plastic cover from the food tray. She picked up the electric control and raised the head of his bed. When he was at what she perceived to be the right position, she asked, "This okay? You dizzy?"

His head actually had felt a little swimmy on the way up, but it quickly passed. "No, this is fine."

Slim picked up his napkin and assessed his meal. His shoulders slumped in disappointment. "There ain't nothing here but liquids and soft stuff, but why am I surprised? Old people's food would be served on the old people's floor. I'd rather have a cheeseburger and a chocolate shake. Don't they know this is one old man who has his own teeth?"

María giggled. "I see Tío is feeling like his old self. But do not worry. The nurse, she said they do not want you to throw up again. When you are better, they will bring you real food."

"No, Marícita, they'll bring me hospital food. I won't be getting any of the real stuff until I go home, which I hope'll be today."

When she quickly averted her gaze, Slim guessed his home-going wouldn't be today after all. "What is it, María? I'm better, aren't I?"

"Oh, <u>sí, sí</u>. You are better, but they want to keep you for...oh, you know, <u>pare mirarle</u>. To watch you."

"Watch me for what?"

María blushed and answered in a small voice. "It is because you are an older man. They wish to know if you are...."

"What? Going to survive?"

"No, no, they want to know why you are so...why you always...."

"Spit it out, girl."

"They are afraid the hit on your head has made you crazy."

"Crazy?"

"No, I am saying this wrong. That was not the word. They said the blow has made you <u>irracional</u>."

"Irrational?"

"Yes, but Raúl told them you have been angry like the bear for many years and the blow did not change you much. But the doctors said when a person is along in their years, perhaps the brain has...."

"Has what? What did they say about my brain?"

she smiled. "It is the chemistry of the brain that changes with the years. There are tests the doctors wish to perform."

Slim sat straight up in bed. "Ain't no Frankenstein doctors running no tests on my brain!"

"But they said--."

"I don't give a lame donkey's backside, what they said. I say no tests!"

María rubbed her arm and sighed. "I have not said this properly."

Slim hated to see how his outburst upset his sweet friend. Here he was lopping off the head of the messenger because he didn't like the message. "Marícita, you said it just fine. Don't worry. I'm ain't mad at you."

"So you will have the tests?"

"No, I won't, but that don't mean you did anything wrong."

"But why, Tío? If they will help--?"

"Look, Marícita, if my brain's too old to function properly, I'd just as soon not know it. At least this way, I still have some hope."

"Will you think about it?"

Anxious to change the subject, Slim pacified María's worry with a "Sure, I'll think on it," but he'd already made up his mind. No tests!

"Now, let's quit talking about this and let me drink my lunch in peace." He fumbled for his plastic spoon.

María picked it up. "Let me help, Tío."

"I guess I can still feed myself. I ain't no baby." When he said the word "baby," he thought about poor little lost Jasmine.

Slim snatched the spoon out of María's hand, scooped up a cube of lime gelatin, and aimed it toward his mouth. Still angry about the proposed tests and feeling a fresh attack of remorse over losing Jasmine, the old man's hands trembled violently. His spastic movement proved to be too much for the jiggling green cube. It hopped out of the spoon like it was trying to escape and landed in the middle of his chest.

María grabbed his napkin and dabbed at the stain. "It's okay, Tío, they will change the sheets soon."

She gently took the spoon from his hand and, humming softly, fed him. Funny thing was, once Slim relaxed and let María do her thing, he didn't much mind somebody taking care of him. In fact, it was kind of nice.

María worked her way through applesauce, chicken broth and a scoop of vanilla ice cream, then gave Slim a cup of juice. He smiled and gulped it down.

After blotting his mouth, his friend repositioned his bed. When he was comfortable, María said in a soft voice. "Tío, I have a message for you."

He leaned forward. "From who?"

"Mamá Dolores."

Stunned, Slim fell back against his pillow.

"She wrote a letter for you, right before she had the stroke. I think she sensed she would not be with us long. You know, from the gift of knowing she had."

"She wrote a letter, and you're just now giving it to me?"

"She said it was not for that time. She said after she was gone, something would happen that would hurt you deeply. How did she say it? Something that would lessen you. You understand?"

His eyes blurring, Slim nodded.

"I thought maybe I should give it to you when you lost permission to carry your Twins, but then my heart said no. Or maybe it was Mama Dolores saying wait. And then last night, when Raúl told me of the girl Katy and the baby, I knew it is time for the letter to be delivered."

She took a pink envelope from her skirt pocket and opened the top drawer of Slim's bedside table. "Your glasses, Tío. Raúl brought them to you from the house."

She placed both items in his hands and walked to the door. "Now I will go to the café to eat. When I return, if the nurse approves, I will bring to you a chocolate shake." She smiled and closed the door behind her.

Slim put on his glasses. His name was written across the front of the envelope in a broad, sweeping feminine hand. After years of invitations, "Thank You" notes, birthday cards and Christmas gifts, he'd know Dolores's handwriting anywhere.

The old man took a long shuddering breath and opened this unexpected message from beyond the grave.

My dearest, most trusted friend,

You must think it extraordinary to receive

a letter from me, someone who has gone to another place, but I feel there will come a day when you will need encouragement from an old friend. I think this because last night I had a strange dream.

I dreamed something had fallen on you,

Slim, something large and heavy. I saw you barely living, because weight of this thing was crushing you, stealing your very heart and soul. Somehow, I knew you would escape, but I also knew you would be only the shell of the man you were.

Slim, do not let the circumstance of whatever has trapped you make you believe you

are less than you are. We have aged, yes, but you are still, at the core of your being,

the same man who came into our lives all those years ago. An honest person with strong values who never violated his friends' trust…even when he saw the truth of their lives…even when he knew they were vulnerable.

You were always my example. How you endured with honor and purpose what you were denied, choosing instead to stand as a friend when you could have run away or tried to undermine. This gave me strength to honor my own vows and commitments when life disappointed me. To survive and carry on when the hurt was almost more than I could bear.

So, dear Slim, I urge you to remember you are a wise, upright man of value who has been salt working to preserve a world of decay. Have faith in your instincts even when they seem they are not to be trusted. And remember, Dolores María Teresa Cruz-Martínez has always counted you as her most cherished friend.

Dolores

Slim wiped his eyes on his sheet and carefully refolded the letter.

He'd always been afraid if she knew how he felt about her, she would have sent him packing, but he'd been wrong. She knew he loved her. She knew and somehow his steadfastness in never acting on those feelings had helped her through her own hard times.

Dear, sweet Dolores, so pure of heart, so faithful, so everything moral and upright, had counted Tucson Slim as wise and made him her example. It was plum humbling.

Dolores always had the ability to sooth him with a word, and today she had applied a much-needed balm to his wounded ego. If she'd believed in him so strongly, shouldn't he believe in himself? Shouldn't he trust the feeling he had way down in his gut? That Katy did not attack him, and Jasmine was her very own baby. Just like she said. One thing he knew. The real Tucson Slim would never walk away from Katy and her baby.

Slim pushed back the covers, slowly inched his feet to the floor and, with one hand safely on the headboard, stood. Slightly unsteady, he moved across the room with his hand on the wall, but the need to hurry weighed heavy on him. If a nurse walked in or María came back, they'd bust him for sure, but he couldn't risk falling down or passing out either.

He found the clothing María brought in the closet and dressed. After combing his hair around his staples, he stuffed all his belongings in his duffle bag, placed Dolores' letter in his shirt pocket, right over his heart, and patted it. He could do this.

Slim slowly opened the door and peeked out. No one was at the nurse's station, and the geriatric ward was as quiet as a tomb. The old man groaned. That was a pretty poor choice of words to be thinking in a place like this.

Creeping across the hall, he bypassed the elevators where someone might see him, and slipped into the stairwell. He stopped on the landing to catch his breath, grateful he had to go down and not up. Three floors down would be a snap. He could do that in a heartbeat. Pulling the loops of his duffle over his shoulder, he snugged the bag under his arm, grabbed the handrail with both hands, and began his descent.

Step down with the right foot. Place left foot next to it. Take a second to steady yourself. Place right foot on the next stair and step down. Place left foot next to it. Steady.

And so Tucson Slim inched his way down the stairs, step by tedious step, hoping he didn't get dizzy and fall, wondering if taking the elevator might have been a better idea, picturing how he would have flown down these stairs thirty years before. When he was safely on the ground floor, he stopped to catch his breath and get his bearings.

Wiping the sweat off his upper lip, the old man straightened his back, smoothed his hair, and walked out into the busy lobby like he had every right to be there. He hoped no one would notice him as he marched across the hospital's entry hall and out into the parking area. So far so good.

Now, all he had to do was find his car. Searching for Queenie's faded blue, he remembered. He'd been carried to the hospital in an ambulance. Queenie wasn't here.

Clinching his fists, Slim refrained from slapping himself in the forehead and possibly worsening his concussion. How in the Sam Hill was he going to get home? He didn't have his wallet, so a taxi was out. And he couldn't walk. It was probably 110 degrees on this fine Arizona afternoon. His knees were weak and shaky, and he didn't have his hat. He couldn't even think of anyone to call for a ride. María and Raúl would make him go back inside the hospital, and there wasn't anybody else he could call.

A tree grew in a nearby parking lot esplanade, so Slim walked over to it and stood in the shade. After several agonizing minutes trying to decide what to do, he glanced back at the hospital entrance. He knew one thing. He had to get out of here before they discovered he was gone. He'd have to walk.

He was halfway across the parking lot when a pristine '82 white Camaro pulled up beside him. The driver tooted the horn several times, and the passenger side door swung open. Slim hesitated. María drove a Lincoln. Maybe it was Katy.

He hobbled over to the car and peered inside.

The car had heavily tinted windows, so the inside was air-conditioned cool and dark. A chubby woman sat behind the wheel. She fluffed her short lavender hair and winked. "Well, hello, you long, tall drink of water. You need a ride?"

Slim blinked. It was that woman from the occult shop. The nice one who'd given him that gris-gris thing.

"Hey, don't you remember me? She sounded slightly offended. "It's me. Opal Oliver, the problem-solver from the Unicorn's Horn."

"Oh yeah, Opal. Sorry, I remembered who you were, but I was having a little trouble with the name."

She laughed. "Do that myself once in a while. Sometimes I don't even remember the person."

A car pulled up behind her, and the driver gunned the motor. Opal glanced into her rear view mirror and motioned for Slim to sit down. "Hey, big guy, I'm blocking the street here. You gonna get in or what?"

It was an easy decision, either walk in the hot sun, or ride with Opal. He'd choose the air-conditioned car. Slim tossed his duffle in the back, picked up a box wrapped in purple cellophane that lay in the passenger's seat, and got in.

As he fastened his safety belt, Opal pulled the Camaro into an exit lane. "What a fortunate coincidence for both of us. I was on the way to see you, and there you were needing a ride home."

"You were coming to see me? How'd you know--?"

"I read all about it in the newspaper." Glancing his way, she winked again. "You're a real celebrity."

As she entered the steady stream of traffic on Hospital Drive, Slim asked, "Why were comin' to see me?"

Opal lifted one hand and motioned to the gift in his lap. "Bringing you a box of chocolates. It's my theory that really good chocolate could cure the ills of the world if properly used."

Feeling slightly nauseous, Slim looked down at the box. "You make this candy in your shop?"

She burst out laughing. "No, silly, I bought it at the Desert Kitchen in Centennial Square. The girl who works there said chocolate-covered cherries are your favorite. She called you Marshal Slim. Should I call you that too?"

"Call me Slim."

"Slim. I like that." Opal suddenly whipped across three lanes of traffic and turned at the next corner. Slim grabbed the bar over the door and hung on.

Her eyes narrowed, Opal pressed her silver tennis shoe down on the accelerator. The powerful car shot down the road, with Opal threading it in and out of traffic like the Little Old Lady From Pasadena. The words, "Go Granny. Go Granny. Go Granny, go," ringing in his head, Slim yelled, "You tryin' to kill us?"

Smiling sheepishly, Opal let off the gas. "I can't resist the thrill of a new love or a powerful car, but if I'm scaring you--."

"It t-takes a lot more than a crazy woman driver to scare me," Slim sputtered as they careened around another corner. "It's just that I already have a concussion. I don't want another one."

He realized that Opal was heading toward his side of town, and he hadn't told her where he lived. Suddenly suspicious, he wondered if the lavender-haired flirt had something to do with his assault. "Don't I need to tell you my address?"

"Oh, honey, I know where you live."

Slim leaned into the passenger door. He didn't like this one bit, and he was jumping out at the next corner.

She reached across the car and patted his arm. "I looked you up in the phone book, silly, just in case you were released from the hospital before I got there. And guess what. You live on the very same street as my cousin Minnie."

Slim did have a neighbor named Minnie. "Her last name Crowder?"

"Yes, don't we live in a small world? Or maybe it's simply kismet." Opal smiled and winked at him again.

Slim wished she quit doing that. They weren't on a date, for Pete's sake. "You never did say why you were bringing me candy."

"Can't a girl visit a good-looking man when he's hurt? You know, to bring a little cheer into his life."

All this banter made Slim's head hurt. He touched the top of Dolores' letter sticking out of his pocket and considered Opal's visit. There had to be more to this than he was good-looking, and Opal was the angel of good-cheer.

As she turned the Camaro onto his street, Slim decided he would find out what was going on when they were safely stopped. He certainly wasn't going to distract her with a bunch of questions when the car was moving. Not the way she drove.

She parked in his driveway, but left the Camaro's engine running, the cold air blasting. "Well, here we are, Big Boy. And please take note, despite your misgivings, I got you home safe and sound."

Hoping to better judge the woman's reactions, Slim turned in the seat so he could easily see her face. "Be honest. Why were you at the hospital?"

Opal hesitated before answering. "I want one thing understood. You didn't hear this from me. Okay, Slim?"

"No one will ever know we talked."

"When I read the newspaper article about you going after that kidnapped baby, I realized you weren't actually looking for your great-granddaughter when you came into my shop. That was a cover story, right? What you really wanted was information."

"That's right."

"Well, I was pretty impressed someone our age being so involved and taking that big a risk. Made me proud I'd given you my guardian fetish, the way it saved your life and all. So I decided I wanted to help you even more than I had.

"Slim, I grew up in Tucson, and I know a lot of folks. Some are real good people like yourself. Some are kinda weird. I started asking those friends a few questions. And believe me, they'd heard things."

The old man leaned closer. "What did they tell you?"

"You're right, Slim. The Scarlet Host is active again. The buzz going around is they're planning a big ceremony up in the mountains."

"What kind of ceremony?"

"One where they'll crown a new leader. My friends say it's done with a blood rite." She hesitated. "Slim, they still have that baby, don't they?"

"Yes, I believe they do."

Her flirty, flip attitude disappearing, Opal twisted her fingers together and looked out the front window. "I couldn't live with myself if something happened to a child, and I could have done something to prevent it."

"You're doing a brave thing talking to me, Opal."

"Not too brave, because now that I've told you what I heard, I'm out of this thing. If the Host finds out I've been working against them, they'll come after me. They've done it before."

"Come after you?"

"No, not me personally, but I've heard things." Opal hung her head. "I'm alone in this world, Slim. The only protection I have are my spells and fetishes. Now, I wouldn't admit this to anyone else, but I'm not sure if what I know is powerful enough to combat an evil of this magnitude."

Slim identified with her predicament. He too was alone in the world and had to depend on what he knew to protect himself. Although he did have more faith in his years of being a lawman than this lady's hoo-doo. "I don't want you to worry, Opal. I ain't tellin' a soul we talked. So if you keep your mouth shut, you'll be safe."

"Oh, I'm gonna make sure I'm safe. I'm going to Phoenix to stay with my sister until this mess is settled."

"What about your shop?"

"I hung a sign in the window saying I was going on a sabbatical. I do that a lot. Go on sabbaticals. I mean." She laid her hand on Slim's arm. "I hope you can find the child before the ceremony's supposed to take place."

"Heck, the moon won't be full again till--"

"Slim, the moon don't have nothing to do with this. The ritual must be preformed on the anniversary of the last leader's death."

Slim stiffened. "When's that?"

"The day after tomorrow. The very stroke of midnight."

# # #

Slim trembled as he watched Opal drive away. He'd thought he'd have more time. Time to come up with a plan, to rest, to heal, but now, he had only one day. How could that be?

One day to save Jasmine. One day to determine if Katy was part of the kidnapping scheme or an innocent victim who also needed his help. Was he up to this challenge? Did any part of the man Dolores believed he was still exist? Or was Tucson Slim as old and feeble as he felt?

He slowly turned and stared at the police tape criss-crossing his front door. Apparently the cops had finally found their way to his house. They must have thought an old man getting mugged was more important than child sacrifice.

Slim's anger flared. And they must have thought he died. Putting all this tape up like it was a homicide scene. He ripped down the bright yellow tape and flung it across the yard. "Well, I didn't die, did I? Sorry to disappoint you, O'Brien."

Unlocking the door with an irritated snap of the key, Slim slammed into his sweltering, silent home only to be stopped cold by the sight of his gun cabinet looming before him as empty as a cocoon casing after the butterfly departs. The floor around it, covered in shattered glass and pottery shards bonded together with his own dried blood, looked like some bizarre mosaic.

His eyes traveled back to the empty cabinet. All the superb firearms he'd collected through his many years were gone. Whether a girl he trusted or a bunch of evil punks had stolen them, they could never be replaced. Three antique black power muskets. Dueling pistols from pre-Civil War New Orleans. The rifle John Wayne shot skeet with. Slim's own prizewinning Twins, his Thunderer hideout pistol, and the Winchester 94 rifle. All gone.

Afraid the Indian women would soon return with their painful, stabbing awls, Slim laid Opal's gift on the hall table, dropped his duffle on the floor, and turned on the air conditioning. Like someone pulled a plug, the strength drained from his body, his legs turned to cooked noodles.

Slim grabbed the doorjamb to keep from falling. When he the weak spell passed, he limped into the living room and collapsed in his Lazy Boy. He managed to push the chair into the reclining position and covered his eyes with his forearm, trying to block a cascading flood of memories. Katy burping her baby. The girl's little victory dance. Jasmine holding his thumb. Katy arguing with Raúl…calling Louie Lamour, Louise…not knowing who MacArthur was…finding his silver dollars….

Slim's eyes popped open. A jolt of adrenalin sent him flying out of his chair and straight to the hall closet where he'd stashed his jar of silver dollars. He yanked open the door, and there they were. Almost three hundred lovely Lady Libertys shining bright in their five-gallon pickle jar, sitting on the shelf in plain view. Katy didn't steal them. If she'd been the one who robbed him, why didn't she take his coins? She knew exactly where they were.

Encouraged by his discovery, Slim hurried into the kitchen, the last place Katy had been before his attack. The table was jammed sideways into the wall. Chairs had been shoved all over the place. His hanging ivy plant, the one he'd nurtured for years, had been ripped from the ceiling and lay sideways in the sink. His old tin canisters were all higgledy-piggledy, the smallest one on its side, drifting cornmeal across the white counter like yellow sand…sand with lines drawn through it.

Slim mimicked dragging his fingers through the meal. Someone had been trying to cling to the slick tile and failed. He turned and scrutinized the room with a skilled eye, taking in every detail. He could almost see the struggle unfold.

Katy had tried to escape. Grabbing chairs and the table. Smashing into his canisters. She'd even latched on to his plant. Maybe she'd wanted to throw it at the intruder, or she might have been trying to--.

Then Slim saw something that erased all doubt from his mind. Now he knew. Katy and her child had been taken from his home by force. He stuck his fingers deep into the spiraling ivy vines, pulled out Jasmine's birth picture, and tried to puzzle it through.

Katy wouldn't have left this picture behind for no reason. Not when she believed it proved Jasmine belonged to her. Why had she hidden it in his plant? Had she hoped he'd find it and figure out she hadn't gone willingly? Did she want him to come for her and Jasmine?

That had to be it! Katy was sending him a message…no…a plea for help. She and Jasmine needed him. It had been a long time since someone really needed him.

Overwhelmed, Slim sank into one of his kitchen chairs and gently touched the sweet faces captured in the photograph. "I'm comin' to find you. I'll come alone, but no matter what, Tucson Slim will bring you home."

Chapter 12

Slim tucked Katy's picture in with Dolores' letter and went to find the only weapon he might have left. And there it was, right in the drawer where he'd left it. The switchblade Luis had given him years before.

Taking out the knife, Slim smiled as he popped it open and tested the razor sharp blade against his thumb. Satisfied, he tugged on his old cowboy boots. These narrow, high-heeled horrors would hurt his feet for sure, but this weapon hidden deep in his boot shaft might be missed if he was caught and searched by the ghouls who'd kidnapped his girls.

No doubt, having his guns stolen put him at a big disadvantage but Tucson Slim was an old-time lawman. He'd been in tougher situations than this before. Like when he came up against Jorge Gonzalez. Those cultists paled when compared to the notorious El Tiburon. The Shark had been a heartless killer with cold dead eyes and a cold dead soul. Slim had made it his own personal crusade to track that monster down and end his reign of terror. Of course, that had been before Miranda. Back in '59, the cops ruled the streets.

Slim suddenly felt old and tired. It had been more than fifty years since he captured El Tiburon. Fifty long years. What if going after the cult proved to be more than he could handle?

He wouldn't admit it to another soul, but he knew how badly he'd been hurt in the attack. What if he forgot some important detail and blew the whole plan. He'd never forgive himself if Katy or her baby got hurt because of him. On the other hand, if he didn't go after them, who would? Katy and Jasmine had only a frail old man to protect them.

Frail or not, he had to try.

Running his hands through his hair, he snagged a staple with his nail. He flinched and cautiously examined his wound with his fingertips. Sore, but seemed okay. Slim glanced at the clock. It wouldn't be long before María and Raúl came looking for him. He had to get moving. His friends would try to stop him and he couldn't let that happen.

The old marshal crammed a bottle of aspirin into his saddlebag, tossed in some beef jerky, and a couple of energy bars he'd bought one day, but never ate. After filling his canteens with water, he picked up his black duster, and before he succumbed to the insecurities of old age or got caught, Tucson Slim got the heck out of Dodge.

He went straight to Hoot Toliver's to do a little off-the-record shopping. Hoot was the kind of man who was always more than willing to bend a rule or two to make a buck. This time he could do it for the good guys.

When he finished with Hoot, Slim picked up some of the Mexican fast food he so dearly loved and rented a room at the Sandy Dune Motel, the old motor court down the road from the Martínez ranch. By the time he finished dinner, his head felt like someone was pounding it with a hammer. He gulped down a few aspirins with the last of his cola and went straight to bed.

Only he couldn't go to sleep. The details of what he needed to do kept whirling through his brain. Breaking down. Reforming. Changing from disjointed and sketchy to full and overblown, then shifting back again. This exhausting cycle of second-guessing fueled by self-doubt would never end unless he wrote it down and emptied his mind.

Slim turned on the light and opened the drawer in the motel's scarred bedside table. Pushing aside the Tucson telephone book, he picked up the short pencil he found and began to make a list in the margin of an old stained menu from a nearby café. When he completed his task, Slim turned off the light and closed his eyes. He had to rest before he moved into the next phase in his plan.

# # #

A few hours before dawn the old man parked his car behind a tangle of greasewood and shut off the engine. Grunting softly, he leaned over and fished around under the front seat. His fingers connecting with smooth cold metal, Slim pulled out his flashlight and clicked it on. Nothing happened. He slammed the butt of the light into his palm several times and tried again.

Dead.

Slim heaved a deep disgusted sigh. He hadn't even thought about batteries. Mumbling to himself, he tossed the flashlight into the back seat, turned on the interior light, and checked his list. If you didn't count the flashlight, so far so good. Maybe he should cut himself a little slack. He had a concussion, for Pete's sake.

Slim looked out across the desert. Well, he had the moon to light his way, and it was still mostly full. He could probably do what he had to do without a flashlight. Getting out of the car, the old man grabbed his duster and quietly closed the door only to see he'd left the interior light on. Perfect. All he needed was a dead car battery when he came back with Katy and the baby. Moonlight wouldn't help that problem a bit. Laying his to-do list on the top of the car, Slim opened the door again, leaned in, and turned off the light.

The wind kicked up. Battling a sudden bout of the shivers, Slim pulled on his black duster. The desert was always so cold at night.

When he was sure all the lights were off, Slim locked his car and reached for his list. It was gone. The wind!

He hurried around the car. Several feet away, something was caught in a patch of weeds. Slim charged through the brush and grabbed for the captive paper, but the wind ripped it from his arthritic fingers.

Slim could only watch the menu, its margins filled with details he needed to make his plan a success, lift high in the night sky, spinning and dancing until it disappeared into the moonlit desert. All his hard work gone, carried away by a puff of air. Well, he didn't have time to stop and make another list.

He'd have to rely on his own memory after all.

Slim's shoulders sagged as he walked back to the car, but when he opened the trunk, what he saw helped to restore his raveling confidence.

Any remorse the old marshal felt about breaking the law disappeared when he picked up the Smith & Wesson .44 Magnum he'd bought from Hoot the gun dealer. Feeling like Dirty Harry, he slipped it inside its leather holster and strapped it on.

The old marshal picked up a Remington twelve-gauge 870 pump shotgun and grinned. This was a gun that would make a big, big hole. He laid the shotgun in the crook of his arm and picked up the last gun in his trunk, a traditional Winchester rifle, Model 94 30-30. Good, solid work guns. Not collectible or flashy or high tech, but substantial enough to make some crazy cultist think twice before taking on the old man who held it.

Slim closed the trunk and carried his new partners to the front of the car. Dumping a plastic bag filled with ammunition across the hood, Tucson Slim the Lone Vigilante, loaded each weapon with quick, precise movements developed from years of experience. When he finished, he holstered the .44 and hooked the two larger guns over his shoulder by their leather slings.

Armed and ready for war, the old man gathered the rest of his gear together and let himself onto the back acreage of Rancho Del Sol through a little-used cattle gate.

With Thunderbolt's shadowy peak as his guidepost, Slim hiked across the moonlit desert. The unusual amount of weight he carried made his back hurt. The muscles in his neck and shoulders cramped and burned. Each step resounded in Slim's head until the dull throb encased there became a sharp pain slicing clear down into his teeth while his tortured feet shot lightning streaks of pain up his legs. It seemed the only place on his body that didn't hurt was right around his belt buckle.

But Slim trudged on, determined to complete his mission despite his discomfort, hoping to make up the time he'd lost picking his way through the dark arroyo he hadn't remembered cut through Luis' property, trying to ignore the annoying doubts chiseling away at his confidence. And he kept feeling like he'd forgotten something besides the arroyo. Something important.

When he finally found Raúl's summer corral and its herd of sleepy horses, Slim gratefully surrendered his burden of guns and gear to a bale of hay and limped inside the dark stable. In a nearby stall, Raúl's dog, Paco, rose up out of the hay, snarling and growling low in his throat. Slim staggered back against the wall, silently cursing himself. Was this what he'd forgotten? That Raúl's ranch dog slept in the dad-gummed barn?

He cautiously offered the back of his hand for the dog to inspect. "Don't you remember your old pal?"

Tilting his head to the side, Paco whined.

"Come on, you know me." Slim patted his leg.

Unconvinced, Paco didn't budge and carefully sniffed the air. Finally catching Slim's scent, the dog lunged again, this time in blissful yipping abandon.

Slim fussed, "Shut your trap, Paco. I ain't got time for any canine foolishness, you hear?"

Although he could feel each second slip away, lost forever, he could do nothing except stand there, stroking Paco's silky ears until the dog settled down. Once their old friendship had been renewed, Slim found the saddle and tack he needed and went back outside to catch a horse.

Like a true herding dog, Paco stayed at Slim's heel and followed him outside.

Afraid the dog would start barking if he saw Slim messing with the horses, the old man opened his saddlebag, took out an energy bar, and ripped off the paper. In a coaxing voice, he said, "Hey, boy, would you like a treat?"

Slim sniffed the bar and grinned at the dog. "Mmmm, apple, cinnamon, and oatmeal, and I'm gonna give you the whole thing. It's so stinkin' hard, it oughta keep you busy for a long time."

Leaning down, Slim offered the bar to Paco.

The dog sniffed the bar, turned up his nose, and looked at Slim.

"Come on, dog, how many midnight snacks do you get?" He offered the bar again.

Slim could have sworn he saw Paco shrug right before he accepted Slim's gift and carried it to the edge of the corral where he promptly buried it.

By the time Slim picked up the bridle he'd borrowed from the stable and slipped into the corral, Paco was back. "Picky, ain't you? Can't say that I blame you."

When Paco realized what Slim was trying to do, the dog went to work. They made a good team and soon, the roan Slim had ridden the last time he went up on Thunderbolt had been separated from the rest of the herd. After saddling the horse with his borrowed tack, Slim loaded his gear. Each time he glanced at the dog, Paco danced with joy.

"Stupid dog," Slim grumbled. "Now I got another danged problem to contend with."

When it was time to leave for Thunderbolt, what was he going to do with his new best friend? If he locked Paco in the barn, he'd bark his head off and wake up everyone. Slim didn't want that. If he left Paco loose, the dog would follow him up the mountain. He didn't want that, either, but what else could he do? He'd have to let Paco tag along. Maybe the dog would soon tire and head back to the barn.

Slim gulped down two more aspirin and mounted the horse. He had a long day's ride ahead of him. It would be a lot easier if his head would quit hurting.

With Paco's help, he chased the rest of the herd out into the pasture and left the corral gate hanging open. If the fates smiled, when Raúl came to feed the stock, he would think the horses had escaped. Maybe he wouldn't even notice the roan was missing until it was time to pen the herd up this evening.

# # #

The blistering sun shining straight down on his head told Slim it was noon. He was only halfway up the mountain. Turning in the saddle, the old man looked back over his shoulder at the desert below. No dust trails. No sign anyone was following him, but still he worried. He'd lost too much time, and the higher the sun rose in the crystal blue sky, the hotter the day got.

Slim had wanted to have everything in place before the heat got too bad. Too late for that.

Behind him, Paco whined.

When Slim glanced back at the panting dog, Paco plopped his backside down in the dirt like he was saying "I'm done."

Poor dog looked thirsty. But if Slim gave him some water, Paco would think he could stay.

Slim sighed. He almost wished Paco could go with him, but it was probably best if he went back home. A yappy dog might give away their position. That would be a disaster, and Slim didn't need any more problems. He pointed back down the trail. "Paco, go home and get some water."

Paco whined again.

"I said go home. You're too hot," Slim yelled.

The dog ducked his head and laid his ears back.

"Paco! Go!"

Slim's new best friend shot him a reproachful look and slinked off into the brush.

Now that he was alone, the old man suddenly felt unsettled, exposed. Like the rocks and cacti surrounding him had grown eyes, and they were all staring at him. And higher up the mountain he rode, the worse it got. It seemed even the roan felt it, twitching his skin and shying at every shadow.

Slim suddenly remembered how the horse had reacted to the mountain the first time they rode up here. Nervous. Ill at ease. Like the poor thing sensed they were headed to an evil place. This must be what he'd forgotten. Too bad. If he had remembered, he would have picked another horse.

Urging the edgy roan across a nasty stretch of rocky terrain, past tall yuccas and patches of prickly pear, the old man heard a warning rattle. Before he could react, the horse screamed shrilly and reared up. Slim grabbed the saddle horn. All he could do was hang on. When the wild-eyed roan finished stomping the snake into bloody pulp, he took off running and sideswiped a yucca plant. The long sharp spikes narrowly missed ripping open the horse's shoulder, but seemed to reach out for Slim and stabbed him in the calf.

When he was able to regain control of his mount, Slim found a patch of shade large enough for them both and slid to the ground. Gasping for air, he leaned his head against the saddle and closed his eyes. All he could hear was the pounding of his own heart and the roan's labored breathing. The wind had ceased to blow, and the desert insects and birds were quiet. It was as if something unnatural had robbed the world around him of life. And he still had the creepy sensation something or someone was watching him.

The old man slowly turned and looked around. Except for his horse, it appeared he was alone. He stood there a moment, uneasily shifting his weight from one leg to the other and realized his leg ached where the yucca had jabbed him. He glanced down. When he saw the dark, wet stain on his jeans, Slim pulled up his pant leg. Crimson blood oozed from several puncture wounds.

This was only going to get worse. Wounds from the yucca always festered.

After he wrapped his leg with his bandana, Slim opened his bottle of aspirin and slugged down four more with a mouthful of water from his canteen. Moistening his handkerchief, he took off his hat and pressed the damp cloth to his face. When he pulled the rag away, the edge nearest his hairline was stained a watery red.

Slim gingerly explored his head injury with his fingertips. The staples were almost buried in the swollen, crusty wound. Now his head was bleeding.

"Great! What else could possibly go wrong?"

Slim's angry voice echoed in a desert devoid of sound. He pressed closer to the horse. Nothing like throwing out a challenge to the furies. Why didn't he just shake his fist and scream out, "Bring it on. Show me what you got."

Slim jammed the aspirin bottle back down in his pack and tried to look busy. He had a hunch he didn't have to issue a dare to incite whatever was waiting for him. He was sure whatever it was had a plan and wouldn't forget a single detail.

With a sigh of resignation, Slim mounted his horse. He couldn't stop because he had a headache, or saw a little blood, or was afraid. If he gave up, the bad guys would win.

And if the bad guys won….

# # #

When the trail played out, Slim tied the roan to a picket line and squinted as he stared up the side of Thunderbolt. He only had a short distance to go. Head and leg be damned. He could make it.

The old man carefully picked his way through searing rocks and spiky cactus, lugging his guns and gear up to the hidden ledge where he'd waited with Raúl. When he was in place, hidden in the deep shadow of the mountain, he put down everything he carried and walked to the edge of the cliff.

Below him, a dust devil swirled across the clearing, disintegrating when it hit the ugly stained altar. He was the first to arrive.

Slim glanced at his watch. Time to go down and find hiding places for his weapons. Picking up his shotgun and rifle, he looked around.

Where was his ammunition?

He ripped open his saddlebag and dumped it. Not there.

Slim frantically searched through everything again. Sweatshirt, food, jerky, aspirin, a new roll of duct tape, but no ammo. Not one single, solitary bullet or shell.

A sudden sinking lurch hit Slim square in his stomach. He could almost see his ammo sitting on the hood of his car. He'd left it behind.

Feeling like the old nincompoop everyone thought he was, Slim choked back a sob and buried his face in his hands. How could he forget his ammo? What was he going to do now? He couldn't face those cultists ill equipped. He, Katy and Jasmine would all die.

But he couldn't go back down the mountain and retrieve his ammunition. There wasn't time. But he couldn't run away and let those ghouls sacrifice that baby. What a mess he'd made. What a horrible, horrible mess.

Slim sat with his head in his hands and berated himself until he ran out of steam and words. Taking Dolores's letter and Katy's photo out of his pocket, he pressed them to his lips.

What was it Dolores had written? "Have faith in your instincts even when they seem they are not to be trusted."

Somehow reassured, Slim reassessed his situation. The cultists weren't expecting him, so he most likely had the advantage of surprise. He had his knife. And he had the ammo already loaded into his guns. Six rounds in the 30-30. Six in the .44. Seven shots in the twelve-gauge with two in the extension tube.

But how would he handle things if more people showed up at the blood rite then he had bullets?

Slim sighed. Didn't matter. Better to die trying, then to live knowing he'd left Katy and Jasmine to die alone at the hands of their kidnappers.

It was time for Tucson Slim to live up to his reputation. Time for him to make a stand. Possibly the very last stand he'd ever make.

# # #

After Slim hid the two larger weapons, he returned to his perch high on the cliff. He absentmindedly massaged his throbbing leg and sat in cool shadows cast by a setting sun, studying the killing field below him. Memorizing every detail, he tried to determine the best escape routes and prayed he wouldn't forget the solutions he found.

When it got too dark to see, Slim stretched his cramped legs and rotated his feet, taking a small amount of comfort in the slight dig the switchblade made against his ankle.

If only he could get rid of his headache.

His hands shaking, Slim struggled to open the aspirin bottle's childproof cap. He'd managed perfectly all day, but now--.

The bottle shot out of his grasp and rolled into a nearby crevice. Slim curled his trembling hands into tight fists and took several deep breaths. How could he shoot straight if he was shaking like an aspen tree?

What he needed was a cup of strong coffee.

Slim's stomach sent acid backwashing into his throat. All that aspirin he'd taken was reminding him he needed to eat.

Unwrapping an energy bar, Slim leaned back against the rock wall. He bit into the dry oatmeal covering and frowned. Man! No wonder Paco didn't want to eat his.

The old man tore off the end of the bar and put it in his mouth. He chewed and chewed and chewed, but he didn't have enough spit to soften the darn thing. The longer he chewed, the harder it was to stay awake. Unable to hold his eyes open another second, Slim spit out the energy bar and gave in.

# # #

The sound of a heartbeat woke the old man. The rapid thud-thump echoing off the rocks, filling his head. He sat straight up and dropped the limp energy bar he'd been eating into the dirt. It was pitch black. How long had he been asleep?

More alert, he listened again. No, not a heartbeat, a drum. Someone was beating a drum in the clearing below. A flute joined in, then cymbals and a gong.

Slim crawled to the edge of the cliff. Peering down, he saw the cultists had arrived. Not only arrived, but they'd had time to bring in a band and build several large blazing bonfires.

A cold shiver slid down his spine like a foul caress. This was really happening. He guessed, deep down, he'd assumed…he'd thought…no, he'd wanted to be wrong. He'd wanted Katy and Jasmine to be safe and for this to be another wild goose chase.

But now it was all too real. Those hideous ghouls were preparing to kill a child. Not just any child, but his own sweet Jasmine! If he lost his nerve and didn't at least try to save the baby, those maniacs would have their blood rite and an innocent life would be lost.

He turned his attention to the small group of musicians near the altar. Two females and three males, wearing black robes with hoods pushed back, playing primitive instruments with great passion. The musicians' young faces seemed to glow with inner light. Slim thought the music the little group played with such enthusiasm was oddly discordant. Discordant, yet somehow compelling.

Three more black-robed individuals, their faces hidden in deep hoods, came into the clearing. They walked from fire to fire, singing and tossing some kind of powder into the flames. Each handful sent multicolored sparks popping and swirling into the sky.

When the band finished their strange song, they flowed right into another. This one sounded like an old Gregorian chant, only sung in English, not Latin. Slim couldn't quite make out the words. Was it "Come park, Lord Jesus?"

No, that didn't even make sense. People who worshiped the devil wouldn't be summoning Jesus to their party. He might show up with lightning or something.

Hey, that wasn't such a bad idea.

Above him, the vivid sparks flamed red and faded into the cold white light of the stars. Slim whispered, "Hey, Big Fella, in case you haven't noticed, I could use a little help down here. How about launchin' some bolts into that pack of monsters? Or send down a few angels with great big swords."

No answer.

Slim sighed. How could God expect one frail, forgetful old man to rescue Katy and Jasmine from all those vicious people down there? It didn't make sense. But here he was, at the top of Mount Thunderbolt, alone, waiting to do that very thing.

The chanting below grew louder.

Slim shoved his doubts aside, cocked his ear, and listened again. His stomach tightened as the song resonated up the side of the mountain.

They weren't hollering for Jesus that was for danged sure. In fact, Slim didn't think he wanted to be around when the being they were calling responded to the plea, "Come, dark lord, lead us."

Two more black-robed cultists, their faces also hidden, came into the clearing. They seemed to float across the sandstone to the altar where they pulled long butane lighters from their sleeves and lit the dozens of black candles someone had arranged along the cliff wall. Several more cultists came into view, followed by what could only be described as a black tidal wave pouring into the clearing. As each one joined the group, they picked up the chant, "Come dark lord, lead us."

An eerie feeling crept over Slim. Except for the musicians, not one showed his face. Maybe the others weren't people at all. Maybe hidden away under those black robes were hideous demons with glowing eyes and razor-sharp claws.

Another cultist came out of the shadows. He lifted a large two-handled urn high over his head and yelled something. Everyone cheered when he took a drink and passed it on. The jug continued through the crowd, each person lifting it high, yelling something, and taking a drink before sending it on.

The crowd's mood heightened. Shrill, raucous laughter echoed up the rock face, and the chanting grew louder, more intense.

Slim slipped on his black duster and wondered what kind of happy juice they were drinking down there. Peyote, maybe. Or some kind of magic mushroom. Whatever it was, he hoped it made them completely addlepated. Then he could slip in, find the girls, and escape before anybody noticed. If he could do that, it wouldn't matter how many bullets he had.

# # #

Knowing the path ended at the altar clearing, Slim slid down the side of the mountain on his backside, slowing his wild descent by digging his heels into the sand and grabbing bushes as he went by. He came to a stop near the cultists' parked vehicles and rubbed his scraped and bleeding hands on his jeans. If he kept hurting himself, by the time he finished this little escapade he might need a blood transfusion.

Slim crept to the edge of the rough mountain road and estimated the number of SUV's and off-road vehicles parked there. Thirty-five to forty. And at the very end of the line was a big R.V. with the inside lights on. There were a lot of people at this shindig, but his best guess would be that Katy and her baby were that motorhome. Good, he'd be heading away from the clearing where the party was still going strong.

Unless while he was on the way down, someone had moved the girls into the altar area. Maybe he ought to take another look. Then if he didn't see the girls, he would check out the R.V. And while he was going down the hill, he would take care of a little crowd control. He didn't want this whole bunch following him when he left with Katy and the baby.

Slim slid his hand into his boot, retrieved his switchblade and popped it open. Two good jabs in each tire ought to do the trick. These cultists wouldn't be going anywhere tonight. He began with the Jeep he was closest to. After making sure the girls weren't in the car, he thrust the switchblade into the tire and pulled it out. There was a quick plip-plip of knife into rubber followed by the satisfying pssss of escaping air.

Moving toward the clearing as silent as a ghost, Slim scurried from shadow to shadow, praying he wouldn't be seen, leaving a line of flat and soon-to-be flat tires in his wake. He worked his way to a large boulder, where he stopped and assessed the rock. Not too close to the clearing. High enough for him to be above the crowd and not be seen. Satisfied, he returned his knife to its hiding place and began to climb.

He was almost in place when the celebration suddenly toned down. In fact, it was too quiet. Afraid of being discovered, Slim pulled himself the rest of the way up, one agonizing inch at a time, until he had a clear view.

A lone worshipper was now standing at the altar with a baby-sized, red-velvet wrapped bundle in his arms.

Slim caught his breath. Was that Jasmine?

He drew his .44. One false move, and that fellow wouldn't be sacrificing anyone tonight, except himself. Only Slim seemed to be the one making all the false moves. His hands shook so bad he could barely hang on to his gun. Steadying the barrel with his free hand, Tucson Slim gulped back the acid churning in his throat, sighted the bundle-carrier's head and took deadly aim.

When a cheer exploded from the crowd, Slim almost jumped out of skin. It was all he could to restrain himself as watched the cultist place his bundle in the center of the altar.

As he carefully took aim for a second time, one of the musicians lifted a ram's horn to his lips and blew a long, ghostly, howling note.

The hair on the back of Slim's neck prickled and the temperature seemed to plunge. Above his head, a flurry of wings erupted from the cliff face and countless screeching birds took off in mad frenzied flight.

The music stopped. In silent unison, everyone in the clearing looked up.

Praying he hadn't been seen, Slim scarcely breathed. When the cultists resumed their chanting, he carefully aimed at his target's head again. The cultist unfolded the velvet wrap and revealed, not Jasmine, but an ornate silver goblet and two knives with curved blades and antler handles.

Weak with relief, Slim tipped his gun back and slowly released the hammer.

The chanting stopped. The crowd parted.

Three cultists wearing blood-red robes, their faces also hidden in their hoods, walked to the altar. The middle one held up a pale green clear glass bottle and removed the glass stopper.

"Dark lord, we sanctify these instruments." His voice was deep and he spoke with great authority, as he sprinkled some kind of liquid on the knives and all around the altar. When he finished, he picked up the goblet and kissed it. The other two followed suit, each picking up a knife and kissing it. Then all three returned the evil tools to their places on the altar and stepped back.

The crowd began to chant in monotone. "Come, dark lord, lead us, come, dark lord, lead us, come, dark lord, lead us," over and over again. Each invocation louder, more passionate than the last, until the words ran together.

One of the girls in the band began to sing. Her song had no words, but the effect was hypnotizing. Slim closed his eyes, riding the highs and lows of her voice. When he realized the unearthly melody seemed to be drawing him in like a siren's song, he shook off its effects.

What was it Dolores used to say? When the devil sings, the angels prepare for war. Well, tonight Tucson Slim could plainly hear la Cancion del Diablo, the song of the devil. And since he seemed to be the only one preparing for war….

He stroked the .44's cold metal barrel. Little did they know the angel of death would soon walk among them.

Then he saw her, standing in the shadows at the back of the crowd, her slight figure hidden by the heavy black robe she wore. Her hood had slipped back. Slim saw her profile. He'd know that turned-up nose anywhere.

Katy.

She tugged her hood back into place. Slim didn't miss the tattoo on the inside of her wrist. Proof positive.

The old man didn't know whether to get mad or cry. The girl he'd come to think of a daughter was actually one of the bad guys. Why else would she be here wearing in that cursed robe?

Mad was edging out tears.

He'd trusted Katy, opened his home to her, battled Raúl, and she betrayed him. Shoot, she'd done more than betray him, she'd stolen his guns and left him to die in a pool of his own dad-gummed blood. She'd probably lied about Jasmine being hers, too.

Slim slid off the rock and ducked behind a saguaro. He'd allowed himself to get sucked in by her little sob story. Let her get under his skin. Well, that wouldn't happen again.

When the baby was safe, he'd find Katy Cleary, a.k.a. Vamp. He wouldn't rest until he'd hunted her down and she was cooling her little ass in the slammer.

The chanting stopped. Another incantation began.

Swallowing back his disappointment and hurt, Slim straightened his spine. He had to find Jasmine, and he had to do it fast. Katy didn't know it, but she had actually made his job a little easier. Now he only had one girl to save.

Chapter 13

Turning his back on Katy and the crowd, Slim crept down the mountain road searching for Jasmine. He looked in each vehicle, slashed every tire, his anger roiling inside him like a volcano fixing to erupt. While he worked, his thoughts strayed to Katy, her crocodile tears, the way she played him, how he planned a future based on lies. Then he would picture her handing Jasmine over to these monsters, and rage would almost sweep him away, forcing him to pause and take several deep breaths to calm the fury.

During one of these brief stops, he noticed a woman inside the motorhome. Backlit by the interior lights, she was only a silhouette, rocking back and forth, swinging her body from side to side, moving in a slow dance Slim knew well. Dolores had moved that same way comforting a fussy child.

His gun drawn, the old man stayed low as he hurried to the R.V. Stopping near the doorway with his back to the wall, he could hear her singing. A lullaby, for Pete's sake. Singing to a baby she was fixing to kill. Slim wanted to rip the door open and shoot her on the spot.

The old man steeled his nerves and called up the marshal within. Holding the .44 in one hand, he slowly opened the door and couldn't believe his good fortune. The woman had her back to him.

He gripped the gun with both hands, stepped inside the R.V. and closed the door.

As she turned around, she asked, "Why are you here so early?" Her hair floated like silver vapor around her sweet unlined face, her cheeks rose petal pink. She held a sleeping Jasmine in her arms, swaddled in a red velvet blanket. She looked so small and vulnerable standing there with the baby in her arms. Like a grandmother in a painting. Only the black robe she wore labeled her "Grandma from Hell."

The woman's eyes widened when she saw Slim and his gun. She gathered Jasmine tightly to her chest. "You!"

Slim smiled his movie bad guy smile. "Yeah, me, your worst nightmare. A really old man with a really big gun."

He closed the heavy privacy curtains behind the front seats. "I want you to put the baby on the table and step away from her."

She defiantly lifted her chin. "Why should I?"

Lowering his voice, Slim added a touch of ice. "Because if you don't, I'll be more than happy to blow your brains all over the place. Now, I'll say it again, but that'll be the last time. Put her on the table."

"Go ahead, shoot me, and the Host'll be all over you before I hit the floor."

"But you'll be dead, so my night won't be a total waste."

She hesitated, seeming to assess him. "What a fool you are, old man. You will never leave here alive. You know that, don't you? There's too many of us. Besides, we have the master on our side."

Tired of her taunting voice, Slim lifted his pistol high and lied. "And I have the law on mine. The police'll be here any minute, so the baby's saved either way. And, hell, I'm so old, I don't give a flyin' fig whether I die or not. It might even be worth it, if I could take a few of you lowlifes with me."

He backed her into the dining table and pressed the barrel of the gun into the space between her eyebrows. The instant the metal touched her skin, her resolve faltered. Fear flickered in her eyes.

"Put the baby down...now!" Slim growled, hoping she didn't see the tremor in his hand. Holding the gun at shoulder level so long was playing havoc with his arm muscles.

Hatred plainly written on her face, she slowly turned. As soon as she placed the child on the table, she slumped, hugged her slight body with her arms, and started to cry.

Slim gripped his gun by the barrel and raised it high over her soft gray hair, but the way she cowered before him, her shoulders heaving as she quietly sobbed, pricked his conscience.

The old man hesitated. Could he actually club a defenseless woman? A small, fragile female? Even if she was bad? Kind of went against everything he'd ever stood for. Maybe he should just tape her up and leave her be.

Slim looked down at Jasmine. The velvet wrap had come undone and puddled around her. Her paper diaper's pastel-colored fairies and stars were a stark contrast to the strange crimson markings covering her body. In the center of her chest, amid myriad squiggles and foreign-looking words, was one Slim recognized…the pentagram containing the head of the goat.

When he saw how they'd marked Jasmine like she was a side of beef waiting to be processed, Slim lost the battle he'd been waging with his unpredictable temper. His fury erupted.

This woman who trembled before him was nothing but a stone-cold child killer. Suddenly, all Slim wanted to do was crack her skull.

Mustering every ounce of his strength, he brought the butt of his gun down on the back of her head. The tiny woman crashed to the floor. A large knife fell from her hand and clattered across the linoleum. Blood matted her bright hair.

Without sympathy or remorse, Slim muttered, "Turn about's fair play, bitch." He kicked her knife out of sight, holstered his gun, and glanced at the clock on the radio.

8:15. The ceremony was supposed to take place at midnight. Plenty of time for him and the baby to get away.

Slim took the roll of duct tape from his pocket. A nice-sized strip over her mouth. One wrapped around her wrists. Another strip on her ankles, and he had Grandma Cultist trussed up like a calf in a roping contest. She wouldn't bother him again.

He returned the tape to his duster pocket and bent to pick up Jasmine. The sight of those obscene marks on her tiny body stopped him cold. Slim spit on his finger and tried to wash one off the back of her hand. No success. He'd have to do it later.

As he wrapped the baby in her velvet blanket, Jasmine woke up. Squinting her eyes against the light, she stretched and yawned and stretched again.

Slim whispered, "You're safe now, darlin'.

The tiny child opened her eyes wide and solemnly studied his face.

"Tío Slim's come to take you home."

Just like she understood every word he said, Jasmine smiled, a wide, toothless baby smile showing off a deep dimple in her pudgy cheek. A smile so innocent, it tore Slim's heart and brought tears to his eyes. He'd give his life for this child.

With Jasmine nestled in the crook of one arm and the gun in his other hand, Tucson Slim took one last look at the unconscious cultist and left the motorhome. Hiding in its shadow, the old man stopped and listened. The party in the clearing was still going strong.

He looked out across the desert at the tiny strings of lights flickering on the highway. He hadn't counted on being this close to the main road when he found the baby. Maybe he should head in that direction and hike to his car.

Made more sense than going back up the mountain and down the other side, didn't it? But he also knew when the cultists discovered their sacrifice was missing, they'd come after him like a swarm of killer bees.

Maybe the safest thing would be to go back for his horse and ride him down to Raúl's like he planned. But Slim had never ridden a horse holding an infant before. And that roan was awful skittish. What if he acted up again? Being thrown from a horse might kill a baby, especially if she hit a rock or something.

But what if she was perfectly safe, and he broke a hip? He and Jasmine could lie out there in the desert until the carrion eaters picked their bones clean.

Besides, Slim wasn't even sure he could get up in the saddle with Jasmine in his arms. When he'd planned this thing, he'd been counting on having Katy there to help him. How was he supposed to know he couldn't trust her? That he'd find himself doing this all alone?

Frozen with indecision, Slim stared down at the infant like she held the answer. What should he do? Highway or mountain?

He took a long shuddering breath. Pulling the switchblade out of his boot, he slashed the motorhome's tires.

Highway.

"Time to go, sweet girl." He kissed Jasmine on the forehead and started down the road.

Flying out of the dark like demons from hell, the black-robed cultists hit him from all sides, grabbing the baby, taking his gun. The last thing he heard before two men dragged him back into the motorhome was a female voice saying, "Well, well, well, if it isn't the Grandfather. Did you find your granddaughter yet?"

She sounded so familiar.

# # #

Slim woke up in the motorhome, handcuffed to the handle on the oven door. He moved his lower jaw from side to side. The pain reminded him someone had punched him. But frankly, he was surprised he was still alive. He had to have ticked the Host off pretty good trying to steal their sacrifice like he had. Why didn't they kill him? And where had they taken the baby?

He glanced at the clock. 8:45 He hadn't been out long. If the Host had to wait until midnight to perform the rite, the baby was probably still alive. All he had to do was get loose, go get his rifle, and find Jasmine.

Slim peeked around the cabinet. No one had stayed behind to watch him. Even the woman cultist was gone. But someone had taken his gun and his duster.

He yanked on the cuff's chain. No way he was strong enough to break the cuff or the stove. He needed a tool. His switchblade might work. He thrust his hand down into his boot and came up empty-handed. He must have dropped it in the scuffle.

The cultist's knife!

Slim looked under the table. Nothing. They must have picked it up when they took the woman.

He ripped through the kitchen, looking for anything he could use as a tool or weapon. The only problem was everything he pulled out was plastic or too small or the wrong shape. Furious, Slim slammed the bottom drawer and searched the cabinets. Every stinking thing in this R.V. was plastic.

"Come on, God," Slim muttered. "Help me out here."

The door opened. A hooded figure slipped inside the R.V.

Wondering what was going to happen to him now, Slim leaned against the cabinet. Composing his face in what he hoped was an indifferent expression, he watched the cultist move quickly through the R.V., closing blinds, pulling curtains. Slim braced himself and waited for the carnage to begin.

When all the windows were covered, the cultist charged him. Slim tried to protect himself with his free arm, but the cultist sidestepped his maneuver. He threw his arms around Slim's neck and sobbed in a girlish voice, "I-I can't believe you came for us."

"Katy?" He pulled back her hood.

She wailed, "I-I knew you were a righteous dude," buried her face in his neck and sobbed.

Slim pushed Katy away. "Get off me."

The girl stumbled backwards, her eyes spilling tears. "Hey, why did you do that? Like, why are you so mad?"

"Do you think I'm so old I'd forget you attacked me in my own home and then gave Jasmine to these monsters?"

Katy's mouth dropped open. "I didn't--."

"I don't forget those kind of things. I don't forgive either."

"But Marshal," she cried. "Alistair's the one who hurt you. He took Jasmine."

"Alistair? Your boyfriend?"

"Yeah, he came to your house to look for that necklace you found."

Slim glowered. "Is that right? Just how did old Al know I had the necklace?"

"I don't know. Somebody, like, told him, I guess."

"I guess somebody, like, told him where I lived too? Somebody like you."

Katy's face fell. She answered in a small hurt voice. "I'd never do that, Marshal."

"Then how did he--?"

"Hey, like your name was in the newspaper. All I had to do was look it up in the phone book, and Al's a whole lot smarter than me."

Slim hesitated. That made sense. And as for the necklace, he had shown it all over town when he was doing his undercover work. Someone could have recognized it. "Then tell me what happened."

"I was in the kitchen bathing Jasmine when Alistair and his brother, Jon, came in through your patio door. Al went after you, and Jon made me put Jasmine's clothes on her."

"How did he 'make' you?"

"He's a drug dealer, remember? He carries a big old honking gun. He made me give him the baby. I didn't want to leave her, but, Marshal, I knew they were gonna kill me because I, like, betrayed them. So, when Jon was taking us out to the car, I ran into your bathroom and locked the door. While he was trying to break in, I climbed out the window and ran."

"Why didn't he shoot through the door?"

"I don't now. Like maybe he didn't want your neighbors to hear. Anyway, they loaded up the baby and your guns and split. I went back for you, but Raúl drove up, and I knew he wouldn't believe anything I said, so I left too."

Slim knew that last part was true. Raúl didn't trust her at all. But something didn't add up. What about the robe?

He blustered, "And now you show up here all decked out in your party best."

She looked down at her robe like she was surprised to see what she was wearing. "Oh, you think-
-.

"You're here waitin' for the big ceremony. I ain't stupid, Katy."

"But I found this robe in one of the cars. Then later, I saw them draggin you in here, so I came to like let you go." She pointed to the handcuff and cried, "But like now I don't know what to do." Katy threw herself on him again.

Slim wanted to be mad. He wanted to push her away again and show her how angry he was, but he couldn't. God help him, he didn't know why, but he believed she was telling the truth.

He tenderly patted her on the back. "Katy, how did you get out here?"

"I-I h-h-hitchhiked," she blubbered.

Slim sighed. He'd hoped she might have some way to get to a telephone. Couldn't he have just one little bit of luck in this deal? Now he had to decide where she would be safer--here with a bunch of crazies or hitchhiking on the highway in the dark? She might find a kind citizen on the road, but if this bunch found her, she was dead for sure.

"Katy, I want you to go back to the main road and flag down a car. You've got to call the police and get'em out here."

She pulled away. "What?"

Rattling the cuff, Slim tried to smile. "Look, I'm kind of stuck, so you'll have to go call in the cavalry."

"No, I'm gonna get you free." She grabbed the chain connecting the handcuffs and pulled on it.

"I already tried that. Now, will you listen--?"

"You pull too."

Too pacify her, Slim helped her pull on the chain. The stove slid away from the wall, but the chrome handle didn't give a centimeter.

Chewing on her lip, Katy let go and looked around the R.V. "Maybe there's a tool box around here. You know, like, for repairs."

Slim suddenly got interested. "I already looked over here. Try up around the driver's seat."

She ran to the front of the coach and slipped between the privacy curtains. "Naw, nothing."

"Look under the seats. Maybe there's a drawer."

"Yeah, there is."

Slim heard a sliding noise.

"Crap," Katy said. "Nothing, but a bunch of papers. Hey, what's this?"

"Did you find something we can use?"

"Naw, just an old book."

The door to the outside opened again. This time a big guy dressed in biker leathers stomped up the stairs and stalked through the motorhome. "Hey, old man, who you talking to?"

Praying Katy would keep her mouth shut, Slim struggled for a legitimate sounding excuse. "I wasn't talkin' to anybody. I was trying to get somebody's attention. I need to go to the john."

"Well, ain't that's too bad, isn't it?"

"No, you don't understand. I need to--."

The biker knocked Slim to the floor. He stood over him, tattooed biceps bulging, a death's head leer on his scarred face. "You think I give a rat's ass what you need? You'd be dead if it was up to me. But, nooo, she won't let me kill you."

"She who?"

He lifted his fist again. "Shut up, and understand this. They won't let me kill you, but if you cause anymore trouble tonight, I'm gonna hurt you real bad." He grinned. "And I'll enjoy every minute of it." He turned to leave.

Slim asked, "Why won't they let you kill me?"

The biker looked over his shoulder. "Cause they got big plans for you, Dad. Big plans."

As soon as he closed the door, Katy came tearing out from behind the curtain. She threw a small leather-bound book on the counter and grabbed the handcuff again. Half hysterical, she whispered while she yanked and pulled for all she was worth. "We gotta get out of here, Marshal. That was Roadkill. You know, that tweaker who works for Al. I told you about him. He's one bad dude." She dropped the cuff. "Shit, this ain't working. There's gotta be something here I can use to break you loose."

The time had come for Slim's own personal sacrifice. He whispered, "Katy, I want you to go. Now."

"No, I'll get you loose, then we'll find Jasmine."

"Even if you can free me, the minute they saw I was gone, there would be a full-out search. It's better if I stay here."

She whirled around to face him. "What do you mean?"

Laying his hand on her shoulder, Slim said, "Do you trust me, Katy?"

"Sure, but--."

"Then do what I say. Go to the highway and flag down a car. If the driver doesn't have one of those cell phones, get them to take you somewhere you can call the police."

Ducking away from him, Katy said, "I ain't leaving until I find Jasmine. You got any idea what they're gonna do to her?"

"I know exactly what they have planned, but I also know there's too many of them for you to do this all by yourself. You have to get help. You are the only hope Jasmine and I have."

"I ain't leaving her to die."

"Katy, Jasmine'll be safe until midnight." He glanced at the clock. "That gives you a little over three hours to get the police out here. Call the Desert Valley Police Station. They know me there."

She kept backing toward the door. "I ain't leaving my baby."

Slim spoke fast, hoping to get everything in before the girl bolted. "Tell them there's a crime in progress. That a crazy old marshal named Tucson Slim is up on Mount Thunderbolt shooting at a bunch of people. Tell them who you are and that you can show them where it's all happening. That'll get them out here faster than if you say there is a sacrifice going on. I kinda wore that ticket out."

She stopped and peeked through the curtains before going out.

"Wait! Katy, have you ever shot a rifle or a shotgun?"

"A shotgun? Yeah. Why?"

"There're three shot-up saguaros just below the road where everybody's parked. I hid a twelve-gauge behind the smallest one. If you can't get down to the road, go for it. It's loaded, so be careful. Close up, it'll make a real big hole, but if you're back some, the shot will scatter and hurt a lot of people. You think you can pump it?"

"My granddaddy taught me good, Marshal." She grinned. "A big fat shotgun ought to convince them to give me my baby."

"No, Katy! Go for the police. Use the gun only if you can't get away."

The girl lifted her chin. "I said I'm not leaving without Jasmine." Before Slim could respond, she opened the door and slipped out into the dark.

The old man sighed. He shouldn't have told her about the gun. He ought to have known she'd think having a weapon would help her get the baby back.

Slim hit the counter with his fist. "Gosh, dang it. Why can't I think before I speak? She's gonna get herself killed."

He jerked on the cuff again. If he could get free, he could stop her. But it was useless. He couldn't find anything to break the handcuff. Oh, for the day he always carried a spare key.

Slim noticed the book Katy had found and opened it with his free hand. It was handwritten, like a diary or a ledger of some sort. Wishing he had his glasses, he pushed it across the counter as far as his arms could stretch and flipped the pages. When he found a map…a map with six little red squares marked on it, Slim decided the little book might be important and stuck it into his back pocket.

He tried not to think about how it would be if Katy went for the gun and tried to get Jasmine. He felt so stupid, so helpless, so old. Maybe Katy would think about what he said before she acted. She wasn't a dumb kid, but she was a kid. So many young people died because they hadn't figured out life was as fragile as an eggshell and could be shattered in an instant.

Outside, people were suddenly running and yelling.

Slim tried to see out the window but his chain was too short. A girl screamed.

Slim cried, "Katy?"

A dog barked. More yelling and hollering. Another scream. A man this time. Then a gunshot. The dog yelped.

Slim had to get free.

Putting his foot on the oven door, Slim yanked...hard. His left wrist cracked like a rotten tree limb. Pain shot up his arm. The old man staggered and slid down the cabinet front to the floor. He'd done it now.

Oblivious to everything except the pain raging through his handcuffed arm, Slim was startled when someone said, "You awake, old man?"

Two cultists stood over him. One, a middle-aged bald guy wearing what was now the all-to-familiar black robe, held a metal cup. The other one, although he looked like someone had beat the snot out of him, must have been a real special cultist. He wore a white robe with blood on one sleeve and had what looked like a priest's stole around his neck. The stole was covered with the same insignias that had been drawn on Jasmine's chest. Gaudy gold drawings that made the guy look like some kind of Vegas altar boy.

The altar boy popped Slim in the back of the head. "Thought you could sneak in here tonight and steal the lamb, did you? If my mother hadn't had to pee--." He looked at his friend. "Can you say pee where your mother's concerned?"

The older cultist laughed. "Not if she can hear you."

While they were talking, Slim studied the altar boy's injuries. Two black eyes and a split across the bridge of his nose, a split sutured with fine little stitches.

Slim remembered his own metal-pinched head wound and narrowed his eyes. Obviously, after Pretty Boy had been clobbered in the face with a big old pottery mug, he'd seen a better doctor than Slim had. The old man smiled, proud that Tucson Slim could still pack a wallop.

Glaring at Slim, Al touched his damaged nose. "You're gonna pay for this."

"So you're Alistair."

"So what if I am?"

"So, now I know who'll be my huckleberry when I get out of here."

"What's that supposed to mean?"

The other man put his hand on Alistair's shoulder. "It means he saw the movie <u>Tombstone</u> and thinks he's Doc Holiday."

"You are a daisy, sir," Slim said in his best Southern drawl. "Only I didn't see it. I was in it."

Alistair responded with a smirk. "And that won't mean squat in a couple of hours, will it, Joe?"

"Nope, sure won't." He put the cup down. "Now quit talking to the old goat and let me take a look at your arm."

Al pushed up his sleeve. His forearm and wrist were bleeding. "Damn that dog. I would have caught Vamp if he hadn't come flying out of the brush like some kind of red and white devil."

Red and white devil? Paco? Could he be the dog they were talking about? Had good old faithful Paco helped Katy escape? Slim let out a soft sigh. Maybe there was still a chance.

"But I got him, didn't I Al?" Joe grinned. "Shot him dead. And I'll get Vamp too. We'll show her what it means to a traitor, exactly like we showed that bitch Chuchi."

Slim clenched his jaws. They'd killed poor old Paco, and they'd killed Chuchi too. Oh, how his hands itched for the Twins. If he were free, Tucson Slim would show these two dog-killing, women-murdering, baby-stealing jerks a thing or two.

"Shut up, Joe, and get the first aid kit and bandage my arm. I have to find Rosie to wash the blood out of my robe."

"Good thing that mutt didn't tear it. Your mama would be real mad."

"You know what I say, what Mama don't know, don't hurt me." Al's laughter turned to a groan when Joe dumped alcohol on his wounds.

Joe worked fast. When he finished, he thrust the metal cup in Slim's face. "You have to drink this."

"Why?"

"Because you, my friend, are about to play a big part in the greatest event in history. In fact, you'll have the best seat in the house."

Al laughed. "Good one, Joe."

"Maybe I don't want to play with you folks," Slim said.

"You are one tough old goat, I'll say that." Alistair leaned closer. "Mom has big plans for you tonight. Drink this and you won't feel as much."

Slim clamped his lips together and refused to open his mouth.

"Okay, we'll have to do this the hard way." Alistair grabbed a handful of Slim's long hair and bent his head back. The rough treatment made the staples tear his scalp and twisted his damaged wrist.

Joe pounced on him like a cat, straddling his legs, pinching his nose shut, cutting off his air. The instant Slim opened his mouth to breathe, Joe poured a glut of foul wine in and covered it with his hand.

It was swallow or choke. Slim swallowed.

Alistair jerked his head around so they were nose to nose. "You're gonna be sorry for getting on my nerves, you old fool."

Despite the roaring pain in his wrist, Slim gasped, "And you, my young friend, are gonna be sorry when I come after you."

Alistair's blue eyes blazed an unearthly green. He growled, "We'll see who's sorry," and slammed Slim's head into the floor.

Chapter 14

By the time Slim heard the handcuff hit the floor he was feeling no pain. No pain at all.

He tried his best not to grin when he looked up at Joe, hanging over him like a huge black cloud, but the old man's mouth wouldn't cooperate. His lips just slid up, and he knew he grinning like an egg-sucking dog. No, that didn't sound right. Egg sucking dogs were bad things. He was grinning like the cat that ate… that ate…that ate something he wasn't supposed to, and it tasted real good.

Slim collapsed on the floor laughing. That wasn't right either, but he didn't care.

"Get up, old man! Showtime!" Now good old Al was standing over him, shining like the rising sun in his white and gold bathrobe. Kinda reminded Slim of a young Liberace.

"Sure thing." Slim giggled. He pictured himself getting up and standing strong, but nothing happened. It was all right there in his head, exactly what he had to do, how he should move, how each muscle would respond, and he tried, he really did, but his body wouldn't co-operate. Al and Joe had drugged him, and he was in big trouble. But he felt so doggoned good he didn't care. Even his boo-boos didn't hurt so much anymore.

Boo-boos. He guffawed. Kids had boo-boos, not Arizona marshals what am vigilantes. He would write a book. Marshals With Boo-boos, a story about grown men wearing guns and cartooned-character Band-aids.

The old man roared with laughter.

"What's he laughing at?" Joe grumbled.

"Aw, he's wasted. We'll have to carry him out to Mother." Al draped one of Slim's arms over his shoulder. Joe stood on the other side and did the same. Suspending Slim between them, the two men dragged him outside.

Amazing. The night air had never smelled so sweet. The bonfires' dancing flames flickered with intense oranges and brilliant yellows.

In the sky above, the stars had changed to dazzling fire wheels. The man in the moon spilled thin cold light like fresh milk across the desert.

"Hey," Slim slurred. "Thought yooou wwas cheeps."

The moon smiled and answered in a voice that sounded like Preacher from Pale Rider, "So it's true then."

"What?" Slim asked.

"What the Good Book says."

"Which part?"

"The part where it says when you are old, someone will dress you and lead you where you don't want to go."

Slim laughed. "Looks that way, don't it?"

The moon's lunar grin disappeared. He narrowed his crater eyes. "I know what your thinking, punk. Did you fire six shots or only five?" Then he laughed just like Pee Wee Herman. "My mistake. You don't have a gun."

The conversation ended when Slim's escorts stopped at the edge of a cheering crowd. They were all dressed in black robes, and they were all waiting for him.

The old man found his feet. He smoothed his black western-cut tux, the one he'd always planned on wearing if he ever won an award. Smiling broadly, Slim waved. "Greetings to my many fans." Only when he said it, the words sounded more like, "Grins to min fas."

Cheering louder, his fans parted, creating a walkway to the podium where a beautiful woman wearing red waited for him.

Slim looked at Al and grinned. "No speese."

"What?"

"No speese prepare. I haf wing it."

Al said, "Whatever."

Slim made a list of who he should thank for his award. His fans, the Japanese, Queenie, General Douglas MacArthur, Patsy Cline, and Dolores, but he wouldn't thank that faithless Luis. No way, Luis.

"What's he mumbling about?" Joe asked.

Al snapped, "Who cares?"

When they reached the podium, Slim realized it was Angelica Huston wearing red. Only her outfit looked more like a bathrobe than a designer gown. Or maybe she was with child. He looked at all the black robes surrounding him. Were they all expecting?

Nervously running his hand over the rough fabric of his own clothing, Slim looked down and saw he was also wearing a black robe. What happened to his tux?

He comforted himself with the idea, that at least he was dressed like everybody else. He wondered if they were wearing underwear. He wasn't. He could tell by the draft on his backside. But if this is what he had to wear to get an award, all he had to do was remember to keep his skirts down and his knees together.

Angelica smiled. "Welcome to our ceremony, Marshal Stevens."

"Gla ta'be here, Anshellica." Then he whispered, "I forget wha cer'mony this is."

"A very important one."

Funny, Angie had an accent. And all this time he'd thought she was true blue American. He squinted hoping to focus his eyes. My God, she had a big black hole between her eyebrows. Did somebody shoot her? She wasn't bleeding. Could Angelica Huston be one of the living dead? Did her daddy know what his girl had been up to?

Angie's face twisted, her yellow eyes blazed green.

"Chain him up, Alistair."

Pushing Slim down into the sand at the base of the podium, Al snapped one end of the handcuff onto Slim's good wrist, and the other to a ring on the sandstone base.

"Hey," Slim growled. Wha kinda awar' show is this an-way?"

Al grinned. "One where I get to kill you."

By the time Slim got his snappy response from his brain to his mouth, Al was gone. Slim saw another winner chained to the other end of the podium. A blond-haired fellow wearing a black robe who looked like a young Alan Ladd. No, a young, sleeping Alan Ladd.

Slim slurred, "Ssson, you gon misss your awar."

When he didn't respond, Slim lay down at Angelica's feet. While he half-listened to her preach some sort of sermon, it crossed his mind that shackling the guests of honor to the podium was unusual. But then he knew from experience Hollywood folks could be a bit eccentric. Mulling over whether he should be offended or not, he absentmindedly traced an engraving on the sandstone base. When he realized what he was doing, Slim rose up on one elbow and brushed away the sand.

The upside-down star with a goat's head.

Slim's mind cleared for a moment. He wasn't at an award show. He was handcuffed to the altar where they were going to sacrifice Jasmine. But what was Angelica Huston doing at a gathering of the Scarlet Host with a hole in her head?

Fading in and out of reality, the old man tugged at Angelica's skirt. She looked down, eyes radiating green fire, smile as cold as death.

With a wave of clarity, Slim drew back in horror. She wasn't a movie star. And that wasn't a hole between her eyes. It was a mole.

The creepy Sonya Szymanski, owner of the Gypsy's Curse, said, "Oh, you know me now. Good, it'll be better for me that way."

Frantic to escape, Slim jerked on the rusty ring embedded in the old sandstone altar.

"No point in trying to free yourself, Marshal. These rings have been embedded here for over fifty years and have had a lot of use." She leaned down. "Before the ceremony begins, I want to thank you, Marshal."

"Thank me for what?"

"For making this night possible."

"How did I do that?"

"For providing all the elements for a ritual I feared we would never have. If you hadn't found the necklace…."

She dangled the demon's claw, turquoise charm he'd found in front of him. "And come into my shop. If I hadn't sent Alistair to retrieve what was rightfully ours, we would have never found his daughter, our lamb. And now here you are, the one who'll give all he has."

"What does that mean?"

"You are the unwilling non-believer who'll give, first, your life's blood to consecrate our new Leader Priest, then we'll burn your heart, liver, brain, and spinal cord at the four points of the compass to sanctify the ground for Alistair's reign."

As bad as all that sounded, a dim hope flickered in Slim's heart. If he was the blood part of this ungodly rite, maybe they weren't planning to kill Jasmine after all. "What're you gonna do to the baby?"

"Why, that doesn't concern you at all, does it?" The woman moved away from him and returned to the business of sacrifice.

His tiny flame of hope died. Whatever these wicked people were going to do with Jasmine, it couldn't be good. He had to get free.

Favoring his injured wrist, Slim shifted his body and discreetly jiggled the ring he was handcuffed to. It was loose. The more he moved it back and forth, the more the stone crumbled, and he could see the ring was connected to a long shaft.

Encouraged, Slim fought the effects of the drug and worked to free himself as all around him, the Scarlet Host prepared for the midnight hour. He tried to shut out all distractions--the strange music, the chanting, Sonya's preaching, the voices in his head--and focused on reaming out the stone where the ring was embedded.

And his concentration held until something heavy hit him in the back of the head, gouging the staples in his scalp into his skull.

When the white heat of pain subsided, Slim realized all the commotion around him had stopped. The night was silent, strangely silent. He opened his eyes. A big bare foot with curled hairy toes swung in front of his face, a foot attached to a thick ankle and muscular calf. Slim looked up. While he'd been working, they'd placed the other captive, the young Alan Ladd look alike, on the altar.

Sonya stood behind the boy and addressed the crowd. "Tonight everything we have worked for these last fifteen years will come to fruition. Tonight we shall usher in a new realm, a new season for the Scarlet Host, one of power and wealth. As most of you know, this ceremony has three parts. First, we shall make an offering to prepare the way for the spirit of our fallen leader, my darling Serge, to return to us. Then we shall sacrifice the lamb and anoint the vessel, our son Alistair. And when the indwelling is completed, Alistair will make his first blood sacrifice as our new Leader Priest." She glanced down at Slim and smiled. "Lucky you. Before you die, you get to witness the first two parts of our ceremony and participate in the last."

Chilled to the core, Slim tried to think of some way to stop her as she reached for something on the altar. But what could he do? He was still trapped, and she was going to kill this boy.

Expecting to see the flash of a knife blade, he was surprised when she held up a silver pitcher. "As I pour the cleansing oil, we shall call forth our fallen leader's spirit. Come Serge, the vessel awaits. Come Serge, the vessel awaits."

The crowd picked up the chant. "Come Serge, the vessel awaits."

Frantic now, Slim jerked on the ring. It gave.

The chanting grew louder. Feeling it loosen with each tug, Slim jerked the ring back and worth. He glanced up at Sonya, standing over the boy, her arms uplifted, a large curved knife in one hand.

Slim braced himself and yanked hard on the ring. To his amazement, the shaft broke free from the sandstone, and he found the ring was attached to a long iron spike.

The adrenaline surging through his body caused Slim to move like a younger man. He leapt to his feet.

Her arms still over her head, Sonya now clasped the knife in both hands and was holding it point down over the boy's chest. When she saw Slim was free, she spun around and stabbed at him. Sidestepping the blade, Slim plunged the spike into the base of Sonya's throat. From the length of the spike and the fury of his thrust, when Slim hit bone, he knew he'd driven the point all the way to the spinal cord. He'd never forget the surprised look on her face as his crude weapon punched through the taunt skin on her neck.

Sonya's serpent yellow eyes widened. Blood bubbled from her gaping mouth, and the knife fell from her hands. Making a funny sputtering sound, she dropped to the ground. Her fall pulled the spike from her throat and left it dangling from the handcuff on Slim's wrist like some kind of evil charm.

Slim was stunned by what he'd done, but not regretful. Here was one woman who'd never hurt another child.

When the crowd behind him roared and surged forward, Slim determined he'd meet his fate head on. He whirled around. Lifting the spike to fight his last fight, Slim thought about Katy and Jasmine. He hoped they'd gotten away.

"Move one more step and I'll kill him!"

The crowd suddenly stopped in their tracks.

His hands in the air, Al stumbled by Slim. Blood from a nasty gash on his forehead had stained the front of his gold and white robe. Katy was right behind him, poking him with the shotgun.

Slim wasn't sure if he was happy to see her or not. If she was here, she hadn't called the police. Help wouldn't be coming. And where was Jasmine?

As Katy moved Al out in front of the altar for all to see, he barely glanced at his mother lying on the ground, her throat a bloody gaping hole, her sightless eyes staring at the heavens above.

A troubling murmur ran through the crowd. They pressed forward.

"Back off," Katy yelled, jabbing her captive again. "Get on your knees, dog."

When Al was on the ground, Slim said in a quiet voice. "Be careful, Katy. You don't want to kill our way out of here, do you? Why don't you let me take the gun?"

"No, tell'em we want Jasmine."

Slim turned to the crowd. "She wants the baby right now."

No one moved.

Katy put the shotgun to the back of Al's head and screamed, "Now!"

His body rigid, his face covered with sweat, Al yelled, "Do what she says."

Still no one moved.

"Do it now!" Al shouted.

A lone figure stepped out of the crowd and pushed his hood back. The man was almost a twin to Al.

This had to be Jude, Al's dope-dealing brother. Slim wondered if he was more upset about his mother's death than Al was.

"Bring the child," Jude said in a tight voice.

"Bro," Al gasped, "I was wondering where you were."

Jude ignored him.

A woman carried Jasmine into the clearing. Still wrapped in her red velvet blanket, the baby was asleep.

"Give her to the Marshal," Katy yelled.

The woman glanced at Jude. He shook his head and took the child in his arms.

Katy bumped the back of Al's head with the shotgun. "I said give her to the Marshal."

"No," Jude said, his voice flat. "We're going to make a trade. My brother and the baby for the old man."

"Jude," Al whined.

"Shut up, Alistair."

"I ain't lettin' Al go," Katy cried. "And the Marshal ain't staying here. Now, give me my baby. If you do like I say, I'll let Al go when we get away."

"Kill him for all I care."

"Are you smoking crack, Jude?" Al said, his handsome face contorted. .

"I said shut up Al. You brought all this down on us when you convinced Mother to move into human sacrifice. You're the one who let this girl get away. Always competing. Always causing trouble. Always Mother's favorite. But now, Mother's dead, and I'm the new leader."

"No, she chose me to be the vessel."

"Shut up!" Katy cracked the end of the shotgun barrels down hard on the top of Al's head. "Or I'll shoot both of you."

Huffing with fury, Al immediately clamped his lips together, but Jude said, "Look, Vamp, I don't want you, the baby, or my brother. Give me the man who killed my mother tonight, and I'll guarantee you get out of here alive."

Katy glanced at Slim. "No, I'm not leaving the Marshal."

Jude laughed. "You always were a stubborn little bitch. Take her."

Roadkill came charging out from one side of the crowd, Joe from the other.

Squeaking like a mouse caught in a trap, Katy scrambled backwards and stumbled over a pile of loose rock. When she hit the ground, the shotgun discharged, blasting the sky. Shot sprayed everywhere, and Al fell forward, the back of his head a red pulpy mess.

Because he'd been standing slightly behind Katy, Slim wasn't hurt, but he hit the ground anyway. Most of the Scarlet Host had gone down, screaming, crying, moaning. No doubt the crowd had absorbed some of the buckshot. Miraculously, Jude was still standing, holding the screaming baby. It appeared they weren't hurt.

Her face white with fear, a sobbing Katy scooted back into the shadows against the cliff face, the shotgun clutched in her hands. Roadkill and Joe crouched in the sand waiting to make their move.

The bonfires surrounding the clearing suddenly blazed brighter. Slim shook his head. When he opened his eyes, he was in a scene straight from The Good, The Bad and The Ugly, when the three gunfighters tried to stare each other down.

Who would make the first move and put an end to this Mexican standoff?

A strange whup, whup, whup sound brought Slim to his feet. As it grew louder, a bright spotlight began to sweep the clearing and a metallic voice from Heaven called out, "This is the Tucson Police. Everyone drop your weapons and lay face down on the ground, hands behind your head."

It was instant chaos. Everyone who wasn't hurt took off, shouting and screaming, running in all directions. Everyone except Jude, who passed the baby to another cultist and charged Slim with a roar of hatred.

Dropping the shotgun, Katy jumped to her feet and took off after the baby.

Slim tried to make it to the gun, but Jude grabbed him by the back of his robe and threw him to the ground. When he rolled Slim over, Slim could see it in the younger man's eyes. Jude was going to kill him. Grasping the spike still dangling from his handcuff like a gruesome charm, Slim jammed it deep into Jude's thigh.

Screaming in pain, Jude jerked the spike out of his leg and tried to shove it into Slim's eye. Jerking his arm, the old man twisted his head to the side. The spike missed Slim's face, but grazed the side of his head with searing pain.

Jude cursed and lifted the weapon again, but instead of bringing it down, he stiffened. The spike dropped out of his hand. When he fell to the side, Detective O'Brien grinned and waved his nightstick at Slim. The good guys had arrived.

Chapter 15

Today was Slim's big day.

Almost everyone he knew was coming to Rancho del Sol for a fiesta grandé to celebrate his birthday.

Slim stared out across the desert panorama of the Martínez ranchland, cradled the cast on his broken wrist with his good arm, and shifted in his chair. As far as Slim was concerned he'd just as soon forget he was turning eighty-one, but it seemed to be a big deal to everyone else he knew; especially since he'd managed to survive that night with the Scarlet Host.

María and Raúl had invited almost everyone they knew. And some they didn't. Like Opal Oliver the Problem Solver.

Slim grinned. He was sort of looking forward to seeing Opal. Lavender hair or not, for some reason that outrageous flirt made him feel young.

The tantalizing aroma of cabrito on the grill drifted by and tickled the old man's nose. Maybe there were some advantages in having a birthday. Raúl was barbequing a slew of goat meat, and Marícita had worked for days, filling her kitchen with tortillas, tamales, chicharones, enchiladas, flan, roasted chiles, tacos; all kinds of good stuff. Slim's mouth watered just thinking about it.

Paco sat up and nuzzled his arm.

"You okay, fella?" Slim leaned down and checked the bandage on the dog's back leg. "Remember, if you mess with your leg, you're back in the cone. And we hate that cone, don't we?"

Paco licked his hand.

Slim absentmindedly stroked the dog's silky ears and thought about Paco's heroic battle, taking on Al to save Katy, and the dog didn't even know Katy. He just had it in his heart that people shouldn't hurt each other.

One thing was sure though: If the dog hadn't intervened…well…Slim didn't want to think about what could have happened if Paco hadn't been there. And if that cultist Joe had been the marksman he'd claimed to be, he would have killed Paco.

The image of him driving the spike deep into Sonya's throat flashed through Slim's mind. He shook his head, trying to distort the memories of that night. A flood of red blood gushing out, the look of astonishment on the woman's exotic face, her pale white fingers grasping at his arm.

Slim shook his head again. Taking Sonya's life had been necessary, but it sure wasn't something Slim liked to think about. He'd had to do it, and under the same circumstances, he'd do it again, but he knew the act wasn't his life's finest moment.

The old man wiped his eyes on his sleeve and scolded himself for being such a ninny. He'd been tearing up like an old woman ever since that night. The doc said it would take awhile to get over the trauma he and Katy had suffered.

"Tío?"

"I'm here, Marícita."

She opened the door and padded outside. "You ready for the party, Tío?"

"Yep."

"Need anything?" She asked.

"Nope, I'm good."

"How you feeling?"

Slim sighed. She'd asked that question at least fifty times a day since he got out of the hospital. "I'm still fine, Marícita."

"Your wrist--?"

"It's itchy but okay." He replied.

"You want water?"

He pointed to his glass. "I've got plenty of water, but I swear, María, you keep askin' me how I feel every five minutes, you can skip the water and bring me a bottle of tequila."

María frowned. "Tío, the doctor said no alcohol with your medicines." She blushed when he grinned. "Oh, you are making fun of María."

"Yeah, won't you be glad when I go home and get out of your hair?"

"No, Tío, I wish you would stay here with us like we asked you to do. We have many empty rooms since our babies are grown and have moved away. Did Raúl speak to you of what he told me last night?"

"No."

"He said he has a feeling, Tío, like his mamá had. A feeling about you living on the rancho."

"A good feelin' or a bad one?"

María laughed. "A good one, old friend. Raúl said for you to stay here will please Dolores up in Heaven."

"That's real nice, Marícita, but like I said you don't need an old man to take care of."

"But, Tío Slim, you are not just an old man. You are part of our family."

And as much as he groused, what she said pleased Slim. It had been a long time since he'd lived with people who really cared for him. Somehow, being in Dolores' home, with all her things, laughing and talking with her children, eased his long-standing grief for his lost love.

Katy came barreling through the door. Dressed in a sweet summery dress and sandals instead of her usual black garb and combat boots, she hardly looked like the same girl he'd met that night at the Square.

"María," she asked breathlessly, "where's Jasmine's new party dress?"

"I will show you." María patted Slim's shoulder as she went back inside.

The old man leaned back and closed his eyes. Things had worked out so well since that night on Thunderbolt. Raúl and Katy had settled their differences, and now he and María were fostering the girl and her little daughter Jasmine.

Katy had proved to be a surprise to all of them; happily trading her heavy metal music, that bizarre Goth look and multiple piercings for her baby, a nice house, new clothes, and a horse of her own. She was even going back to school when all this was settled.

And school would probably be a struggle for the girl. She'd been out for a long time and was pretty far behind, but at least she was trying. Couldn't ask for more than that.

As far as Slim was concerned, life was good. He'd accomplished what he set out to do. He'd completed the task God had given him and saved Katy and her baby. He'd shown the world just because a person was old didn't mean he was useless, and today he'd see all his good friends and eat until he couldn't hold another bite. Yep, life was good.

Slim sat on the porch and dozed until the guests began to arrive, and then he and Paco held court. Two injured heroes, sitting in the shade, sipping on iced tea, basking in the glory of a job well done. Everyone rewarded Paco with tidbits of food and lots of petting, while compliments and admiration fell on Slim's withered ego like spring rain in the desert.

Detective Mark O'Brien even came by to pay his respects and give an update on the legal end of things. He called them all together on the porch.

"Folks, just wanted you to know that Officer Diaz is getting a commendation for rescuing the baby before that cultist got away with her. Raúl, do you think you can bring this bunch to the ceremony?"

"Sí," Raúl answered, "if they will come."

"We'll be there," Katy said. "I'd like to thank that guy again."

The red-haired cop grinned. "Great, now Slim, guess what? They found all your guns in the Host's weapons cache."

"The Twins, too?" Slim asked.

"The Twins, too."

Slim grinned. "That is good news," he said. "When can I pick'em up?"

"As soon as the case is closed. It'll be a while but at least you know where they are and that they're safe. Now, about that notebook you found."

Slim leaned forward. "Did it help?"

"Help? It made the case for us. It was Sonya's notebook. She kept a detailed record of everything the Scarlet Host did, every deal they made, and hopefully, every crime they committed. She gave us enough information to prove they'd kidnapped those missing college students and where they'd buried them. As horrible as all that is, it's given a lot of people closure."

Slim scowled. "They sacrificed those kids, didn't they?"

"Yeah, looks that way. And they would have Tommy Gallagher, too, if you hadn't stopped Sonya."

María crossed herself. "Why would they do such a thing?"

O'Brien rubbed his freckled jaw. "They thought it would give them power. By the way, Slim, Tommy and his parents would like to come by sometime and say thanks. I made sure that kid knew how close he came to losing his life. Maybe he'll stay away from those raves now."

Katy, who had been standing back watching Detective O'Brien and Slim talk, stepped forward. "Did that woman write anything about my friend Chuchi Ruiz in that notebook?"

"No, Katy, she didn't. But we did locate Miss Ruiz's boyfriend Booth Reynolds. He told us he left the group when Roy Nagle--."

Katy interrupted. "Who's that?"

"Nagle's street name is Roadkill. You know him, don't you?"

She nodded.

"Nagle claims Alistair Light murdered Miss Ruiz."

"I knew it." Katy's face crumpled. "Did he kill her because she helped me?"

He shrugged. "We simply don't know. We did find out that Al was the one who introduced his mother to the art of black magic. Seems she kind of lost her mind after her husband Serge died. One thing led to another and the two of them decided to incorporate what they'd learned about the black arts into what the Host believed. From there it seemed to be an easy jump to human sacrifice. Nasty business."

"What about the drugs and the baby selling?" Slim asked. "How does that fit in with all that false religion stuff?"

"That one's easy. They were filled with greed, Slim, pure unadulterated greed. Jude spilled his guts and told us all about how that transpired. He thinks if he cooperates, he'll do less time. Ain't happening, but we're not telling him that. Between the notebook and what Jude's telling us, we're roundin' up all that's left of the cult, plus their contacts in the drug business, their illegal gun running, and the baby schemes."

"What happens to all the other babies they sold?" Katy asked.

The detective shrugged. "The legal system will have to decide that, Katy, just like they'll decide if any charges will be filed in the deaths of Sonya Szymanski and Alistair Light."

"Have you heard anything?" Slim asked.

"No," O'Brien answered. "But I'm not too worried. I believe you and Katy will both be exonerated. There's only one little loose end left, but it's probably not important."

"What loose end?" Slim demanded.

"That necklace you told me about. The one you said Sonya was wearing when she died."

"Yeah, what of it?"

"It wasn't on her body when she got to the morgue. I sent my men back out to the site, but no one could find it. Seems like it disappeared again."

This bit of news made Slim uneasy. What if that necklace fell into the wrong hands? What if they came after Jasmine again?

"Oh, yeah, I almost forgot." O'Brien pulled a piece of paper out of his inside coat pocket, unfolded it, and gave it to Raúl. "This came from family court. They've assigned the guardianship of Katy and Jasmine Cleary to María and Raúl Martínez. Congratulations, Katy. You've got yourself a real home."

Katy slipped her arms around María's ample waist and hugged her. "So it's official. Me and Jasmine are all yours."

Mark O'Brien stood. "I better get on back to the house. Good to see you all. Slim, I want you to know I'm sorry I didn't listen to you when you needed me. I'm glad everything worked out as well as it did." He gave a little salute and walked toward his car.

"Detective?" Slim called out.

The cop stopped and looked back. "Yeah?"

"So…now can you get the-powers-that-be to let me carry my sidearms again?"

"Sorry, Partner. Not in this lifetime."

Slim shrugged. "I didn't think so, but it don't hurt to ask, does it? It is my birthday."

Although he was a little disappointed, the funny part was, as Slim looked at Katy and María, wearing his guns didn't seem like such a big deal anymore.

"No, I guess it doesn't hurt to ask, but you have a happy birthday anyway, okay? I'll keep you posted on the case."

Slim watched O'Brien get in the car and drive past a red convertible coming up the road. The red car stopped in front of the house. The man driving smiled, his unnaturally tanned face cracking to reveal unnaturally white teeth.

Where had Slim seen him before?

The man got out, dusted his khakis off, and adjusted his red tie. "Mr. Stevens? Remember me? Gary Mason from the <u>Daily Star</u>?"

That's who he was. The reporter from the Square. The one who caused all that trouble with Carter and got Slim fired. "Katy, why don't you go inside?"

"Why?"

"Because he's a reporter, and Tucson doesn't need to know where you live."

The color drained from the girl's face. She slipped back inside the house.

"Mr. Stevens," the reporter called out again. "Do you have a minute for the press?"

"No!"

Mason obviously had a hearing problem, because although Slim said "No," the reporter took a camera bag out of the back seat of his car. "I heard it's your birthday and thought it would be the perfect time to do a cover story for the Sunday paper about a real Tucson hero. Complete with photos of the whole family and the dog. My editor agreed, so do you think you might have some time for an interview?"

"I said no," Slim snapped. "Not the way you fellas at the Star twist things."

Mason's face flushed. "How about I give you final approval on the story before it's printed?"

Slim thought a moment. "Final approval means if I don't like something, you have to take it out, right?"

"Yes sir, but you're going to like this article. I want to tell your life story. I want our readers to know the old-fashioned Western cowboy still exists in Arizona. That even now there are men who wear white hats and live to defeat the evildoers."

Trying to appear nonchalant, Slim examined his fingernail. "Okay, as long as I get to approve every word. I want that in writing." He looked at all his friends. "And you are all my witnesses."

Mason had his camera out. "No problem. Now, for our first picture, let's have you, the girl, the baby, and the dog. That was Katy Cleary who ran inside the house just now, wasn't it?"

Slim frowned. "Don't matter. You said you wanted to do a piece on me. In fact, you better not mention Katy or her baby in your article, understand? I mean it. They haven't brought in all the Host last I heard." He paused. "How about a picture of me and the dog?"

Mason shrugged. "Whatever you think is best, Mr. Stevens."

"Why don't you call me Slim?"

"I'd be honored, sir. Now give me a minute. I need to change my camera lens."

Slim smiled and leaned back in his chair. What a difference a few weeks made. He'd repaired his damaged reputation and taken Tucson Slim from senile old fool to revered hero.

"Tío, let me fix you up for the picture." After María turned his collar down, she straightened an errant strand of his hair. Her loving gestures warmed the old man's heart. Dolores' family was now his family. He guessed he'd better get over his mad about his old running buddy Luis. Looked like in the future they'd be seeing a lot of each other.

Paco nuzzled his arm again.

Shoot, even the dog loved him. Maybe he should stay out here on the ranch like María and Raúl wanted. He could rent out his house in town, and it wasn't like he was a complete invalid. When his wrist healed, he would be able to help Raúl. After all, the boy was getting older and probably needed a full time ranch hand, especially a good one.

And the best part was if he lived at the ranch, he'd be near Katy and the baby. He'd see Jasmine take her first steps, hear her first words. He could help Katy with her homework. He could teach her all about World War Two and General Douglas MacArthur.

As far as he could tell, they needed him almost as much as he needed them. Besides, with that necklace still out there somewhere, one day Jasmine and Katy just might need their old Uncle Slim to come to their rescue again.

Who knew? In the life of an Arizona Marshal, anything was possible.

About the Author

I have a wonderful job with a major airline; a magnificent husband, three exceptional children, seven amazing Grandchildren, and one brand-spanking new Great-Grandson. Now really, who could ask for anything more?

I hope you enjoyed Slim's Last Stand and that you will take a look at my new novel, Walking the Monkeyboard. Thank you, and God bless.

62874202R00233